Praise for Sue Lawrence's novels:

"Breathless pace, unexpected eve[nts]... up late." *E.S. Thomson*

"A fascinating slice of Scottish history packed with high stakes power-play and bloody revenge. Chock full of gasp-inducing twists and turns!" *Sarah Smith, author of Hear No Evil*

"Absorbing and vividly imagined. Clan feuds, love and betrayal, violence and vengeance … Who can ask for more?" *Sarah Maine*

"A rich atmospheric novel, giving voice to the women of Scotland's past." *Ailish Sinclair*

"All the ingredients of a thrilling read – royal jewels, a secret compartment, family intrigue, ghostly superstition and a treacherous husband." *Sara Sheridan*

"Brilliantly evokes the lives of the women around Mary, Queen of Scots … Beautifully written. I loved it." *Elisabeth Gifford*

"From Jacobite intrigues to Scotland's dark and sea-battered islands … eye-popping. An amazing story." *Sally Magnusson*

"Swept me along breathlessly … what a story!" *Dr Annie Gray*

"Fascinating … utterly compelling." *Undiscovered Scotland*

"A haunting, moving story." *Kirsty Wark*

"Enthralling. It's a cracking story beautifully told." *Lorraine Kelly*

"Plenty of intrigue, there is much to enjoy here … smart twists … particularly strong descriptions … her characters are all distinct individuals." *Louise Fairbairn, Scotland on Sunday*

"Excellent … Intriguing … Full of fear and danger [and] page-turning … many twists and turns." *Historical Novels Review*

"Lawrence's parallel plotlines advance in lock-step with each other over alternate chapters … until they're entwined to great effect towards the end." *Sunday Herald*

"A gripping tale." *Daily Record*

"Fascinating … Lawrence's skill of storytelling allows for the tension to really build throughout." *Scottish Field*

Also by Sue Lawrence:

Lady's Rock

The Green Lady

*The Unreliable Death
of Lady Grange*

Down to the Sea

The Last Train

Fields of Blue Flax

Whispers in the Glen

SUE LAWRENCE

CONTRABAND

Published by Contraband,
an imprint of Saraband,
3 Clairmont Gardens
Glasgow, G3 7LW
www.saraband.net

Copyright © Sue Lawrence 2025

All rights reserved. No part of this publication may be
reproduced, stored in a retrieval system, or transmitted,
in any form or by any means, electronic, mechanical,
photocopying, recording, or otherwise, without first
obtaining the written permission of
the copyright owner.

ISBN: 9781916812437
eISBN: 9781916812475

1 2 3 4 5 6 7 8 9

*In memory of my father Bob Anderson
and his brother Frank ('Unc'),
who instilled their love of Glen Clova
into three generations of the family.*

Prologue

A loud knock at the door made her jump. She put down the glass she'd been wiping and looked around the shadows of the deserted bar. She'd been on edge since the last customers had left; the locals from down the road had gone ten minutes before.

The noise rose to a hammering. Anxious, she picked up the hurricane lamp and walked slowly to the door. There had been talk all night about a crash. The thrum of a plane had been heard over the village at lunchtime, then the sound had disappeared abruptly after a distant bang. One of the older men said it could have been a German plane.

It was pitch black in the corridor. She approached the door, turned the key in the lock and pulled it slowly towards her.

A tall figure stood there, fist raised. He lurched forward, collapsing onto her lamp to the sound of tinkling glass. She gasped in terror as the light went out.

PART 1

Nell

Chapter 1
May 1942

Nell leant against the door, gazing towards the hills. The low, threatening clouds from earlier were clearing to the south and a bright sky was lighting up the glen. She tilted her head upwards to where she'd heard birdsong in the tree. The high trills of a thrush were breaking the dawn silence.

She took a sip of her tea and returned inside. The only noises in the kitchen were the tick of the clock and the porridge plopping on the stove. She rushed over to take the pan off the heat, hoping it hadn't caught on the bottom. Her sister was always complaining that she burnt the porridge and never had time to clean the pan. She spooned it into two bowls, then scraped at the gloopy layer on the base with the spurtle. For once, it had not burnt.

"Effie," she called, filling the pan with cold water, "breakfast's ready." She had just sat down at the table to eat when her sister walked into the kitchen. She sniffed loudly. "Burnt or normal this morning, Nell?" Effie raised an eyebrow, then grabbed a spoon from the drawer and joined her sister.

"*Comme il faut*," she said, dunking the hot porridge into the bowl of cold milk at the side.

"Dear Lord, Nell, did you put any salt in it at all?" Effie screwed up her face. "It's sugar that's rationed, not salt."

"If you're so fussy, make it yourself." Nell scooped up the last spoonful and downed her cup of tea. "And by the way, I'm the one who can drink my tea with only one spoonful of sugar. I know you're still sneaking in a second helping."

Nell picked up her jacket from the back of the chair and headed for the door. "See you later."

Effie swivelled around to look at the clock. "It's not even half past seven. Why are you off so early?"

"There are lots of things to do at the post office before my deliveries. Mrs Bell needs a hand with the sorting." She grabbed her postbag from the hook and went out, slamming the door.

She got her bicycle from the shed and cycled down to the road, then turned right towards the post office. She leant the bike against the stone wall and turned around to look down the glen. The sky was now clear, with only a few high clouds over the hills to the south. She looked west towards the mountains where some heavy grey clouds were lingering. Hopefully they weren't a sign of rain to come towards Glen Doll; she'd been soaked the day before and only had one other dry pair of uniform trousers and jacket.

"Come away in, Helen," Mrs Bell shouted as she pushed open the door of the little sub-post office. Even though everyone else in the village called her Nell, Mrs Bell had insisted on using her full name since Nell had taken over doing the postal deliveries from Mrs Bell's son Jimmy. He was one of the first boys in the glen to sign up and had been away since the start of the war. A lot of the locals had scoffed when Nell said she was to be the new postie, at her age. But she was only in her forties and fit as a flea. The hills were never a challenge to her. Last summer she was first up to Loch Brandy for the Sunday School picnic with Wee Janie, leaving those much younger behind, including her sister, who certainly was not as fit as she used to be.

"I've just started to sort the mail, if you could take over here while I get some things together round the back for Mrs Harper at the youth hostel?"

Nell took off her jacket and began to sort the mail.

"There's tea in the pot, if you want."

"Thanks, Mrs Bell, but I've just had some."

The older woman nodded and pointed at a pile of letters on the desk.

"There's one for your sister there, by the way."

Nell shuffled through the pile until she came to an envelope addressed to 'Miss Euphemia Anderson, The Schoolhouse,

Clova'. She turned it over. Just like the one she delivered a few weeks before, there was no indication of who had sent it, and she couldn't make out the postmark. Her sister had not shared the contents of the last one. Nell slipped it into her jacket pocket and carried on placing the mail into piles before finally arranging them all, in order, into her postbag.

"See you later, Mrs Bell. I've not got too far to go today; I should be back by early afternoon." Slinging the postbag over her shoulder, she went out to her bicycle and set off up the glen. She overtook a tall, slim man wearing solid boots and knee-length shorts with a pack on his back. He was clearly heading towards Mayar and Driesh.

"Morning," she called. "Nice day for a climb."

"Isn't it?" he shouted after her.

She hadn't gone far when she saw another man coming down the road. This man was more formally dressed: it was the minister. She stopped her bicycle and smiled as he removed his hat.

"There's nothing from Sandy today, sorry Mr Johnson," Nell said.

One of the minister's sons was a prisoner of war in Germany, and he and his wife were overjoyed whenever they had news from him.

"It's fine, Nell. We had a letter last week, remember?"

Nell nodded. "How's Mrs Johnson doing?"

"As well as can be expected. Jimmy's finished his training so he'll be starting to fly sorties soon. And you'll have heard about Willie Robb?"

Nell nodded. "Hopefully he'll be all right. His mother said his injuries weren't too bad?"

"I'm going to see her later. Well, I must be on my way."

Nell jumped on her bike again and set off up the glen. At least today she had no telegrams with her. That was the worst part of this job: delivering bad news, and to people she had known all her life.

* * *

"Honestly, the mess you left behind you this morning," Effie muttered as she bowled in through the front door. "I had to scour the porridge pan, do all the dishes as usual, then try to find the bed under your piles of things." She shook her head. "How can two sisters be so different?"

Nell poured her sister a cup of tea and reflected on the fact that this diatribe about untidiness was delivered almost every afternoon. Their relationship never used to be so fraught. Nell wondered whether Effie was perhaps too old for teaching; she seemed continually grumpy these days. "So, what did you do at school today?"

Her sister sat down and sipped her tea. She looked exhausted. The class was bigger than usual at the moment, and it must be a strain teaching children whose ages ranged from five to eleven years old.

"Well, I'd planned a nature walk along the river after lunch – we'd seen frogspawn the last time, so I was hoping today they could find some tadpoles. But then the rain started after playtime."

"You don't need to tell me about that, Effie," said Nell, pointing up at her postal uniform jacket drying on the pulley.

Effie grinned. "But I must tell you about Mrs Cameron this morning."

"Presume she's still cooking up a storm?"

"Yes. And today she arrived, all apologetic, saying she couldn't get much in the way of meat; she could only get neck of mutton for the stew. But when I asked about pudding – I've told you it's the highlight of the children's day, having a hot sweet pudding – she told me she was going to make a rhubarb sponge."

"You told her to take our rhubarb, didn't you? We can't possibly use it all."

"Of course. But then she said there was a problem with the

eggs – we've already used up the school's weekly rations."

"So how was she planning on making her sponge?"

"The minister's wife had told her the manse hens don't understand rationing, so she gave Mrs Cameron three of their eggs."

"Well, well, the nefarious goings on in Clova village," Nell said, raising an eyebrow. "Anything else to report, Miss Anderson?"

In the past, Nell had made the mistake of forgetting to ask her sister about her day in the classroom and had been told she was selfish and uncaring as she sat there reading the paper when she came back from her work. Somehow Effie forgot that Nell's job entailed cycling for miles along mountain tracks and carrying her bike over muddy fields in all weathers to deliver the post. But just to try to keep Effie sweet, she made a point of asking about her day, even though the ins and outs of the classroom didn't interest her one jot. They used to be so close, but somehow over the years they'd drifted apart, even though they lived in the same house.

Nell placed her finger on a sentence in The Courier and looked up, feigning interest as her sister spoke.

"Elspeth Falconer fell out of the big tree at afternoon playtime."

"Was she all right?"

Effie shrugged. "Wee Janie was supervising them."

"Will she ever get called anything other than that by the way? She's fifteen and nearly six foot! It does seem ridiculous nowadays. It was fine when she was five."

"She doesn't seem to mind. Anyway, she came rushing in to get me. She said there was no blood, just a graze, but she wondered about getting the nurse."

"Bessie's on her day off though, isn't she? I saw her up at the Hendersons'."

"Yes, so I went out to the playground to see. The girl was a bit upset, but nothing visible. I was just bringing her inside to have a seat while I cleaned up her knee when Wee Janie suggested I get you."

"Me? Why?"

"Exactly. Why you?" She tutted. "She seems to think that just because you spent three years in a French hospital, you're medically trained. Honestly."

"Effie, I did have some basic training, you know."

"I thought you were just an ambulance driver," she retorted and flounced off to her room.

Why did she always try to demean what Nell had done in the First World War? The way she spoke, you'd think that if Effie Anderson hadn't been teaching in a tiny village school in Glen Clova everything would have fallen apart and the Germans would have won the war. Besides, Nell was not 'just an ambulance driver'. Sadly, the job entailed a lot more.

Chapter 2

October 1915

Nell left the woodland path and cycled straight ahead, looking up at Royaumont Abbey in admiration, as she did every time she approached. She had just leant her bike up against the wall outside the cloisters when she heard a voice bellow down from a window.

"Miss Anderson, can you drive?"

She looked up to see Dr Gibson peering out from the window.

"Well, I've been in the driver's seat of a motor car but…"

"Come on upstairs, would you? I'll meet you in the ward."

The window slammed shut and Nell went through the solid wooden door in the thick stone walls of the ancient abbey. She leapt up the worn steps two at a time and entered the first-floor ward where Dr Gibson was standing at the side of a patient's bed with a nurse.

The doctor came to meet her. "I'm about to operate – an amputation – so I can't talk for long." She turned to tell the nurse she would be back later, then said, "So you've driven before, Miss Anderson?"

"Well, not really. I've been in a motor car, as I said, and had a short drive around the nearby estate, supervised by the laird's son, but…"

"But your father must surely have one? You live in a house in the country, do you not?"

Nell shook her head. "Pa's only the headmaster, he's not gentry."

"Never mind. We're expecting a rush of patients in the next few days and we're short of an ambulance driver." She looked up at the large clock on the wall. "I must go into theatre now, but find Miss Nicolson. Tell her I said she has to teach you how to drive.

And fast. I need you driving by tomorrow."

She headed towards the door.

"But what about my duties as orderly?"

"We've plenty of orderlies at present. I've decided you are the best one to join the chauffeuses and your fluency in French will be an advantage. See to it, Miss Anderson."

Nell was about to protest that she was only twenty and didn't the drivers need to be twenty-four, but the doctor had already turned away and was striding off towards the stairs.

She went out and along the dim corridor, thinking how extraordinary her life had become since she had arrived at Royaumont Abbey some ten months earlier. Like the others, she'd been thrilled to be selected to join the Scottish contingent leaving Waverley station for France in December 1914.

At Royaumont Abbey, thirty miles north of Paris, an exclusively female-run hospital had been set up, and Nell was one of the seven orderlies on the staff. As well as seven doctors, there had been ten nurses at the beginning, though over the months the number of orderlies and nurses had increased.

The 'Scottish Women's Hospitals' project was conceived by Dr Elsie Inglis, who wanted to establish hospitals run by women as a means of supporting the war effort. Royaumont Abbey had been chosen by the French Red Cross to accommodate the hospital.

When they arrived at the abbey after the long journey from Edinburgh, even though they knew it wasn't far from the Front they had expected a modicum of comfort in their surroundings; an abbey, even one that was centuries old, sounded rather grand. But the women found themselves in terrible conditions, with inadequate lighting, heating and water supplies. By the time they received their first patient in January 1915, they had made the place slightly more respectable, but it was never anything less than freezing – and dimly lit. The Germans had seen to it that fuel was a continual problem, and the first winter in France had been bitterly cold.

Along with the other women, Nell discovered she was hardier than she had thought, and she soon became used to the awful stench of gangrene, the abominable moans of those in pain and the hopeless whimpers of the dying.

* * *

"Bella, is it meant to make that noise?" Nell asked as she cranked the ambulance from first gear into reverse.

"Yes, that crunching sound usually happens when you change gear. You're maybe a bit heavy on the throttle mind you, but apart from that, I think you're all set."

"What, to go solo?" Nell frowned as Bella Nicolson opened the passenger door.

"Yes, it's baptism by fire at Royaumont, as you know." She winked and beckoned Nell out of the car. "You'll need to change out of your orderly uniform. Come on and we'll get you kitted out as an official chauffeuse."

She had just tried on a khaki overcoat in the storeroom when she heard a tapping noise on the flagstones outside. She peered round the door and saw Paul, the injured French soldier who now worked in the kitchen.

"*Bonjour* Belle Hélène," he said, his smile revealing those beautiful dimples.

"Hello Paul." He always called her that, and it never ceased to make her smile: if there was one thing she was not, it was beautiful. "What are you cooking today?"

"Rabbit. One of the chauffeuses was given a sack of them by a farmer on her way back from the railhead with the injured yesterday. I'm going to make a casserole with some red wine, garlic, thyme..." He grinned and pointed out the window at the bright sun high in a cloudless sky. "I know, it's too hot for that kind of dish, but it's filling and good for the patients."

Nell nodded.

"Why are you wearing that?"

"I'm a chauffeuse now, Paul. I've been taken off orderly duties starting today. I've to leave for Creil this evening."

His eyes opened wide. "That's some change, Hélène, and so sudden. Just like me: one day I'm a soldier fighting for France, a couple of days later I'm an amputee."

Nell frowned and grabbed the hand that was not on the crutch. "Paul, you are so lucky – you're alive! And you were allowed to stay on working at Royaumont, cooking delicious food for the patients and for us." She forced a smile, even though she knew he did not feel lucky.

"Hélène, one of the few things that has got me through these past few months has been talking to you. You know that. But as for lucky?" He shrugged. "Luckier than Bertrand and the others, for sure, but…"

Nell was used to him talking about fellow soldiers who had died, but she always tried to change the subject. She usually asked him to tell her about his home in the south – are there mountains near Arles as there are near Glen Clova, what do they eat for dinner in Provence? Just as she opened her mouth to speak, a shout was heard along the corridor.

"Nell! All the drivers are needed. You're to come now!"

She turned to see Bella marching towards them from the courtyard.

"I thought you said we were collecting the injured tonight?"

"We've just had some news; it's all change on the Front. Get yourself over to the stables, we're leaving now. Since it's your first time, you're to follow my ambulance."

Nell turned back to say goodbye to Paul, but he had already started off towards the kitchen, the tap-tapping of his crutch fading away as he hobbled along the cold, dark passageway.

* * *

Whenever she got a letter from home, she waited till bedtime to read it alone, in the dark, with only a candle to see by. She needed to get away from the noises and the smells, to try to imagine herself back in Clova. She just hoped the bell wouldn't ring; that was the command for her to jump into the ambulance and drive off for more wounded troops. The past few days had been exhausting and draining, the sight of the injured soldiers harrowing – some with severed limbs, all with blood over their filthy uniforms.

Bella had told her she'd get used to the sight of the carnage as she arrived at the station at Creil and helped load the injured into the back of her ambulance. And in a way she did; she had no choice. But it was the noises. She could not cover her ears as she drove. All the way from Creil to Royaumont, there were low moans, shrieks and sobs. And there was nothing she could do for the poor men other than drive as carefully as possible along the potholed road to the hospital.

Dear Nell,

I hope things in France are not too bad.

As I said in my last letter, I'm back home in Clova from Prosen now. I'd hardly taken off my coat last night when Pa told me he wanted me to take over teaching the younger pupils. The class is now quite large since there's a new family with five children. The ages of the children are too disparate. I told him I'm not even eighteen (I think he's forgotten my birthday's next month) and don't think the parents would be happy with someone who's never had any training teaching their children.

You can imagine his response:

"Of course they are. There's a war on! Besides, the piano's been neglected since your mother's time. You can play it for the children. They enjoy singing."

I hadn't realised it's five years since Douglas became Pa's assistant dominie. How can it be that long since Ma died? I still feel sad when I think about her.

Nell sighed. There wasn't a day she didn't think about her mother, and for her to have died so suddenly and unexpectedly made it even more tragic. Since the absence caused by her mother's death, Douglas Harrison had been working with her father, and things seemed to run pretty well at Clova School. Even though the class seldom had more than twenty pupils, the wide age range meant the older ones often got neglected, so that was where Douglas had stepped in: he concentrated on reading, writing and arithmetic with the little ones while Pa taught Classics to the older pupils.

But Douglas had enlisted as soon as war was declared and was now with the Black Watch. According to Pa, everyone missed him. He was a popular young man, her father had insisted, though Nell had never really taken to him. It was hard to pin down exactly why.

I asked Pa if there was any news of Douglas, and he said he knew only that he was with the Black Watch. He said we'd have heard if there was bad news, even though he's 'not a Clova boy'.

I did point out to Pa that he was hardly a boy. He must surely be in his late twenties by now? He just ignored me, as usual, and carried on, saying how personable and talented Douglas was, so very good with everyone.

I couldn't help but think back to the previous summer. Remember I told you how he called at the schoolhouse one lovely warm day to see if I wanted to walk with him along to Corrie Fee?

Nell did indeed remember hearing about it, in detail, from her sister. She had been surprised that Douglas had chosen a day she was away in Kirriemuir shopping and her father, in his position as session clerk, was with the minister on parish business in Cortachy.

The way her sister had told her about it, almost breathlessly, made her a little concerned. She always tried to look out for her younger sister, who was naive about everything. At only sixteen, it was the first time Effie had walked anywhere alone with a man, apart from with Pa. Effie had told her later that she and Douglas had walked along the road to Glen Doll and then through the forest towards the corrie. At Glen Doll, they'd met Mr Fraser the blacksmith, who'd tilted his cap and walked on, ever a man of few words, saying nothing. Nell often wondered if he'd told his wife afterwards about seeing them walking out together.

When they eventually got to Corrie Fee, Effie said, of course they'd stopped to gaze at the view. And that's when Douglas told her all about the terrain with the glacial erratics and moraines. She was clearly smitten by the man's knowledge – and probably by his attention. He was a good-looking man, and Effie was a young innocent.

As we looked at the stunning view, I remember he told me how he loved geology and that he'd wanted to take the older children there to tell them about the Ice Age, but Pa didn't think that was a good idea. And it actually is a long way for children, I suppose. Nell, when the war's over, you and I must walk along there. I'd forgotten just how beautiful the corrie is, like a natural amphitheatre, and that waterfall over towards the Knapps of Fee so lovely.

'When the war is over' – how often did she and the other women at Royaumont say those words when they had finished yet another gruelling day's work.

Sitting against the rock gazing at it all with our picnics was memorable. I remember all I had was some fruit cake, but he shared his pieces with me. And his water flask.

The fact that Effie was still recalling these details all these months later was more than a little unsettling. She remembered her sister had also begun to read Susan Ferrier's novel Marriage about that time. She'd clearly not got beyond the first few chapters, when the heroine was still blissfully happy, having eloped with her handsome, penniless lover. Nell remembered her gushing about how romantic it was, even though she told Effie to read on to see what happened next. Effie only saw idealised love in every relationship; evidently she hadn't scrutinised their own parents' marriage.

But back to my conversation with Pa. He told me I'd have to concentrate fully when I was a teacher and stop daydreaming. He asked me about my year over in Glen Prosen with Aunt Winifred after supper, which as usual was eaten in complete silence. Tell me, are you allowed to talk while you eat in France? I'm sure I can remember chatting at table when Ma was alive.

Yes, they did indeed talk at meals here in the abbey, though depending on how awful the day had been, sometimes silence was preferred.

I told him a little about my time with Aunt Winnie, but I don't think he was that interested; he just felt he ought to ask me something about where I'd been for the past year.

Effie had just returned from living for a year with her father's younger sister, Aunt Winnie, over in Glen Prosen. Her two elder sons had enlisted, and as a widow she'd been struggling to continue running the farm, even though the younger son, Allan, was allowed to stay on the farm to help.

I was telling him about our cousins and he asked which service Allan was going to join, so I explained that he was exempt from military service. There was still an awful lot of work with the sheep, there's hundreds of them up on the hills.

He said he'd no idea Allan was exempt at eighteen, but I told him the rules meant farms have to carry on producing food. I'd already mentioned Allan was at the farm in my letters to him, but clearly he wasn't interested enough in my news. I saw a stack of your letters to him on his desk this morning, so there's no need to worry about him not cherishing yours.

Here she goes again: Effie, the least favoured child, the one who's always in her big sister's shadow. She always was so needy.

He asked me to tell him more about the Belgian refugees. Remember that was one of the reasons I returned home, a few months after they'd settled in; I wasn't needed any more. He'd read in the paper about them arriving in Perth last October but I suppose, like everyone else, he'd never imagined they'd end up in the glens.

Yes, she'd mentioned the Belgian family at Aunt Winifred's farm in previous letters.

Pa was interested in why they were on Aunt Winnie's farm. He seems to have little idea just how much work goes into running a farm these days, which is surprising since he was brought up on one. Apart from their baby, obviously, the Belgians were all able to help out, clipping the sheep, milking the cows and so on. The older boy used to muck out the lambing sheds and help Allan with the haymaking.

I suggested to Pa that the six-year-old girl could come over to Clova School, since Mr Forbes at Prosen School doesn't speak more than very basic French and I thought it would be good for her to be taught by a French speaker. But you know Pa, it's all about him. Where would she stay? he asked. There's no way he wanted a pupil living in the schoolhouse with us. He told me I should just concentrate on our own glen and our own children and leave the Belgians to make do in Prosen.

After he'd finished his tea, he stood up and looked over at me. I thought I was going to get a telling-off for something as I always used to, even though I'd been away for a year. But no – wait till I tell you what he said. He told me the house had 'lacked a feminine touch' and he was pleased I was back. (I confess I'm not convinced that I'm too pleased.) He then said I'd 'gone away a girl and had returned a woman'.

I was taken aback, it was so unlike Pa. Was this a compliment or, I wondered, could he detect a difference in me? And it actually made me want to cry, but I pulled myself together and turned back towards the sink to do the dishes so he couldn't see my tears.

Please write soon, Nell. Your letters brighten my day.
Yours lovingly,
Effie

Chapter 3

August 1942

The sisters walked away from the congregation gathered outside the church and headed up the road. Both tall and slender, they looked almost identical from behind, their dark hair swept up under their hats and each in their best Sunday frocks and stout shoes. But from the front, the sisters were different. Nell always had a twinkle in her dark brown eyes, her lips constantly twitching into a smile, her outgoing personality evident. Effie was far more serious, anxious, a frown embedded onto her forehead. Though she had always been deemed the prettier sister when they were younger, now her wary nature somehow made her seem the less attractive one.

They strolled up the road towards the hotel and paused to take in the view down the glen. Beyond the grazing sheep they could just see the large haystacks in the fields by Inchdowrie.

"The stooks seem to be really tall this year, or is it just the perspective from here?" Effie held her palm above her eyes to block out the sun.

"No, I thought that too when I came back on the bus from Kirrie last week. I've no idea why..." Nell looked up. "Can you hear a plane, Effie?"

Her sister stopped and looked towards the hills. "Oh, is that what that low thrum is?"

"Must be, I can't see anything though. It's a bit cloudier up towards the north."

Effie grabbed her sister's arm. "It can't be a German plane, can it?"

"Don't be daft. Why would they bother with us in the glens? It's the cities they target." She tilted her head as if to hear better. "Besides, someone said German engines sound harsher." She chuckled. "Like their language."

Effie bit her lip. "So you think it's another bomber setting off for Germany?"

"Probably." Nell sighed. "This bloody war, honestly, when's it going to end?"

"Mind your language, we're about to have the minister for lunch."

Nell shrugged. "All I could think about during the sermon was if I'd put enough liquid into the rabbit stew. I hope it's not too dry."

"But you added loads of water, it can't be."

"I know, but the liquid should be red wine, not water. There's not much call for wine around here though, is there?" Nell grinned.

"We're much later than normal. We should've known that when there's a baptism, the service is always longer."

"Yes, and everyone wants to gaze adoringly at the squirming little thing afterwards. I practically had to push past Mrs Caird to get out."

"Effie, it was an adorable little six-week-old baby. I thought he was quite cute."

"If you like babies, I suppose so."

The sisters were about to cross over to the schoolhouse when they saw a black motor car coming up the glen.

"That looks like the police car. What's Tam Campbell doing up here?"

They stood on the verge and waved as the Clova policeman approached. He rolled down his window. "Nice day, ladies," he said, smiling, then continued to drive off towards Glen Doll.

"Where could he be going? Must be something important to drag him up here from Dykehead on a Sunday." Effie was frowning.

Her sister leant in. "I heard there've been poachers on the estate; maybe the laird wanted someone official to get involved."

They crossed over the road towards the schoolhouse.

"Who knows, he might be checking in on us later, asking where we got our lunchtime rabbit from." Nell winked.

"I thought you said Willie along at Braedownie shot them, but he's a farmer so…"

"I'm just teasing, Effie. Of course he's allowed to shoot them, they're on his land. Rabbits are a nuisance."

She flung open the door and breathed in. "Mmm, that actually smells all right, doesn't it?"

"All I can smell is the rice pudding," Effie said, sniffing. "I hope I didn't overdo the nutmeg." She looked over at the clock. "They'll be here soon. I'll set the table."

"Hopefully they don't linger. Remember I'm on duty over at the hotel bar at five."

"I hardly think they'll stay beyond three. We'll have run out of village chat by then."

* * *

The sisters were seeing Mr and Mrs Johnson out after lunch. The rabbit hadn't been dry at all and the rice pudding had a satisfying, nutmeg-flecked, burnished skin that the sisters both liked.

"Thank you again for lunch. It was a pleasant change," said the minister's wife. Nell had known Mrs Johnson for long enough to feel this was a great compliment.

"Yes," the minister agreed. "It was just fine. Thank you." Another paean of praise from her husband – the word 'fine' such an accolade here, Nell mused, as she thought back to the way, many years ago, that Paul described certain dishes from his home in Provence in rapturous tones.

As they all stepped out to cross the playground, the noise of a car speeding down the glen made them all turn to look.

"That's Tam Campbell the policeman. I wonder what he's doing up the glen on a Sunday," Mr Johnson said, frowning.

They all walked towards the gate and the car screeched to a

halt. The policeman got out and rushed towards them.

"I'm glad I saw you, Mr Johnson. I think you'd better know: we may need you later." The stout man breathed out slowly. "There's been an accident."

"Where?" They all leant towards Tam Campbell, who was now speaking in a loud whisper, clearly aware he could not divulge information like this lightly.

"There's been a crash up in the hills. They think an aeroplane's gone down."

The sisters gasped while Mrs Johnson raised both hands to her mouth.

"What can I do to help, Mr Campbell?" The minister's voice was grave.

"Well, depending on what – or who – we find, and in what state, we may need prayers and, well, possibly more than that, but we can't say till we've been up there."

"D'you know where it crashed?" Nell asked, glancing at Mrs Johnson, whose face was white.

Tam Campbell shook his head. "The crew of another aircraft saw it go down – somewhere over the back of Ben Tirran, they said – and they think they saw someone trying to climb out of the rear turret, but it was difficult to see anything up there."

He started to go round to the driver's side again. "I must go. I'm meeting two of the estate gamekeepers down at Wheen farm. We'll set off for Loch Wharral and see what we find."

The four of them stood in silence as he shut his door, then Nell banged on the passenger window. "Mr Campbell, you could be gone a while, have you any food to take up there?"

He shook his head.

"Give me five minutes, I'll run and make you some pieces."

"I don't have time to wait, Miss Anderson, but that's very kind."

"Let me at least fetch some bread and cheese?"

He nodded and Nell sprinted to the house and was back within a couple of minutes, thrusting a bag into the policeman's hands.

"Thank you."

"I'll be at the manse awaiting news, Constable. Let me know if I can help in any way at all," said Mr Johnson.

Tam Campbell started the engine and the police car sped off down the glen.

Effie shook her head. "Is there any way the crew could have survived, d'you think? I mean, hopefully there's at least one man if they saw someone trying to get out, but…"

Nell shrugged. "Until they get up there, they won't know. It's quite a climb; will they take the ponies?"

"I imagine so," the minister said. "They're used to carrying stags off the hills, so they can help with any…" he swallowed, "… any injured men."

He turned towards his wife, who had not moved nor said a word since the policeman gave the news. "Come, my dear, we shall await news at the manse."

"It could be a lad as young as Jimmy," she whispered, dabbing her nose with a handkerchief.

"But he is not here in Scotland, Elizabeth. Besides, this is not a time to think of ourselves." He took her arm. "Let us go. We shall sit at home and wait till we hear more."

He tipped his hat and guided his wife over the road.

The sisters watched them head towards the manse. Nell turned towards Effie. "If it's the back of Ben Tirran, it could be several hours till anyone hears anything." Nell was frowning. "It's a really steep climb up, and then there's that wide-open ridge at the top."

She turned and looked north-east towards the hills, now veiled in ominous cloud.

Chapter 4

November 1915

"I had no idea there was so much administration for the men we bring in," Nell said to Celia, the hospital clerk.

Nell had delivered six patients to the abbey earlier and was now in the clerk's office handing over the information she had about them to Celia.

"Oh, you've no idea. Each man needs at least four documents completed by the French military authorities, each one recording different pieces of information, though there's a lot of repetition. Look at these – same patient, almost identical material in each document." The clerk raised a finger. "Oh, Nell, your French is better than mine. How do I translate that?" She pointed to a couple of words one of the doctors had written in the patient's notes.

Nell shook her head. "It's Dr Gibson's handwriting that's tricky, not the translating." She peered at the letters. "Does it say 'corneal abrasion'?"

"Think so."

"Well, that would just be *l'abrasion de la cornée*, I think, though I'm wondering if *l'écorchure* is a better word." Nell frowned. Either would do, I suppose. How long does all this take you?"

"Depending on how many patients, hours sometimes."

Celia dipped her pen in the inkwell and wrote the words into the blank space, then pressed down on the document with blotting paper. "Nell, while you're here, I want to ask you something. What do you think about a Christmas party?"

"For the staff?"

"For everyone – doctors, nurses, orderlies, drivers obviously," she said. "We could wheel in any patients who can sit in wheelchairs – and also invite the locals who help out in the garage and the kitchens?" Celia beamed. "I could perform some of the play I've been writing." She was an actress and playwright when home in London.

"Sounds like a nice idea. Though most of the Scottish staff here won't be used to celebrating Christmas that much. Hogmanay's our big party time, or at least it was before the war. But yes, why not?" She shivered. "Though since we can only use electric lights in the theatre and x-ray rooms at the moment, it could be a dark old do. And cold…" She pulled her scarf tightly around her neck. "Will candles be enough to light a stage or wherever you're going to perform?"

Celia held up her hands. "Who knows what could be happening in three weeks' time. I was just wondering what you thought."

"I think it would definitely help morale," Nell said, rubbing her hands together. "Celia, do you happen to know if it's still fortnightly baths for us?" She was staring at her filthy fingernails.

"I've no idea but presume that's not changed."

"Nurse Fraser found fleas on the patients who arrived yesterday, and the nurses and orderlies are scared they're going to get them again."

She was turning to go when a loud horn reverberated outside the door and throughout the building. Celia sighed. "Another load of poor patients arriving."

"Yes, that'll be Bella's ambulance. She was a couple of hours behind me. I'd better go, I may need to go back to Creil."

She walked out and stood aside to let the stampede of nurses and orderlies rush past her. Nell watched as they lifted the stretchers out of the ambulances and began to carry them carefully inside. As they passed, she tried to hold her breath: the smell was, as usual, dreadful. One man's arm dangled off the stretcher before a nurse gently lifted it and placed it on top of his body; Nell could tell by the angle the arm lay that it would probably need amputating. Another man was clutching a bloodstained cloth to his head, his face contorted in pain.

On the next stretcher, a man was trying to sit up. He was delirious, yelling that he had to get out, to leave – presumably he meant the fighting, not the hospital. She put her hand over her nose as he passed. These men had come straight from the trenches, and they stank, primarily because they hadn't washed in weeks, but there was also the pervasive smell of terror and despair. She tried not to look as the stretcher passed close by and the orderlies attempted to restrain the poor man.

She stepped outside and took a gulp of cold fresh air. Bella was picking up a cloth from the dashboard. She waved when she saw Nell.

"Will there be many more coming in?"

Bella nodded. "I had to leave some there. I was about to go back once I've given the cabin a good clean out."

"I'll go," Nell said.

"But you were driving all night."

"It's fine. I'll set off now. Let them know I'm on my way, would you?"

* * *

"Were all the men badly injured, or are some going to be able to walk out of here fully healed?" Paul asked as they sat in the candlelight in the cold dark kitchen.

Nell put down her fork. "Dr Gibson hasn't seen them yet, but when I was in the ward just now, Dr Nicholl was saying she reckons there's one who'll need to be operated on. They were just waiting for the x-ray to process." She didn't want to mention that the doctor had told her the patient would probably lose his leg below the knee.

"Can the x-ray machine also detect bullets and shrapnel and things in the body?"

"More or less, yes."

"You know I can't poach a whole salmon now, even if I could get one? The fish kettles from the kitchen are in the x-ray room."

"What?"

"Yes, they're used as cisterns to develop the x-ray films."

Nell shook her head. "I had no idea. Well, I'm sure you have other ways of cooking salmon, in case you ever get any." She scraped her plate clean with a hunk of bread. She sighed. "That was good, Paul. Is it the garlic that makes your beef stew so much better than ours back home?"

Paul chuckled. "How would I know, Hélène? I was brought up with garlic; all my life I've had it. Thank God I started growing it out the back; it's not as easy to get it here in the north." He shrugged. "Well, nothing is easy to get now. Though did I tell you that Monique, who delivers from the bakers every morning, is managing to get some extra loaves for us now?"

"Is she the pretty young one with the curly fair hair?"

"I suppose she's quite attractive, yes."

Nell finished her drink, then got to her feet.

"When are you next going to Creil?"

"Tomorrow, I think, but I might have a later start since I've driven for three days back-to-back now. The roads – if you can call them roads – are terrible, so full of potholes, you just can't avoid them. I'm used to being flung around in my seat, but I feel so sorry for the patients being hurled around in the back."

"How near are you to the battlefields, Hélène?"

"They seem to be closer now than when I started as a driver a few months ago. You can see bomb holes not far from the road now, and at night it's all a bit scary." She sighed. "But still, at least I can drive away from it all; the men can't."

Paul hobbled around the table to her. He grabbed her hand just as she was about to put on her other driving glove. "Hélène, please be careful. If anything happened to you…" He shook his head.

"Don't be silly, Paul, I'm fine. They make strong women in the glens, you know." She started towards the door but turned around. "Oh, Celia is hoping to organise a party at Christmas.

That should lift everyone's spirits, don't you think?"

He nodded. "Will there be dancing?"

Nell tipped her head back, laughing. "I hope so, but probably more sedate than what I'm used to back home. Ceilidhs are pretty raucous. But when I come to think about it, I know one of the doctors plays the fiddle. We usually have an accordion playing at our dances too..."

"I can play the accordion – my father has one at home, he taught me. If I can get hold of one, could you teach me some of your Scottish tunes?"

"That's more my sister's speciality; she's much better at music than I am, but I'm sure I could find someone who can read music." She yawned. "I must get off to bed now. Oh, would you be able to make any special food for the party, with all the rationing?"

He looked around the kitchen. "Something sweet and fragrant would be good, different from all the usual savoury flavours. I know, I'll make dessert *fougasse*, we have that at Christmas in Arles. But I'll need more sugar than I'm allowed, and also orange flower water, but I can try to make that myself." He smiled again. "As you say, Hélène, a party should raise the spirits."

She said good night, then turned towards the door before setting off towards the chauffeuses' dormitory above the garage. She so hoped she would sleep for hours and wake up refreshed, but the blaring noise from the bell was bound to wake her in the middle of the night, alerting some poor chauffeuse to rush to her ambulance. She just hoped it would not be her.

Chapter 5

August 1942

Nell walked out of the gate and up to the hotel. All her life she'd lived next door. And though her sister was rather snooty about her evening job working in a bar, Nell enjoyed it. It was good to be in the place her mother had spent so much time in her childhood.

Because her father had never been keen on going into the hotel when she and Effie were young, they'd got out of the habit, even though it was mere minutes from their front door. She remembered he had discouraged Ma from popping in to see the staff, saying it was not becoming for someone who was now a teacher at the school. Honestly, the way their father described the tiny village school, you'd think he was the head teacher at Eton.

When the man who'd run the bar enlisted, Nell had offered to help out after she got back from her post rounds. Effie was horrified. "You can't possibly work in a bar, Nell. What will everyone say?"

"Effie, don't be such a snob. It's the war, everyone's doing different jobs. It'll be fun, I'll get all the local gossip," she'd said, winking. "You know what they're like after a few pints."

Nell wanted to add that her sister had never gone further than Glen Prosen to help the war effort, and surely that had not been exactly hard, though the farm work must have been challenging. They were never really in any danger, in the glens, of being bombed or attacked by the Germans.

She opened the main door of the hotel and let out an elderly lady wearing a greyish brown fur hat. It looked like the fur was mountain hare – dear Lord, surely that was rather hot to wear in August? Nell was about to speak to her, but the woman pulled the hat down over her ears and strode along the road towards the bus stop without glancing back.

"Afternoon, Helen," said Mrs Mackie the cook, who was buttoning up her coat as she rushed towards the door.

"I thought you were always off on Sundays?"

"Usually, but we were stuck. There's no one else to do lunch today and they were sending down some guests from the big house since their chef's sick. I couldn't let Mr Noble down."

Nell shook her head. "I bet you've never been ill in your life."

Mrs Mackie smiled. "No time to be off my work. Just like your granddad. When I trained in his kitchen all those years ago, he was never off sick. He wasn't always punctual, admittedly, but he always got the dinners ready in the end." She smiled and grabbed her hat from the stand. "Bye then, love. Have a good evening. Hope the bar's not too busy and you can get home early. Are you all right to put up the blackouts?"

"No problem." Nell turned to go, then paused. "Mrs Mackie, there's been no news of an accident, has there?"

"What sort of accident?"

"Oh, nothing, it was just something I heard earlier." Nell didn't want any misinformation to get out and for locals to start worrying. Everyone in the glen knew someone who was involved in the war in some capacity. "See you later."

Nell opened the pub door and entered what had always been called the 'Climbers' Bar'. It wasn't anything like the smart bars in bigger hotels, but it was cosy and clean. In the summer they had lots of hikers coming in after climbing Driesh and Mayar or walking over from Braemar on Jock's Road. They'd come in for a welcome drink before they set off home. Now, in wartime, there were far fewer climbers. And more of those who did come had a sense of guilt, even though they were too old – or too young – to enlist. They felt it was an indulgence to be in the beautiful hills when so many people they knew were endangering their lives in the war.

She went to fetch the hurricane lamps from the reception where old Mr Noble sat.

"Good evening, Miss Anderson. Thank you for helping us out once more."

"Pleasure," she said as he handed her two lamps. It was as if the owner was unaware that she was in fact paid to run the bar, though admittedly it was a pittance.

"You shouldn't need them till after eight o'clock. Sunset isn't till 9. But make sure the blackouts are in place first."

Nell smiled weakly. Even though she had known the hotel owner for years, he still treated her as if she were a child. "I will," she said, aware that he too seemed ignorant about the possible crash. She set off along the corridor to open up the bar.

Soon the customers started to come in, and she began to pull pints and wash the glasses in between orders. When one of the men teased her that it was so gloomy he couldn't see his beer, she realised she couldn't delay putting up the blackouts any longer. She headed over to the windows, and as usual the men rushed to help her secure the wooden shutters, even though she was perfectly capable of doing it herself.

"Wait till I've lit the lamps," she shouted, as two of them started on the final window.

***

Most customers had already left, leaving only two stalwarts sitting at the bar near the beer, the drams and the light.

"So you heard, Nell, that there might have been a crash in the hills?"

"Well…" She turned round to replace the top on a bottle of whisky.

"Were you outside about lunchtime?" one of the locals asked. "You might have heard a plane going overhead?"

"Yes, just after church. But it sounded all right." She didn't want to tell these two men, who'd had several pints, about the conversation with the police constable.

The men cowered in, their faces ghoulish in the lamplight.

"That lad who was in the corner over there at opening time, remember? He left about an hour ago to get back to Dundee. He was up Ben Tirran and had headed along the ridge to the north of Loch Wharral. He said that while he was walking he was convinced he heard a loud bang and then some sort of smashing or crashing sound."

"But I told him it was really windy up there, and misty; it could have been anything. It could even have been thunder from further north."

"So you think there was a crash then?"

The men leant over the bar towards her. "As we were walking along here, we met the head gamekeeper's wife. She said her husband had been called away urgently – with PC Campbell." He stretched out his hands. "It all makes sense now."

She sighed.

"And," one of the men whispered, "I reckon it was a German plane."

"Why?" Nell frowned. "Could it not have been an RAF plane flying overhead? Doing some high-level training or something?"

The men downed their pints. "We just don't know, do we?"

They struggled to put on their jackets and headed for the door.

"Make sure you only open the door a crack when you leave, don't let any light out," she yelled after them.

"There's no light in here anyway, Nell," one of them muttered as he stumbled over a chair leg and staggered towards the door.

Chapter 6

December 1915

In the run up to the Christmas party, Nell was even more exhausted than usual. The injuries were not just from shelling and artillery, but now more and more from gas. The gassed men could hardly breathe and there was no point in driving slowly to avoid the ruts and holes all along the roads. In fact, the chauffeuses had to drive as fast as possible; the men needed oxygen. The gas also caused a lot of eye injuries, which meant the men could not stand light of any kind. When her ambulance finally arrived at the hospital, emerging from the darkness in the back of the ambulance and into the light was agonising for them. There were wails of anguish while they wondered if they had been blinded.

The orderlies worked so hard dealing with truly awful scenes, but a couple of them had confessed to Nell at breakfast the day before that emptying the crachoirs had become the worst thing they had to do. These were for the gassed soldiers to spit and cough into, and both the sounds from the ward and the contents of the spittoons were indescribably vile.

However horrific these injuries were, shell shock was another matter. The doctors and nurses had begun to notice that when soldiers appeared to be healing, their mental state was often dire, even for those who had not suffered head injuries. Some men could not speak, could barely eat, their hands shook so much. But it was the glazed blankness in their eyes that Nell found most chilling.

* * *

By early December, all the staff were weary, so the prospect of having some kind of celebration at Christmas would bring welcome festive cheer. Paul had just heard he was officially seconded to Royaumont as chef for the duration of the war, and Nell could not believe the difference in him. Even his limp seemed less pronounced as he planned his meals and managed his budgets.

"Apart from the desserts I've planned, what shall we eat at the party, Hélène?" he asked, his dark eyes twinkling by the candlelight as they stood with their backs against the large range. Nell was cold after her night shift and she'd come into the kitchen to try to warm up.

"Can you get turkeys anywhere?"

"I'm going to try. And if so, I could stuff them with veal, pork, walnuts and thyme... if I can get the meat. I have plenty of walnuts and thyme."

"Oh, well that sounds delicious, Paul. Back home it's usually chestnuts and sausage meat for the turkey, but yours will be wonderful."

She turned around to look at him. He was losing the haggard look he'd had since he arrived so badly injured. His face was less sallow, his cheeks now had a healthy glow. "You look so much better these days, Paul." She smiled. "You must be pleased now you know you don't have to go back to the Front?"

"It's not about that. I feel guilty that I'm still here. But I'm delighted I can carry on working at Royaumont. At least I feel I'm helping the other soldiers a little."

"More than a little, Paul. They love your food. The ones who've been here a while can remember the difference in the meals and how much better the food is now. Your meat dishes are so good and your potatoes are the best."

"Maman's always had a way with potatoes. She adds a good sprinkling of herbes de Provence just before they roast. She's great with meat too, but it's so difficult to get decent meat these days..." He shrugged. "But there's a farmer nearby who has turkeys, so I am hopeful for those."

"You must miss your parents, Paul."

He nodded. "Leave just isn't possible; Arles is too far. I'm resigned to not seeing them for a while, which makes me sad, but letters help of course."

"Oh, I agree. I've just got another from my sister. I'm looking forward to reading it tonight."

He grabbed her hand. "Though I miss my family, I feel so blessed to have you here, Hélène." He gazed at her. "Some mornings, when I wake up, I momentarily forget I have only one leg. Then as I swing my good leg over the side and the memory comes flooding back, the only thing that makes me able to face the day is the thought of seeing you."

He released her hand and raised his to stroke her cheek with a tender touch.

"Well, it's lovely to have such a good friend," Nell said, unsure how to react to the caress. To her, Paul was a friend, nothing more. She pulled herself away and forced a smile. "See you later, Paul. Thanks for allowing me to warm up against the cooker."

"Anytime, Hélène," he said as she headed out the door.

* * *

Dear Nell,

At last, winter has come to the glen. I am looking out to snow flurries and it's beginning to lie. The branches are already clothed in white. School finishes in a week and I have to say I shall be glad. Teaching can be so rewarding, but working in the same room as our father every day is wearing. This morning, while I was on one side of the classroom with the little ones, I had to listen to him chanting 'Amo, amas, amat, amamus, amatis, amant' while beating his tawse in time against the desk. I really wish he wouldn't do that; it terrifies the younger children. Actually, it scares all the children, especially since it's more likely to be the older ones who're given the belt. Despite having the younger ones at the other end of the classroom, they're so easily distracted. I have to reassure them that he won't belt them.

I do think Pa's lack of patience is even worse than usual. He has always had a temper – well, we saw that in the way he treated Ma sometimes.

Nell shivered as the memories came back – the unpleasant evenings when their mother began to answer him back when he criticised them. She always stood up to him, until the day she no longer could.

And I just don't think it's conducive to teaching. I've tried to tell him he mustn't take it out on the children, but of course he never listens to me.

When the snow began today, coming down in thick, solid flakes, the children were so excited and straining to see out the window. But he just bellowed at them to sit down and they all slunk back into their seats.

Remember how you and I used to love the snow when we were younger, Nell? I completely understand the little ones being desperate to get out to play in it, but he was having none of it till break time. He seems to find joy in very little these days.

I was just finishing up with my five-, six- and seven-year-olds, shortly before playtime, when I saw him put down the tawse, thankfully, and storm towards me. I could almost feel the little ones tremble. He said we would assess the situation during break time, in case we needed to finish school early. Usually it's just the ones from far up the glen who need sending home early if the weather's bad, but today the whole glen was covered in white.

Nell was lying in bed, reading by candlelight in the dorm above the garages. It was so cold she could see her breath. But there was no snow yet, thank God. She had no idea how the ambulances would manage if there was deep snow.

I worry about some of the pupils being cold. So few of them have good coats. Only Chrissie Muir has a warm coat, scarf, hat and boots. And as you know that's because her mother's a maid up at the big house and she gets cast-offs from Miss Amelia. Oh, guess what: her governess, Miss Carnon, came along at the end of school yesterday to ask Pa for advice on which books to use to teach Latin to Amelia and Master William. I thought he'd be livid, but he was affable and helpful, bringing her into the classroom to show her our selection. She is an attractive woman, it has to be said. In fact, I often wondered if she was sweet on Douglas and that actually her coming to ask Pa's advice was her way of seeing him, before the war. I still think of him often you know, Nell. I can't help it.

When would she put that man into her past and forget all about him? Though Effie hadn't told her, as well as that day up at Corrie Fee, Nell had found out they'd met up once more before school started, and again when she and their father were out. The hotel housekeeper said she was sure she had seen them heading up to Loch Brandy together. When Nell had confronted her about it, she denied ever having seen him.

Apart from no winter coats, little Sandy Smith didn't even have boots on today. When I asked where they were – I was sure he usually wore them – he told me his brother Alec needed them because he started his job up at the big house today. Apparently they told him he could start when he was ten. He said there were no more boots or shoes at home that fitted; his sister Janet has really tatty hand-me-down boots, but she's smaller than him. You'll remember they live along the road towards Glen Doll, so I was starting to worry about him trudging home in the deep snow barefoot.

But then I looked out the window and noticed the blacksmith's horse was tied up outside the hotel. I ran over to ask if he could take Sandy home on the horse and he agreed. He said he was just about to finish up in the stables and he'd be right over. Sandy was so excited to be given a lift home on the back of a horse. His sister insisted on joining him, of course. And Mr Fraser almost smiled, Nell – he seemed delighted to have a couple of children on the back of his horse. I've never seen him do more than grunt or scowl.

Nell grinned. The blacksmith was indeed a curmudgeonly man, always grumbling. His wife was so sweet though, it was very odd. But then, look at her own parents. Ma had been so caring and kind, though also forthright. And Pa was always strict, uncompromising, looking for fault.

Once we got home, Pa said we'd have to decide what to do, whether to keep the school closed if the snow was too thick for the children to get in. As he said, the weather forecast in The Courier was not likely to mention the glens specifically, so we just have to hope it won't last too long. It's a pity as I was going to play them Christmas carols on the piano after playtime.

After we'd finished our tea, Pa said he had something to discuss with me. He started by saying of course we don't celebrate Christmas as they do down south, but still, he was thinking of inviting his sister Winifred over from Glen Prosen for a few days over Christmas and the New Year. He thought it'd be good for me to have some female company, while he could catch up with his younger sister. He'd not seen her for such a long time.

You perhaps can't understand why I was hesitant about that. It was fine while I was living over at her farm, far away, but I just don't feel I could have her here for that long, in case anything was said about my stay. My time there was perfectly adequate, but it was hard work and, I have to admit, our aunt and I never always saw eye to eye. So I told him she'd be far too busy with the farm and couldn't possibly leave Prosen for such a long time.

He said why couldn't Allan and the Belgians run things in her place? I reminded him Allan is only eighteen and what a huge undertaking it would be as they've hundreds of sheep now – and there are also four cows to be milked twice a day. And Aunt Winnie could not possibly expect the Belgians to run her farm if she wasn't there.

But he ignored me as usual, and the last thing I saw was Pa sitting at the writing desk, inviting his sister over for Christmas. I now hope the snow lasts and she can't make it. I'm pretty sure she won't. In fact, perhaps even the post won't get through if it continues to snow heavily and she won't even receive the invitation. I also mentioned to him, what if she made it over here then got stuck? Remember those floods we had over New Year one year?

Nell thought back to that winter when they were little, when the South Esk had flooded and practically the whole glen, from Gella all the way up towards Glen Doll, was covered in water. Luckily their house is up the hillside a little, but so many of the other homes were flooded. There was no way of getting from the schoolhouse to anywhere other than the hotel except by boat, and there were obviously none of those up the glen. That was one of the few times Pa didn't mind them going to the hotel as they were beginning to run out of food.

You can imagine his response when I tried to argue that the invitation wasn't a good idea.

"'You never used to answer back, Euphemia,",' he said, then went on and on about the fact that he is my father and he makes the decisions for our family, diminished though it is at the moment.

And I thought back to when I'd just returned from my stay in Prosen and he called me a woman. Do you remember I told you that? Now he was back to treating me like a child – or worse, like one of his pupils… though thankfully it's a while since he's used the tawse outside the classroom.

Nell, there's nothing more to say; that's all my news. I so look forward to yours when you have a moment.

Yours lovingly,
Effie

Chapter 7

August 1942

A loud knock at the door made Nell jump. The bar had been so silent since the last customers had left. Maybe it was just the wind. She picked up the glass she'd just washed and had started to wipe it when there were more knocks. There was no mistaking it, there was definitely someone at the door.

The keepers from the estate down the road must have forgotten something. Honestly, why did they allow themselves to get so drunk? She moved the lamp above the tables to see what they could have left, but saw nothing. Why was she so anxious? The suggestion that a German plane had crashed was ridiculous. If, sadly, there'd been a crash, it would have been one of ours. And when she thought of that possibility, she felt wretched.

There was another hammering at the door. Perhaps there were several men there. Why was her heart beating so fast? She had seen so many terrible things while she was at Royaumont; she was frightened of very little. But somehow, something like this happening in her home village was scary.

Carrying the lamp, she ambled towards the dark corridor and headed for the door. The knocking was now starting to sound feeble. Perhaps it was just one man there, one of the keepers, after all. She set the lamp down at her feet and reached into her pocket for the key. It was her job to lock up when she was on bar duty; Mr Noble was always in bed early.

She put the key in the lock and turned it. She pulled the door towards her and peered into the gloom. A figure was standing there, stock still. As she tried to make out his face, she realised his fist was raised. Dear God, he was going to hit her. She jumped back and leant down to grab the lamp, but just then the man slumped forward and collapsed on top of it. There was a tinkling sound of breaking glass, a mighty thud as he hit the floor and a pungent smell of paraffin.

It was now pitch-black inside. She pushed the door wide to try to see by the moonlight. In the faint light she could make out a uniform. And a flying helmet. He was clearly from the crash. But was he British or German?

She leant over him and put her fingers to the inside of his wrist. She could feel a pulse; thankfully he was still alive. She had to get help, and soon. She staggered along the dark corridor, hands on the walls at either side, till she found the stairs. She went as fast as she could up to Mr Noble's bedroom and hammered on his door. Soon a bleary voice said, "I'm coming, wait a minute."

The door opened and he stood there in his dressing gown, a candle in his hand.

"There's a soldier downstairs, he's injured. We need to get the doctor."

He followed her down the stairs, both of them trying desperately not to trip and fall in the poor light from the candle. When they reached the reception, he shuffled around behind the desk searching for another hurricane lamp. He lit it quickly, then motioned for her to follow.

Together they headed for the door, Mr Noble leading the way. The man was still there. He was now moving a little and his eyelids fluttered open.

"Don't move," shouted Mr Noble. "Who are you?"

There was a silence and Nell bent down and asked, *"Wer sind Sie?"*

Mr Noble turned towards her and even in the shadows, she could see panic in his eyes.

They both stared down as the man raised his shoulders and opened his mouth.

"Plane went down. No survivors," he whispered, screwing up his eyes. "Just me."

He collapsed once more onto the floor. Thank God – the man

was British, not German.

"Have you got a first aid kit?" Nell asked Mr Noble, lifting the man's head. "And can we have more light on? I can try to see if there's anything I could do before the doctor gets here."

"I'll light some more lamps, then go and phone Dr Geddes." He looked up at the clock. Hopefully he won't be in bed yet."

Once the lamps were lit, Nell could see the man properly. He still had his helmet on, his uniform was torn and there was mud all over it. How on earth did he get down here by himself? It's challenging enough coming down the hills and into the village when you're uninjured.

He had drifted back into unconsciousness, and she'd just begun loosening his clothing when Mr Noble arrived. "The doctor's on his way. He should be here in half an hour or so. That's an RAF uniform, isn't it? I'll go and see if I can find a number for the nearest air base and let them know."

Nell nodded and continued to tend to the man, tilting his head back so he could breathe more easily. There didn't seem to be any broken limbs, though she didn't want to move him much until the doctor arrived. She went to grab a blanket from one of the unoccupied ground-floor bedrooms and enveloped him in it, trying to keep him warm.

She recalled what they used to do at Royaumont if someone was sliding in and out of consciousness and began to speak loudly to him, trying to keep him awake. She remembered patients who looked as if they had already died telling her weeks later, once they had recovered, that they recalled hearing a soothing female voice, even when they were deemed unconscious.

Soon he began to look agitated, his mouth was opening as if he wanted to speak, he was trying to lift his hand. She asked if she could get him anything, and he kept tapping his side pocket, so she removed his hand gently and put hers inside. She pulled out a tattered photo of a dark-haired woman; was it his wife? She was certainly too young to be his mother. She showed it to him, and he flicked away her hand. When she tried to put it back in his pocket, he shook his head.

"Keep it safe," he hissed. "Don't let them see it."

She placed it in her pocket and kept watch as he drifted in and out of consciousness again, but she kept up her inane prattle until the doctor arrived. Dr Geddes had just begun to examine him when two men from the RAF base at Edzell arrived. Once he had been placed on a stretcher, he was taken away in the RAF vehicle to the hospital in Stracathro with the doctor following close behind. As she stood at the door peering into the darkness, listening to the last rumbles of the engines along the road out of the glen, she patted her pocket where she'd tucked in the photo. Heading across the road for home, she felt exhausted and yet strangely exhilarated. It took her back to Royaumont and the feeling of doing something useful.

* * *

The next day, Nell had just changed out of her postal uniform when she heard a knock on the door.

"Come in, door's not locked," she shouted, looking around for her sister.

Effie appeared from the back door, a pile of firewood in her arms.

Nell went to the front door and saw Bessie, the district nurse, propping her bike against the wall. "Want a cup of tea, Bessie? I was just about to put the kettle on," said Effie, washing her hands after having deposited the wood in the basket by the fire.

"I'd love one, thanks, I'm parched. What a warm day."

"Presume the midges are out in force at the top of the glen?"

Bessie nodded. "Luckily they never bother me, don't know why. Maybe tiny insects just don't find me attractive."

The three women sat down at the table. "Though every time I see a child with nits," Bessie said, "I can't stop scratching my head. All the Craik children have them, you can practically see them jumping about in their hair." She shuddered. "I see so many unpleasant things as a nurse, but honestly, there's something quite hideous about head lice."

Effie scratched the nape of her neck where her hair hung loose. "You've got me at it now, Bessie." She grinned. "Thank goodness there's two more weeks till school's back. Have you heard how the harvest is going?"

"Pretty well I think, nearly all finished. You can see the farms further down the glen already have their stooks. The fine weather's been such a bonus." Effie was carrying on as if nothing had happened last night. Nell tried to interrupt and ask Bessie if she'd heard anything, but her sister continued.

"That may mean all the children will be here for the first day of school for once, and not helping their parents get the harvest in."

"How many pupils are you expecting this term?"

"Only ten, but to be honest, that's enough when someone as disruptive as Johnnie Craik's in the class." She rolled her eyes.

"I can understand that," said Bessie, delving into her sizeable bag. "One of the reasons I popped in – apart from the fact I was gasping for a drink – was to see if you needed anything for the school first aid kit? I seem to have lots here and new supplies are coming later this week."

"Funnily enough, I was just looking at it yesterday while I was starting to get things ready in the classroom. We're low on dressings and iodine, but I was going to order them. Won't you get into trouble if you give me some of yours?"

Bessie grinned. She'd been Effie's friend since primary school and knew her well. "Always a stickler for rules, Miss Anderson." She riffled around in her bag. "There's a war on, Effie, we have to help each other out." She brought out some gauze dressings and a bottle of iodine.

"You've known me since we were five, Bessie – I've always been Miss Goody Two-Shoes."

Nell gave her sister a sidelong glance and raised an eyebrow.

She coughed. "You'll have heard about the crash, Bessie?"

She nodded.

"Everyone in the village was talking about it yesterday," said Effie. "And then last night, Nell…"

"I can tell Bessie myself," Nell interrupted. "I was shutting up the bar when the survivor arrived at the door, then collapsed. So we called out the doctor. Has Dr Geddes mentioned anything today? Presume you've seen him?"

"Yes. Well, that's also why I called in. I met Dr Geddes up at Mrs Lindsay's earlier. He was going to pop in to see the minister after he left her, so they'll know by now at the manse." She downed her tea and pushed the cup and saucer away. "You know how Ben Tirran is up here," she said, tracing an outline of a map on the table with her finger, "and Loch Wharral's here," she said, pointing. "Well, it looks as if the plane was on a test flight from RAF Lossiemouth before a mission over Germany planned for later on Sunday. Something happened with a part of the cowling I think he said – it dislodged, damaging a propeller, and there was engine failure."

"So it did actually crash up there in the hills?" Effie asked.

"I told you that this morning, Effie." Nell shook her head; honestly, her sister was exasperating.

"Dr Geddes said Tam Campbell had told him the pilot might have been trying a forced landing, but then obviously…" she shrugged. "Well, then it crashed." She continued to trace a line with her finger on the wooden table. "On Muckle Cairn, somewhere over here."

"What kind of plane was it?"

"A Wellington bomber."

"So what did they do? Did Tam Campbell not have a couple of other men with him?"

"Yes, two of the gamekeepers from the Cortachy estate. They found four bodies. I think that's why it's taken so long for anyone to hear what happened, they had to let the families know, obviously. Three of them were Canadian air force, one RAF."

She pointed her finger at Nell. "But there was that one survivor, who you saw, Nell. Did he say anything?"

"Not really, he was in shock."

"Was he the pilot?" Effie asked.

"Don't think so, I didn't see wings on his uniform."

Bessie shook her head. "I think Dr Geddes said he was the rear gunner, I suppose that's how he could have got out relatively unscathed. But he must have been injured?"

"I gave him a quick look over but couldn't really see if anything was broken. It was too dark, and I didn't want to move him till the doctor arrived. But now you're saying it crashed up at Muckle Cairn, that's a hell of a climb down to the hotel. How on earth did he manage that?"

"Would he have seen lights?"

"There shouldn't have been any lights, I had the blackouts in place, but I have to say, Mr Noble sometimes forgets he also needs to put them up when he goes to bed upstairs. So the man could have seen those if he was walking down from Loch Brandy, his bedroom's at the back."

"So where is he now? Still at Stracathro?" Effie asked.

Bessie nodded. "Yes, Dr Geddes said he's still in hospital."

"Hope he's all right." Effie sighed. "That's the first time the war's come to the glen."

"I know," Bessie agreed. "It must have taken them ages to get up there and then to come across that awful sight. I wonder if they had to leave the bodies there or if they managed to bring them down yesterday." She shook her head.

"Nell, you've been up there. How long would it take to get down from Muckle Cairn to the hotel?"

"No idea, if they were bringing down four bodies. I wonder if they were taken on stretchers or on ponies." She shuddered. "And the survivor… I reckon he must have gone from the crash site along to Green Hill then dropped down the east ridge, skirting

Loch Brandy, then straight down to the hotel from there."

"And it was getting really dark by the time he got to the hotel, surely?"

"Yes, I had no idea at first if he was one of ours or a German. I couldn't really see."

Bessie let out a long breath, then pushed back her chair. "I'd better go, I've got to go and see old Bill Fraser at the smithy."

"Thanks for the first aid things, Bessie. And for filling us in with the news." Effie shook her head. "Just awful, so sad."

Bessie opened the door and pulled her bike off the wall. She put her bag in the basket at the front and was about to step onto the saddle when she turned back. "What happens to that man now, Nell, the survivor? Presume they have to let his family know. I wonder if he's got a wife or girlfriend. Would anyone from his family be allowed to visit?"

"Who knows," Nell said. And as they watched Bessie wobble down the road on her bike, she could not help thinking about the photo she had been given the night before, and the words that were written on the back.

Chapter 8

December 1915

Nell had just returned from Creil and had spent some time helping the nurses and orderlies unload the injured. Instead of only a few having symptoms of being gassed, today every single man had them. It was shocking to see and hear, and as she walked into the abbey to have a wash, she looked up at the stunning vaulting and elaborately decorated pillars of the ancient building. She usually smiled as she marvelled at the beauty of the abbey, but today she just felt despair. How many more men would die or be injured in such hideous circumstances?

She passed a couple of orderlies helping two soldiers out into the December sunshine. It was still not as cold as the previous winter, though that could all change soon. "*Salut*," she said, greeting the men. One was Senegalese, one from Algeria. They both smiled in return. Though the majority of their patients were French, there were now many French colonial troops, as well as some from the Foreign Legion. She had not yet met any British soldiers at Royaumont, though as the fighting got nearer, the doctors all said it was only a matter of time.

She headed for the kitchen, hoping to get something to eat as she'd not eaten since the night before.

"How are the preparations for the Christmas party going, Paul?"

He lifted his head from a large pan and shouted over to her, "*Pas mal*, Hélène, but those turkeys I managed to get are ancient birds, I'm going to have to give them a long slow roast."

"They'll be wonderful in your hands, Paul," she said, coming towards him. He hobbled towards her, holding onto the table for support.

"You're not using your stick. That's good, isn't it?"

"I'm trying, I'm determined to walk normally as soon as I can." He winked, then lifted his arm and clenched his fist.

Nell stepped back as two of his cooks stepped in front of her, carrying a huge roasting tin between them.

"Careful, don't let the jus slop over the side," he told them as they passed. "Thank you." He was always so polite and kind to his cooks, unlike the chefs Paul used to work with before the war. He told her all they ever did was shout; they'd been terrifying.

"Am I right in thinking you Scots will want some kind of thickened gravy with the turkey?" he asked, smiling at her.

"Would you not usually do that?"

"We'd never make a flour-based sauce from the juices, we'd just add some wine and reduce it down a bit, then serve it as it is."

"Well, we are rather partial to gravy, that's true. But as I said, everyone will be more than happy with whatever you produce, Paul. I presume you'd never make gravy in Provence?"

He chuckled. "Why on earth would we want a thick, heavy sauce when the sun is shining and warm on your neck?"

"Even in winter?"

"Even at Christmas the skies are usually beautifully blue, and it seldom gets really cold. Well, certainly not in Arles. These grey skies here in the north get me down." He sighed.

"What news from your family?"

"My sister's still young at fifteen, but she hopes next year to start training as a nurse."

"And what does your mother think about that?"

"Maman is all for it. Papa, though, thinks she should just stay at home and help them with the farm. The olive harvest was difficult this year, there were too few people to make the oil. What about your family back in Scotland? What's your sister's latest news?"

Nell sighed and leant in towards her friend. "She's mentioned that man Douglas Harrison again, remember I told you about him? I had hoped she'd forgotten him. But she wrote in last week's letter how Pa said one of the Black Watch battalions had moved to Mesopotamia, but she was sure Douglas's battalion had gone to France. She never asked Pa if he knew if Douglas was in France; he might wonder why she was asking about him. I thought she'd moved on from the crush she clearly had, but it seems not."

"You're not keen on him, are you?"

"Not really, it's difficult to pinpoint why. He could be a bit cocky, maybe it's that." She grabbed a piece of bread from the counter and started chewing.

"I can make you something to eat if you want, Hélène?"

"It's fine," she said. "Thanks. Oh, but Effie's other news is that it's started snowing in the glen. There's already quite a lot of snow lying. In fact, I'm amazed the mail coach is getting through to Clova with the post. Effie's actually delighted; they'd had to close school early the afternoon she wrote to me."

"I've only seen snow here in the north, not in Arles."

Nell nodded. "Effie said they'd spent most of the weekend drying out the sphagnum moss the children had collected the week before, for the Red Cross; it's for bandages. So she feels she's helping the war effort somehow."

She looked up at the clock. "I have to go and get ready. I'm hoping there'll be some hot water left after Bella's washed. I can't go to the party with dirty hair."

"Everyone's got dirty hair here, Hélène," Paul said, chuckling. The hiss of liquid on the hot stove made him turn around, and she watched him lurch towards the cooker to rescue a pan of stock that was boiling over.

* * *

Celia was rushing around the room, lighting as many lamps as possible for the party. They had erected a makeshift stage for her play, which Nell had helped translate into French. Celia had insisted she would play most of the parts, even though her French accent was terrible. But because she was a professional playwright and actress in London, the doctors said she could do whatever she wanted. Anything vaguely entertaining would be such a relief.

Dinner had been superb, and only one alarm bell sounded during the meal. Edna had insisted she would do the drive over to Creil since she'd been off sick for the last few days. Celia and her fellow actresses performed the first act of her new play, and even though Nell was sure none of the men had a clue what was going on, they seemed to love watching the women dressed up and performing on stage.

Then a gramophone was brought out, and Dr Gibson sat there putting on record after record while the nurses and orderlies danced with any of the patients able to dance. Some of them were even whirled about in their wheelchairs.

Nell had just returned one of the Senegalese men to his seat when she saw Paul coming her way. He was smiling and she grinned back. "What a triumph dinner was." She gave him a kiss on his cheek. "Are they finished clearing up the kitchen?"

"Nearly. They won't be long."

He reached out his arm to her and took her hand. "I've been practising dancing. It's not easy, but if you don't mind, shall we give it a try?"

They shifted uneasily across to the dance floor, and when the next tune began, they began to move in time to the music. "You see, it's not that hard, is it, Paul?"

He had left his stick at the side so she was supporting him a little, but they were moving slowly. His face was full of concentration, as if he was terrified he would tumble.

"Don't worry, Paul, I won't let you fall," she said, beaming. She had a good grip on his waist and shoulder.

"I feel safe when you're holding onto me," he said, hobbling around the floor.

At the end of the tune, he stayed put, clearly wanting another dance.

"I've got to go and ask another patient now, Paul. Sorry, we've got so many patients to dance with. But you can dance with Bella?"

"I don't want to dance with anyone else," he said, leaning in towards her lips.

She turned her head a little to let him kiss her cheek, then walked him over towards his stick. "Aren't you getting your accordion out for later?"

He nodded and limped off towards the door. Nell sighed: he was such a good friend, the person she confided in most at the hospital, but there was nothing more to it. She headed towards one of the French patients whose head was almost completely covered in bandages; there were two holes for his eyes.

She took his hand, and they started to dance. He was light on his feet and could really move well. She laughed as he twirled her around and, as she was spun gracefully towards the door, she spotted Paul standing there glaring at them, his whole body slouched over his stick with the air of a dejected man.

Chapter 9

August 1942

She sat on the grassy knoll above Loch Brandy and gazed towards the north-east where the bomber had crashed almost a week before. It was such an awful accident, with four of the crew dead, but sadly that was nothing compared to the numbers injured and killed all over the world in this terrible war. She'd finished work early that morning and decided she needed to get up into the hills to try to clear her head.

On her rounds earlier, she'd met a couple of the gamekeepers down near Wheen farm and had found out more about the crash.

"How're you doing, Miss Anderson?" Bill Muir had asked. "Still enjoying being a postie?"

"Loving it, thanks. What about you two – how's the shooting season going?"

"The stag season's just begun, but it's quiet, really slow. Not like it was before the war." He shrugged. "Well, nothing is, obviously."

"How's the crash site looking?" Nell asked. "Someone said all the parts of the plane are still there?"

John Craig nodded. "Yes, we were up there yesterday. It's such a sad, sorry place. You can see huge pieces of propeller, engine, fuselage... there's so much debris. The tail section's pretty intact though; I suppose that's why the injured man was able to walk away from it."

"Let's hope he makes a full recovery."

"Absolutely. We'd have heard if he'd died, surely."

"Where was the plane heading?"

"It was on a training mission from RAF Lossiemouth, it'd only been out for a couple of hours, so we've no idea if it was heading home or carrying on south," Bill Muir said, shaking his head.

"It's always a bleak part of the hills," John Craig said, "but with all the wreckage up there, it looks even more desolate."

"Can you see the wreckage from Ben Tirran?"

"No, you've got to carry on over that ridge after the summit, down the other side, over the burn, then up the hill there, towards Muckle Cairn. On a good day, you could probably see it from the edge of the ridge."

"Think I'll just avoid that area, for now anyway. It must be such a dismal place. There's so much tragedy everywhere."

"That there is, Miss Anderson," said Bill Muir, tilting his hat as they both headed towards the hills.

Looking over the tranquil water now, she felt so removed from it all. Was that selfish or just a survival tactic? What about the men's families? They must still be grieving. Three of those killed were Canadian – did that mean they weren't able to travel to even bury them? She shook her head. It didn't bear thinking about.

The sound of birdsong made her look around. It was a wheatear chirruping its staccato cheeps right behind her. She tried not to move as she watched it peck at the worms in the grass. She'd already seen grouse on the way up the hill from Clova, and as she watched scores of them fly low over the heather, she wondered if they were now living longer, with fewer men joining shoots since the war began.

She turned her head to look again at the loch. It was crystal clear. She could see the stones under the surface from the shore to far across the loch. The green corrie at the other side was reflected in the water, even though the sky was darkening a little.

She opened her pack and took out her buttered scone. Though she was a terrible baker, the one thing she could make – God knows how – was a treacle scone. She bit into it and grinned as she thought of her mother, who could turn her hand to anything in the kitchen apart from scones. She used to say she could just never get them right, and it was true. At all the church fetes and harvest teas, the women would ask her to bake sausage rolls; they insisted they could do all the scones and pancakes themselves.

Her mother knew, of course, that it was a polite way of telling her she could not bake, but she produced the sausage rolls anyway, adding some mountain thyme to the sausage meat as if to show the glen ladies that she understood proper cooking and good flavours, even if she couldn't bake a scone.

Nell popped the last bite into her mouth, then watched as some ripples appeared on the water in the middle of the loch. Probably trout. Damn, why hadn't she brought a fishing rod? They could have had something more exciting to eat that night. But no, it was potato pie again. Effie was convinced it was actually very tasty. On this, as with everything else these days, the sisters disagreed.

* * *

The following day, Nell swung her bike into the playground and leant it against the schoolhouse wall. She'd had such a busy morning, which was not unusual, but today's deliveries had been particularly bulky. She couldn't get them all in her postbag. She always put Mrs Macdonald's messages from the grocer's van in her saddle bag, but today there was also a large hat box for the big house.

She had wobbled along the road, trying to balance the box on her handlebars, until she'd got up to the big house, where she had a proper look at the label and realised it wasn't, as she'd thought, for the laird's wife, but for the governess. What did she need such an enormous hat for? It wasn't as if she'd be asked to open a fete or cut a ribbon any time soon. Could she not have brought her own hat back on one of her many shopping excursions to Kirriemuir?

She went into the kitchen and lifted her postbag off her shoulder, then turned it upside down on the table.

"What on earth are you doing, Nell? That tablecloth's clean, look at all the debris coming out of that filthy bag," Effie grumbled as she walked towards her sister.

"Nice to see you too, Effie." Nell swept the bits and pieces from the table back into her postbag, picking up a letter that had fallen out and placing it in front of them both.

"Now, is that an E or an H there?" She pointed to the letter between 'Miss' and 'Anderson'. "I've had it in my bag all day, but I didn't have time to take a good look. You teach handwriting – what d'you reckon?"

Effie peered down. "It's terrible writing. If the sender was one of my pupils, they'd get a severe ticking off."

"But you don't ever belt them, do you, Effie?"

Her sister shook her head. "It does no good at all – it didn't help when we were at school either or when our father used to do it. I threw out his tawse, remember?"

Nell nodded.

"Well, I think it's an H and it's for me." She lifted up the envelope and put it in front of her sister.

Effie shook her head. "Not sure, let me look more closely." She grabbed the letter from Nell and looked at the back.

"There's nothing from the sender on the back." Nell grinned. "Ah, you think it's another of those mysterious letters you've been getting, don't you?" Nell reached out to snatch it back, but Effie held tight.

"I'll go and open it, I'm sure it's for me. I'll give it back if it's not."

Nell sighed. "You're so childish. All right, but open it here."

Nell sat down and looked up at her sister, who picked up a knife from the drawer and slit it open. She scanned the letter before saying anything. She was frowning.

"Well?"

"Well, it may be addressed to you after all, but I don't see why…"

Nell leant over, snatched the letter back and read it. "Well, this is rather poignant. I was just speaking to a couple of gamekeepers yesterday about the plane crash. And now here's the Imperial War Graves Commission wanting me to go to Fettercairn Cemetery on Friday for the funeral of those three Canadians." She shook her head. "It's all so sad."

"Why d'you think they'd ask you?"

"The dead include French Canadians, so maybe I'm to interpret what the minister says?"

Effie frowned while Nell continued speaking. "I don't know. Both of us speak French, but I was the one who spent nearly four years in France in the war and spoke French every day." She pointed to the letter. "Maybe Mrs Blair at the council told the cemetery people about me being a French speaker… or actually, when I think about it, perhaps Dr Geddes said I'd helped with the surviving soldier. I suppose he might be there, if he's fit enough?" She shrugged. "And even though it says Dear Miss Anderson, the envelope has an H on it – that's not an E, Effie. It's clearly for me."

"And you don't think my French is as good as yours? I'll have you know…"

"Effie, this is a pointless argument. The letter's for me." She skim-read it again. "I have been invited to the military cemetery in Fettercairn for those soldiers' funerals. What an honour."

"How do you intend to get a day off your postal duties? I'm still on school holidays, I could easily go instead."

"I'll get Wee Janie to do the rounds, she's helped out before. Remember when I had that awful flu?"

Effie stomped over to the range and flung open the oven door. She brought out the pie and slammed it onto the pot stand. "Set the table, Nell. Supper's ready," she hissed.

"Yes Miss!" Nell said, standing to attention and trying not to laugh at her sister's sulking.

Chapter 10

August 1942

On the few occasions she had been to a funeral, Nell always thought about her mother. As she bumped along in the bus towards Kirriemuir, she wondered again what had happened to her. There was no grave in the Clova cemetery, and her father had explained that she was buried back at her own family home instead. But because they had never been to where her parents had come from, Nell had no idea where that was. She could remember her grandfather vaguely, but she was only a child when he'd died. She wished she had pushed her father more about it, but he always closed down the conversation when she enquired. She used to think he was just too upset to speak about it, but she'd started to wonder if he was hiding something.

A few weeks after her mother had died, a couple of the boys from the farm along the glen had followed her on her bike. She was fifteen and taller than them, but they were more than merely annoying; the Cumberland boys were known for harassing anyone they felt they could pick on.

"We know why your Ma isn't buried at the kirk," one of them taunted.

She tried to cycle on, but they caught her up.

"The minister wouldn't bury her, you know why?"

She held her head high and continued on, but they swung their bikes around so they were in front of hers. "It's because she killed herself. You're not allowed to get buried in the kirkyard if you do that."

Her whole body tensed up, but she clamped her teeth together and forced her bike through them and sped up, leaving them laughing and mocking in her wake.

When she told her father about the confrontation, he had

been very still.

"Helen, do not listen to any of those urchins' gossip. Your mother is buried in a fine cemetery in her parents' hometown. I've told you before."

"But how did she die, Pa?"

His eyes narrowed as he leant towards her. "I have told you this; she had a sudden pneumonia." And off he had stormed.

But all these years later, Nell still wondered about her mother's place of burial. She and Effie never talked about it with their father. He had instilled into his daughters the mantra of her death being both sudden and tragic; no more questions should be asked.

Effie had said Mrs Wilson once asked her why their mother wasn't buried at Clova, and Effie had repeated their father's explanation. It didn't seem to appease the woman, who was known to be a gossip. Nell remembered telling Effie the village gossips could fabricate all sorts of theories, but the sisters knew their mother was buried near her own family home. Though recently she had begun to wonder if that was true.

Nell got off the bus in Kirriemuir, then began heading to the railway station where she was meeting the minister's wife, who had offered to drive Nell to the cemetery where her husband was conducting the ceremony. The Fettercairn minister was overseas as a chaplain, and Mr Bain, the Kirriemuir parish minister, often took his services.

As she passed the school in Reform Street, she remembered Effie telling her the week before about how evacuees were now pupils there. There were not only children from Dundee, less than twenty miles away, but there was also a girl from Edinburgh and a boy from Glasgow. The poor things, they were such a long way from home.

When she arrived at the station, she saw someone waving to her. She went over to shake Mrs Bain's hand and took a seat beside her.

Just before they set off, she turned to Nell. "Before I forget, my sister-in-law sends her regards."

"Your sister-in-law?"

"Yes, she was a friend of your mother's before she died so tragically young. Her father was the minister here at Kirriemuir and now her brother, my husband, is minister."

"Oh." Nell shrugged. "Please send my best wishes back, though I'm ashamed to say I didn't know my mother had any friends."

"Anyway dear, it's so good of you to come to this funeral. I think my husband wants you to say the Lord's Prayer in French, but he'll brief you when we get there." She shook her head. "It's an awful business, isn't it?"

"It really is."

"Angus is also going to speak about the men's gallantry and say prayers on Sunday at church for their families in Canada. At least the RAF lad will have his family near his grave in England."

Nell nodded. She didn't know what else to say. "Thank you for the lift."

* * *

As they walked into the cemetery and began to climb the gentle slope towards the graves, Nell realised she was the only one not wearing black or in uniform. She didn't have anything black, but she'd borrowed a dark navy coat from Effie, whose mood thankfully was better that morning. Once she'd had a few words with the minister, she took her place at the first grave.

While they were waiting for the ceremony to start, she looked around. It was a bright summer's day, and the cemetery was pretty enough, with flowering bushes hanging over the stone walls and some birdsong from the trees behind. All three graves were up against the wall, and as she looked into the long holes dug in the earth, she thought of the survivor. Would he be here? Or perhaps he was still not well enough to leave the hospital. There was no way of finding out, she did not even know his name.

The noise of commands being barked out made her turn around. Soldiers were marching in from the gate carrying the coffins, each covered in a flag. She bowed her head as the soldiers stood in front of each grave and lowered their coffins. And as the minister started the service, she looked around. There were only men in uniform, and the minister, his wife and herself there. Presumably it was too soon for the men's families to be able to come over to Scotland from Canada. Perhaps they would come over when their gravestones were ready.

She'd been told that only two of the Canadians were French speaking, from Quebec, but she was to recite the Lord's Prayer after all three were buried. At the minister's nod, she began, faltering at first then finding her voice. After she had finished, the minister spoke some final words, and then a bugle sounded the Last Post and the firing party took their positions. As they fired into the air, she thought of the survivor, whose name she was never told. He had been too badly injured the night he came to the bar for her to ask. Also, though he was British, how come he had a photo with an inscription in French on the back? Was it even his photo?

She walked down to the gate to wait for Mrs Bain and took out the photo from her pocket. The woman's dark hair was rolled up around her forehead and down the sides in loose curls. She didn't appear to have any rouge or lipstick on, but she looked naturally pretty. She was staring directly into the camera, smiling rather coyly. Nell flipped over the photo to read once again the words: *'Ensemble pour toujours.'*

Chapter 11

July 1916

The bombardments on the Somme had begun at the end of June. And because both French and British infantry were involved, going over the top to advance towards the German lines, they were inundated at the abbey with injured soldiers. The Great Push, as they called it, had begun, and with it came thousands upon thousands of casualties.

Since Royaumont was less than thirty miles from the firing lines, the cases reached them fairly quickly, which of course meant a better chance of survival. Nell and her fellow chauffeuses sat in their ambulances at Creil railway station and waited for the men. No sooner had they driven them back to the hospital than they had to return for the next load. Trains were arriving from the Somme one after the other, all full of injured men.

The staff at Royaumont worked harder than ever, with hardly any breaks and very little sleep. The doctors were operating nonstop and sending men for x-rays in between. Everyone worked through the long nights, and when Nell passed one of the doctors, nurses or orderlies in the corridors, no one had time to chat; they simply continued with their work, faces grim and determined.

Most of the injured had gas gangrene, and though shrapnel had to be removed if at all possible, the most crucial thing was to clean the wounds to prevent the gangrene from spreading. The stench was almost unbearable, but still the doctors worked on. There were no spare beds, and the operating theatres were hardly ever empty, apart from when the orderlies went in to clean between operations. There was so much blood to be scrubbed away.

Nell had never been so sleep-deprived in her life and often had to shake herself to keep awake on the long bumpy drive to collect the patients. Usually, she felt cold in the driver's seat, even in summer; the vehicle cab only had half doors so the drivers were exposed to the elements. But with her overwhelming fatigue, the fresh air was useful in keeping her awake. On the way back, the noises of the men in the cabin behind kept her alert.

By early July they were receiving between seventy and 100 injured men a day, and if time permitted, Nell helped the orderlies get the men to the operating rooms or into a ward for assessment. They were so short-staffed. Eventually Dr Gibson managed to get some more help from the Scottish Women's Hospital in Corsica.

Nell hardly saw Paul during those frantic weeks of the Somme Push. Sometimes she managed to snatch a few words when she rushed in to eat something before her next trip to Creil. He had been rather subdued over the past months, and she didn't like to ask why. She thought she knew the reason: he had perhaps been in love with her, but sadly it was not reciprocated.

* * *

One afternoon, Nell was helping a stretcher case into the abbey and upstairs to the operating ward. The orderly at the other end of the stretcher whispered that the soldier was British. Underneath the rough blanket, she'd seen that he wore a kilt. Nell was peering down at him, trying to see him more clearly, but he had his hands over his face as if protecting his eyes. Poor thing, she thought, he was clearly one of the ones suffering from that awful mustard gas. Hopefully, if they rushed him to surgery, the doctors could save his sight. At the top of the stairs he began to mutter incoherently and shake his head, pressing his skull with his two fists.

They laid the stretcher down on the floor in the corridor outside the operating room where there were three other men, all lying unmoving on their stretchers. This man was shifting his whole body about, clearly in agony.

"I'll stay with him until the doctor's free," Nell said. "He's too agitated to be alone."

The orderly nodded and ran downstairs to continue unloading the other patients.

Nell bent over him, trying to ignore the smell. "It's all right, you're going to be fine, the doctor will see you soon, then you'll be right as rain."

"I want to go home," he mumbled, and as he continued muttering, she began to make out a Scottish accent.

"Where are you from?"

He had screwed up his eyes again and was wiping blood from his arm over his face, as if trying to wipe the poison from his eyes. She removed his hand gently and bent down as he whispered, "I'm from Kirriemuir, I need to get home."

"What's your name?" Nell smiled, but had no idea if he could see anything. There was silence as he kept trying to rub his eyes.

"My name's Nell and I'm from Clova, not far from Kirrie."

He stopped moving and blinked. His eyes had been brimming with tears as they spoke, but now tears ran down his bloodied cheeks. "My name's Douglas," he said as his head flopped backwards and he suddenly became completely still.

Chapter 12

August 1943

"Nell, come and listen to the radio. The Allies have invaded Sicily!"

She rushed into the kitchen and sat down beside Effie at the fireside.

"When did it happen?"

"Just listen, Nell, don't speak!"

They sat in silence till the end of the broadcast.

"So it began a couple of weeks ago and presumably they're continuing up into Italy?"

Nell shook her head. "It's just Sicily so far, but if they take all of Italy then that's a really good sign. Surely the war will be over soon."

"Is Jimmy Bell not one of the troops down there?"

"I think he might be, actually. I know he's in the Marines. I'll ask Mrs Bell when I'm in on Friday. The papers'll have more about it tomorrow, I imagine."

"Can you maybe get another paper when you're in Kirrie tomorrow? *The Courier* might not have as much information as *The Scotsman* or *The Times*, if you can get one of those."

"I'll do my best."

"What time are you leaving in the morning?"

"I've to be at Fettercairn by eleven so I'll be away early. I'll get a lift with Billy on the post bus at 7.30, that should give me plenty of time."

Nell had again been invited to the cemetery as a French speaker, this time not to recite a prayer but rather to translate the memorial service for the French Canadians' families, who were due for the one-year anniversary of the crash.

Effie pointed to her sister's head. "What are you trying to do with your hair, Nell?" Half of her hair was pinned back with hair clasps, the other dangling down her neck.

"Those big rolls you've done in your hair before, but mine doesn't seem to want to curl up, it's too frizzy."

"You've got to wet it first, then pin it with kirby grips. If you sleep on it, it should be fine by the morning."

"Well, I won't have time tomorrow, so it'd better be."

Nell got up and went into the bedroom again.

"D'you want me to do it?" Effie shouted.

Nell popped her head back round the door again. "If you're not too busy, Effie, thanks."

Effie put down her knitting and went in to her sister.

"Right, sit on the chair while I get some water to dampen it down." She returned with a basin of cold water and proceeded to wet her hands, then attempted to smooth down her sister's wavy hair. Nell's hair was not as thick as her sister's, whose hair was heavy and glossy. Though they both had their mother's colouring in hair and dark brown eyes, it was Effie that everyone used to say was more like their mother, whom many said had been beautiful. Nell just changed the subject if anyone talked about appearances, it was all so superficial. Was it really important how anyone looked?

"That's freezing, Effie. Could you not have warmed the water a bit?"

Effie shrugged. "Do you want me to do it or not?"

Nell sighed and shivered as Effie shook dribbles of cold water all over her head.

"It's dripping down my neck, d'you need to use so much?"

"That's it all wet now. Right, where's your brush?"

Nell pointed to the dressing table and her sister got to work.

* * *

She stood in the cemetery at Fettercairn with an umbrella over her head. All the way there, she'd been hoping the rain would clear up for the ceremony. It would be such a pity for the families if it was still pouring. But water continued to drip from the overhanging bushes as the rain persisted. The men in uniform had no umbrellas, but the families huddled under theirs.

It was the same minister, Mr Bain, who was leading the commemoration service, and he had asked her to interpret his words if necessary. No one knew if the Canadians all spoke fluent English as well as French. As he began, she looked at the headstones which were now in place. The most striking fact was their ages. They were aged twenty-one, twenty-two and twenty-four: far too young to die, and such a long way from home. Their gravestones each had a simple line from the Bible at the foot, in English or French.

As the minister continued, she looked directly at him in case he needed her, but it seemed as if the families could all understand. There was a woman about her age, perhaps one of the soldiers' mothers, and two women who looked in their twenties, perhaps wives or sisters. Their expressions were all grim, eyes downcast. There was only one man not in uniform, a gentleman who looked in his sixties, perhaps a father. Of course, if there were any brothers, they were likely away fighting.

As the short ceremony came to a close, the minister said a final prayer, then asked if they had all understood. They nodded as they wiped away their tears. Thank goodness the rain had stopped; the umbrellas were folded, and the families stood by the graves.

Nell went to ask the minister if there was anything she could do.

"Just go and speak to them, Miss Anderson. Kindness and sympathy are all we can give."

She held back until they'd had some time at the graves, then went to offer her condolences to all three families.

She'd just said goodbye to one of the French-speaking families and had gone up the slope a short way to allow them time for themselves when she noticed a figure at the far end of the cemetery. She walked slowly towards the woman, who was dressed in black and had a neat hat with a wide brim over her face. Nell wondered why she was apart from the others. She didn't want to get too close, it didn't feel right, so stood a short distance away.

When the families began to wander back down towards the gate, the woman headed slowly towards the graves. Nell looked at her as she passed. She looked up at Nell, then quickly back down to the ground. But in that brief glance, Nell thought she looked familiar.

The woman looked towards the gate, where the last family member had just filed out, then went to stand by the first grave. She bowed her head and clasped her hands together. As Nell began to walk down to the gateway, she suddenly realised where she had seen her before: she was the woman in the photo.

PART 2

Effie

Chapter 13

October 1914

She arrived at the pretty white church in Glen Prosen and stopped to look around. She hadn't been to her aunt's house since she was a child, so had little memory of the village. She looked all about her: the hills were less striking here, and there seemed to be more woodland than in Clova. There were none of the impressive corries that Glen Clova had.

The long journey from home had meant traipsing over moorland and through forests. Amongst the trees, she'd seen red squirrels darting along the branches, and at one stage she'd looked up to the overcast sky to see a buzzard circling overhead.

It was a six-mile walk along the Minister's Path from Clova over to Glen Prosen, a route her father explained had been used in the past by the minister at Prosen, who also had to take services in the Glen Clova church. In years gone by, he would have used pony and trap. Now there was a minister in each church, so there was no need for this long trip.

When she asked Pa why they hadn't walked over here more often, he said that if they'd wanted to visit his sister when she and Nell were small, it was easier for them to go in a horse wagonette via Dykehead, rather than walking all the way there and then another six miles back, especially if the ground was wet. But they were often too busy, and so seldom ventured over to this neighbouring glen.

She turned right and walked along the narrow road lined on both sides by tall beech hedges. She hoiked her bag up over her shoulder again; it was not heavy, just awkward to carry. She had very little in it apart from some clothes, an indoor pair of shoes and her journal. She had not seen Aunt Winnie for such a long time, she wondered if she would even recognise her. But her father had insisted she go to help his sister on the farm now that two of her sons had enlisted. Nell was off very soon to help in the war effort, so life would be quiet at home.

Nell had told her she thought their mother and their aunt had not got on, but neither of the sisters knew anything more and it was certainly not something they could speak to their father about. When Effie had once asked him why they could not visit their mother's grave, he gave her short shrift, telling her that visiting graveyards was sentimental nonsense.

There were a couple of young lads leading a horse along the road ahead, and she stood aside to let them past.

"Excuse me," she said. "Is the Lindsay farm near, do you know?"

They slowed the horse down to a stop and one of them turned around. "You see the bend in the road there? There's a gate in the fence on the right, go through that and there's a track up to the farm."

Effie smiled. "Thanks. Where are you off to with the horse?" It was a beautiful creature, tall and sleek.

"We're going to the blacksmith's, she needs new shoes."

"Don't we all," she said, looking down at her tatty outdoor boots before continuing along the road.

At the end of the farm track she was able to see the farmhouse. She could hear dogs barking round the back. Her stomach was churning; she had felt rather out of sorts all along the walk from Clova, slightly queasy. She was so nervous. She remembered her aunt as a formidable, no-nonsense woman, and here she was, coming to stay with her for an indefinite length of time. Being a mother of three boys, she was not used to having girls around. Effie hoped she would not disappoint her aunt. And hopefully the war would not last long and she'd be back in Clova as soon as possible.

* * *

The door opened and a lanky woman with an apron and a bonnet on scowled out from the dark interior.

"Uhuh?" she muttered, peering at Effie with a steely stare.

"I'm here to see Mrs Lindsay, my aunt."

"Oh, you must be Euphemia. Come away in. I'll tell her you're here." She pointed to a door. "Go into the drawing room. She could be a while, she's out milking."

Well, that was a surprise, her aunt having to milk her own cows. But presumably there were very few farm hands now, with the young men all enlisting. She put down her bag and went into the room. She shivered; it was cold and draughty. She sat down and looked around. There were some old portraits around the walls, presumably her father's ancestors, since Aunt Winnie had inherited the family farm when Effie's grandfather died. Her husband Robert Lindsay had run it with her till his own death. Pa never wanted the farm. He was only ever going to be a dominie, though goodness knows why; he had little patience for children, or indeed anyone.

Most of the people in the portraits had the dark ginger hair of her father; anyone who didn't was presumably a wife or husband. Their skin was freckled, like Pa's, and their noses long. She and Nell looked so unlike him; they were much more like their mother, with dark hair and a duskier complexion.

It seemed unbelievable that it was four years since Ma died. Four long years of just having one parent, no one to mitigate her father's tempers and moods. And though her sister had somehow found a way to avoid confronting him by leaving the room or changing the subject, Effie sometimes still could not help trying to placate him if he was cross, even though that usually made matters worse. And while she was not looking forward to this stay with her aunt in the neighbouring glen, she had to admit she was not unhappy to be leaving her father.

"Ah, Euphemia, come over here, let me look at you," a voice boomed from the doorway. She got to her feet and went to kiss the cheek of the short, stocky woman before her. That was another attribute she and Nell had inherited from their mother: her height.

"You are paler than I recall, but then you haven't been outside in all weathers working from dawn to dusk as I now find myself having to do." She pointed to the chair. "Sit down. Betty will bring us tea." She turned around and instructed the woman. Then, as the door shut, she turned to face her niece.

"So, my brother tells me you are able to assist here on the farm."

"Yes, I will do as much as possible, Aunt Winnie."

"Good. Since first Ewan and then just last month Donald decided to join up, I am left with only Allan, who at seventeen is hardly qualified to run the whole farm. We have some five hundred sheep on the hills, so both lambing and shearing time are hectic. The shepherds need a lot of help then. I don't imagine you would be up to those tasks – how old are you again?"

"I'll be seventeen next month, Aunt Winnie."

"I see," she said, gesturing toward the table as the maid brought in the tea. She peered at the tray. "Are there no scones left, Betty?"

"You didn't ask for any, Mrs Lindsay."

Her aunt sighed. "Please fetch some scones and butter. My niece has had a long journey." She turned back to Effie. "How was it underfoot?"

"Very wet and boggy in places. I'm afraid my boots are rather dirty. Sorry."

Aunt Winnie shrugged. "We're a working farm here, Euphemia, no time for airs and graces." She poked a strand of stray ginger hair into the tight bun at the back of her head. "So, I think you can start working in the milking shed while I help Allan and the shepherds with the sheep, and we've a couple of old men in the village who've said they'd help, though they'd have to fit us in around tending to their own flocks." She handed Effie her tea.

As Betty brought in the scones, Effie was aware her aunt was studying her face. "You have more of a look of your mother since

I saw you last, but that was years ago. Does your sister have that too?"

"We do look like our mother, everyone says."

"Well, never mind, you can just count your blessings you're an Anderson."

Chapter 14

August 1943

Thank goodness Nell was away all day at the memorial service in Fettercairn; Effie had time for herself. And once she had tidied up the mess her sister made every single morning, she went to sit at the window and removed the letter from her pocket. This was not the first letter she had received from him, but she still felt she needed to keep them a secret. Her sister would judge her as usual.

My dear Euphemia,

I explained in my previous letter that I thought once more of Clova and my happy times teaching at the school when my wife's death notice was in The Courier alongside your father's nearly four years ago. But I must tell you that I have thought of you often over the years.

Did he mean since his wife had died, or when she was alive? Effie wondered.

I think back to our wonderful walks – or rather, the one up to Loch Brandy was more of a hike, wasn't it? Do you remember it was such a beautiful day, and we had to go and paddle in the loch to cool down our feet, hot from the climb? I remember you yelping, not because of the freezing cold water, but because the stones we'd to stand on at the lochside were so painful to perch on. Your feet were – and surely still are – clearly so much softer than my gnarled old ones.

And then afterwards, with not a care in the world, we enjoyed not only the stunning scenery of the Clova hills and corries, but each other.

Effie felt a shiver through her whole body. How could she ever forget that afternoon? She also remembered worrying about having to lie to Nell about where she had been, but thankfully she had been so preoccupied with her day out in Kirriemuir that she never asked. Besides, Effie could not have told her about either what happened up at Brandy or back at the schoolhouse on her return; she had been too ashamed.

As I've written before, where I live near Forfar is not a grand house, indeed it's more of a farmhouse, but it is rather beautiful on a good day. Today as I write, I am looking over a field of cattle under a clear blue sky to Restenneth Priory, which, though it has existed in some form since the twelfth century, is more of a ruin these days. There was some restoration, including the magnificent spire, during the last century, but there is still work to be done. Did I tell you that Robert the Bruce buried his infant son there in the early fourteenth century?

I do hope you don't find me a history bore? My late wife used to tell me I was so clever with all my facts about geography and geology, but I do find these days I am interested in history too. I still adore discovering more facts about geology, as you will recall. Perhaps the interest in history was brought on by the dreadful circumstances we find ourselves in these days. I do hope your family are all safe and well? And on this subject, I never had the courage to ask before, but now I must.

Dear Lord, what was he about to ask her?

You must have married, Euphemia – you were always too pretty and lively not to. But I believe you and your sister now live alone in the schoolhouse, so I imagine that perhaps, like me, you have been tragically widowed? I do hope you have no sons serving in the war. It's a cruel and wretched business. And even though the Allies are making progress in Italy, there's still a long way to go, isn't there?

Effie continued reading more about his thoughts on the war, till the end of the letter. The last paragraph made her gasp.

I wonder, dear Euphemia, if you might consider meeting me at some stage. I think you are now sole teacher at the school, so you will be busy, but perhaps before the summer holidays end – or indeed during the Tattie holidays next month, we could meet somewhere. Perhaps Forfar – or if that is too far for you, Kirriemuir?
I look forward very much to hearing from you.
Yours,
Douglas

Chapter 15

November 1914

"So where are the Belgian refugees going to stay, Aunt Winnie?"

Effie was out in the milking shed with her aunt. She was carrying the buckets of milk to the door to be uplifted, trying not to spill the milk onto her boots.

"That cottage over there," she said, pointing to a tiny croft at the other side of the courtyard. "It's just a but and ben, but it should do them. There's two children – and a baby, I think."

"Do you want me to help get it ready for them? I could maybe clean it and tidy it up a bit if it's not been lived in for a while?"

"We can do it together, Euphemia. Tomorrow after morning milking. I've been waiting for delivery of some material to make them curtains and it just arrived earlier, so I can start sewing this evening if there's time. Hopefully they will help make the cottage feel a little less cold."

Effie's opinion of her aunt had changed since she'd arrived a few weeks before. She was a hard-working woman who never seemed to tire and whose patience was exemplary, compared to her brother. Perhaps she enjoyed Effie's company, or perhaps it was because her sister-in-law was no longer there. Her comment the other day made her think that what Nell had said about them not getting on was true.

"And both the parents will be able to help with the animals, will they?"

"Well," said Aunt Winnie, "the mother will be busy with the baby I suppose. I've no idea how old it is. But the boy is about twelve I think, so he can certainly help Allan with his chores. The girl is only six, so I suppose she had better go to school, though she won't be able to understand a thing."

"I can help her with English, maybe?"

"Ah, of course, you and your sister speak good French. Well, that'll be most useful; it may make them feel less out of their depth."

"Why are the Belgians coming to Scotland?"

"When the Germans invaded their country, they had to leave. The soldiers were brutal, there was no choice. So several thousand of them landed in southern England. And just last month, Scotland started taking lots of them too."

Effie nodded and yawned. She put her hand over her mouth. "Sorry, I don't seem to have as much energy as you, Aunt Winnie. I'm always sleepy."

Her aunt stared at her, frowning. "Did you see Allan bringing in the tups earlier?"

"Are they the rams?"

She nodded.

"Is it because of the weather?"

"No, they've stayed out in snow some years. For now, they're put into a separate field, then they'll be put into the field of ewes. Then it'll be only five to six months till lambing." Aunt Winnie kept staring at Effie, a strange look on her face.

Effie opened her mouth to speak, then turned away.

"Euphemia, I have something I want to ask you."

The two women were standing at the shed door side by side. Effie turned to look at her aunt.

"Betty says she has had no monthly rags to wash from you."

Effie looked away and held her breath, waiting for the next question.

"I only had boys to bring up so obviously have no idea if things have moved on, but in my day, monthly rags and cloths were washed. Are there more modern or fashionable methods of dealing with monthlies these days? It's not the sort of conversation I can have with the village ladies over tea at the big house."

Effie found she could hold her breath no longer. She let out a long sigh and lowered her head. Still she said nothing.

"Euphemia, I am a farmer, I see what the animals do; it's nature. I am also a mother, I was a wife, I know what happens…" She peered round at Effie, who still hung her head.

"I am also my brother's sister, and if anything happens to his daughter on my watch, I shall be the one to be blamed." Aunt Winnie took hold of her niece's chin and gently pulled her round to face her. "Well?"

"I have not had my monthlies for three months now. But I am sure they'll return, it's probably just the strain and the stress of everything." She attempted a smile.

Winnie continued to study her. "I see." She opened her mouth to speak again but instead cupped Effie's face between her hands. She leant towards her and spoke in a low voice. "Euphemia, you know you can tell me anything. I am not your father, with his strict ways. I am your aunt, whose primary concern is your wellbeing." She raised her hands. "I also don't care two hoots about what other people think. Your mother didn't either, but strangely that did not bond us together."

"Were you and Ma not close?" At last Effie could ask.

She shook her head. "Little misunderstandings – silly things – got us off to a bad start when she married your father, and we never quite got back on track. And then there was…" She turned to look away. "Then, sadly, she died."

She shrugged. "Anyway, Euphemia, if and when you want to talk about anything, come and find me."

She turned back into the shed and shouted back, "Why don't you leave the heavy buckets of milk, I'll do those myself later. You can go to the pantry and ask Betty to show you how to make the butter, so she can get on with the laundry." She strode onwards, shouting over her shoulder, "Time to get back to work."

Chapter 16

September 1943

The first weeks of term after the summer holidays were always challenging, and since the schoolhouse was now busier than usual, it was a little stressful. But thankfully the Tattie holidays were looming. Sometimes she wondered if she was getting too old for teaching. It was relentless, though she had to admit it was also rewarding.

That morning, her first class after playtime had been handwriting. She'd written some sentences on the board for the younger ones to copy and she was going around the desks, stopping to check their spelling and writing. She stopped at little Angus Hunter's.

"What's that word meant to be, Angus?" she asked him.

"Turnip, Miss."

"That doesn't look the same as the one I've on the blackboard though, does it?" He'd missed out the final P. He looked back at the board, screwing up his eyes.

"Oh yes, Miss. I'll put that there now." He bent over his desk, tongue sticking out as he concentrated on adding the P. She watched him and made a mental note to see if she could organise an eye test somehow. She'd speak to the doctor. She was sure he was short-sighted, but she knew his mother would tell her they could not afford an eye test and certainly not a pair of spectacles.

He laid down his pen on his desk. "We got a letter from my daddy yesterday. Miss Anderson delivered it!" He was beaming. "Mummy said it was the first letter he'd been able to send from the camp."

Angus's father had been in a prisoner of war camp in Germany since the summer.

Effie always tried to discourage talk of the fathers away in the war after Ena Mackie's father was killed, but the boy continued, in his extremely loud voice, to tell the whole class that his father had said he and his fellow prisoners have turnip jam in the camp. "They have bread and margarine and turnip jam for breakfast."

All the other children looked around, most grimacing.

"What do you think that would taste like, Miss?"

Effie shrugged. "I have no idea, Angus. We could maybe ask Mrs Cameron to make some for us when she can get more sugar."

"We get lots of turnips in our field, for the sheep in the winter," said Francis Harper, then they all put their hands up to say, "Me too, me too."

"Back to your letters, children," she said. "We can discuss turnip jam another day."

She looked up at the clock on the wall. "It's not long till dinner time. Mrs Cameron's got a lovely pudding for you all today." She looked at their expectant faces. "It's bramble pie."

"Will there be custard?"

"If you're very lucky."

After dinner, her plan was to take the children out to collect sphagnum moss. The last time they did that, though some of them enjoyed it, most had hated it, and today was wet and miserable so she did not have high hopes. But she started in the classroom with a lesson about why the sphagnum moss they collected was so crucial for the war.

She placed some dried moss in a bowl then got the children to add water to see how it was absorbed. "It's urgently needed for wound dressings, for the injured men," she said as she handed each child a cup of water. "It restricts any bacterial growth because of its acidity, and it can absorb up to twenty times its volume in liquid." She then explained what "bacterial" and "acidity" meant.

"My daddy was in a hospital when he was injured, he maybe had one of those dressings," Joan said.

Effie nodded and continued. "There's lots of it in our glen as it likes to grow in boggy areas. And we've got plenty of those here in Clova."

A hand shot up.

"Yes, Lizzie?"

"When I told my mummy we were going to be collecting the moss soon, she said she did that when she was at school, when her daddy was in France fighting."

Effie nodded. "Yes, it was used a lot in the last war too. And in fact, I remember your mummy – and Joan's daddy – coming to collect it with the class when I was a girl."

After the children had left at the end of the day, Effie set about removing the twigs and leaves, then laying the moss out to dry on tables at the back of the classroom. Once it was dried, she would get the children to help her pack it into sacks to send to the Red Cross, who would supply the military hospitals. They'd sent nine sacks the year before, and she was determined to try to get even more this term. She sighed as she wondered why she was so determined to beat her own record; she hated the fact she had inherited her father's competitiveness.

* * *

After she had sorted the last batch of moss to dry, she headed next door to the schoolhouse. Nell had to work in the bar at the hotel that evening, so they'd planned to have an early supper. It was Nell's turn to cook, so goodness knows what delights there would be. In fairness, her stew the week before hadn't been too bad, considering she'd used scrag end of mutton.

At least in two days' time, at the start of October, when the pheasant shooting season began, she could make game pie. The keepers often brought Nell a couple of birds when she was working in the bar.

Effie still did not think it becoming to work there, even though she knew her sister was – just like delivering the post

– only doing jobs the men would normally have done. Also, the hotel was where their mother had her own first job from an early age.

"What time will you be back tonight, Nell?" Effie had asked as she started on the washing up. Supper had been surprisingly fine – well, you can't go far wrong with a tin of corned beef and some potatoes.

"I don't know, depends how many customers I have. If they're all gone by nine, I'll come home then. It's not as if there are many hotel guests. Mr Noble was saying the weekend will be busy though, he's expecting an overspill of guests from up at the big house, some sort of party to celebrate the young laird returning on leave."

"Is that appropriate?"

Nell shrugged. "What do we know about the kind of things the gentry do? I've a feeling young William would prefer just his own immediate family, but they're coming from all over the county to see him."

"How long's he been away now?"

"He's not been back since he first enlisted, so over three years?" Nell went to grab her coat. "See you later, Effie. Presume you're just doing school preparation this evening?"

"What else would I be doing, Nell? Having a party in the middle of the blackout?" She raised an eyebrow. "No, it's just preparation for harvest festival and listening to the nightly bulletin on the wireless. And I might practise my new Chopin piece if there's time." She stared at her sister, willing her to leave. "I won't be idle, don't you worry, Nell."

Once she was sure her sister had gone and the house was quiet, she went over to the writing desk. It still felt strange to sit there. It had been their father's special place, where only he had been allowed to sit. But ever since Pa had died, she had used it.

She got out a piece of paper and dipped her pen in the ink.

Dear Douglas,

I've been thinking for a while about your kind invitation to meet, hence my delay in replying. I've not been ignoring your letters, merely taking time to consider my response. At first I was not sure it was altogether a good idea. It's nearly thirty years since we last met, and we have both had so many things going on in our lives – you with your wife and your son, me with my teaching and running the school single-handedly.

I was actually wondering what would be the point of meeting, since our lives have taken such different paths. But because, shamefully, I have never visited Restenneth Priory, I came to the decision just yesterday that in fact I would like to visit, perhaps to see the priory since it is so near your house.

But how would that work out? Do you have an automobile? I could get the bus to Kirriemuir then change for the Forfar bus, if necessary.

The Tattie holidays would probably be best, if this is going to happen.

But you will detect in my words a little hesitation, and I am sure you will understand why.

I look forward to hearing from you.

Yours,

Euphemia

Chapter 17

December 1914

Effie had just posted her weekly letter to her father and continued on down the road towards the school. She'd left Gabrielle, the little Belgian girl, there earlier, telling her she'd collect her after lunch since it was only her second day. At the school gate stood a well-dressed lady with a beautiful fur hat that was brown with a silvery-grey tinge. Presumably she had a child in school, but when Effie approached, the lady had only glanced at her, then turned and strode down the road towards the village.

Effie opened the school gate and looked around the children in the playground. Glen Prosen's school usually had about the same number of pupils as Clova's, but this year Mr Forbes the dominie had told her there were twenty. Her father had written back that though he only had twelve pupils on his roll this year, they were each getting more individual attention, as if he was in competition with the school in the next glen.

She looked to her right and left, but still could not see the little girl, so she went into the classroom, knocking gently on the door first. Mr Forbes, who, with his bushy beard and white hair looked more like Father Christmas than the dominie, stood up from his seat.

"Ah, Miss Anderson, I'm glad you've come. Gabrielle has been a little better today but is still rather shy with the others." He pointed to a desk where the little girl sat drawing. She beamed when she saw Effie and ran over to her, taking her hand.

"*Ça va, chérie?*" Effie asked. "Did you have a good morning?"

Gabrielle told her about the lessons they had had and that she ate mutton at lunch.

"Can I come back to the farm with you now and see Maman?"

"Yes, you can. Go and get your coat."

While she ran into the cloakroom, Effie spoke to Mr Forbes.

"Do you think she understands anything yet?"

"Very little, but it's early days. I wish she would play with the others at playtime. But they can't communicate yet. Are you still teaching her some basic English words?"

Effie nodded. "Hopefully by Christmas she will be a little more confident," she said as Gabrielle came back into the room. "I'll bring her in on Monday morning as usual. Have a good weekend."

All the way home, Gabrielle chattered away. Effie felt the little girl was gradually getting used to the village, though she had been through such a lot in the past few months. Aunt Winnie had told her the Belgian families all had to leave in a hurry, with barely time to pack their clothes and belongings, before the Germans invaded.

The baby was only a couple of months old when they left, so it had been especially challenging for the family. At least the father and the older boy were settling in well, helping Allan with the farm work.

They went up the farm track and saw Madame Dubois in the field, the baby strapped to her back. She waved and Gabrielle ran over to her. Effie stood and waited, then when she saw she'd begun helping her mother with the weeding, she headed for the farmhouse for lunch with her aunt and cousin.

* * *

"Is Allan not joining us today, Aunt Winnie?" Effie asked after Betty had served them their soup.

"No, he's taken a piece up the hill. He's repairing fences today. Monsieur Dubois is helping him."

She took a first sup of soup, then laid down her spoon.

"Euphemia, I must once again ask you what I asked last month: is there anything you would like to tell me?"

Effie stared down at her soup plate, then looked up towards her aunt. "Aunt Winnie, I now find I have missed four of my monthlies." She opened her mouth to continue but then was silent.

Her aunt took a little more soup, then spoke again. "You are getting fatter too, Euphemia. I see your waistband is tight. What could be the cause of that?"

"I don't know, Aunt Winnie."

"I think you do, Euphemia." She finished her soup and was about to speak when Betty entered the room to clear the plates.

Once she had gone, they waited in silence until their main course was brought in. "Shut the door over for me, Betty, will you? Thank you."

Once the door was closed, Aunt Winnie looked directly at her niece. "Are you with child, Euphemia?"

Effie's eyes grew wide, and she sat completely still before starting to mumble, bowing her head. "I'd heard from one of the village girls in Clova that she was expecting a baby, and I asked her how she knew – and how was it possible as she wasn't married. She told me she felt sick and was missing her monthlies. She was sixteen, same age as me then, but a week later she told me that she and one of the gamekeeper's sons were getting married very soon."

"And so, to return to your situation?"

"I don't actually know how you get to be with child."

Her aunt threw herself against the back of the chair. "What, you've never seen sheep or cattle mating? Dogs?"

Effie shook her head.

"You were too young when your mother died for her to have told you some facts of life, but did your older sister not explain the basics?"

She shook her head again. "She told me what to do when I started my monthlies, but that was all."

"How can such a bright girl be so ignorant?" Aunt Winnie shook her head. "Let me tell you what it takes…"

She went on to explain how a woman becomes pregnant. All

the time, Effie became paler and paler.

"I presume you have experienced what I've just described, Euphemia?"

Effie looked around at the door, checking Betty was not about to barge in. "In the summer, something like that did happen to me, but I didn't, well, I didn't understand what was happening." She began to clench her fists.

Aunt Winnie frowned. "Did he force himself on you?"

"I'm not sure, he did hold me down, yes. But, the thing is, I just didn't know what to do, whether to tell him to stop, if it was a bad thing or…" Her knuckles were now white.

"Of course it was a bad thing if he held you down. That is called brute force, it was against your will." She tutted. "I presume you put up a struggle?"

"Yes, but he kept forcing me down, I couldn't move under him…"

Aunt Winnie let out a long breath. "Some men are animals. To have done this to one as naive as you, who had no idea what was about to occur. Dear Lord, only sixteen years old! He took advantage of your naivety, your trusting nature." She sighed.

"You do not have to disclose who the man was, unless you want to, but I presume you are no longer in contact with him?" She raised a finger. "And that this did not happen more than the one time?"

"No, he went off to join up a week or so later. He's now away fighting with all the others." Effie sniffed. "What shall I do, Aunt Winnie?" she said as tears began to trickle down her face.

"There is much to discuss. We have to make a plan. And with some haste. You have missed four months? So you have another five to go." She counted on her fingers. "The baby is due in May."

Effie was now sobbing, head bowed over her plate. Her aunt reached over to take her hand.

"I have had time to consider what can be done; I think you know I have suspected this for a while. Here is what we are going to do: you will have the child. I shall have a family ready and willing to take it, preferably far away from our two glens. If there is any delay, Madame Dubois, whose baby will be just about a year old by then but still not fully weaned, could stand in as wet nurse. Then, once you are fully recovered, we can all get back to normal, and this sorry episode will be forgotten."

"What if Pa finds out?" She whimpered. "Or Nell?"

"Whether you tell your sister or not is up to you, but your father will never know. He will not ever come here to visit, and by the time you go back to Clova, you will be thin again and the baby will be with a loving family. Oh, and from today, you shall not take the Belgian child to school or indeed go anywhere in the village unless you are wrapped in a large coat to disguise the fact you're getting fat. Thank God it's winter. Apart from that, you will stay here on the farm. I shall speak to Betty about the matter but no one else."

"What about Allan? We three always have our meals together."

"He won't notice, and if he does, he will say nothing. I know my son."

Aunt Winnie leant towards her niece. "Do you understand everything we have discussed, Effie?"

She glanced over at her aunt, who saw such fear in her niece's eyes. Effie nodded and wiped her tears on her sleeve. Her aunt handed her a handkerchief, and the door began to open.

"Not now, Betty," she boomed. "We are not finished yet."

And they both turned to listen as the footsteps faded down the corridor.

PART 3

Nell

Chapter 18

August 1943

Nell waited at the gate while the woman stood, head bowed, by the grave. Everyone else had left and she had a bus to catch, but she knew she had to speak to her. Nell turned to look the other way as she saw her step away from the grave, dabbing her nose with a handkerchief. She started to wander down towards the gate.

When she reached her, Nell smiled. She had wondered whether to speak in English or French but recalled that the woman had been at one of the French Canadians' graves.

"*Bonjour, Mademoiselle,*" she said, looking into the stranger's face. She was definitely the woman in the photo. "I was here today as an interpreter for the families for the service. I hope you understood everything?"

"*Merci,*" she began, frowning at Nell. "I was not with the families, I stood apart, but I... I wanted to be here."

Nell nodded. "Were you related to one of the men?"

She looked down. "Not related, not really." She took a deep breath.

"You don't have to tell me anything, but..." Nell checked her watch. She was about to miss the Forfar bus anyway. "Would you like to have a cup of tea or coffee, if we can find a tea shop?"

The woman shrugged her shoulders. "Why not?"

As they walked along the High Street, Nell talked about how beautiful the service had been and how fortuitous it was that the rain had stopped just in time. The woman was silent all the way to the tea shop, which thankfully was open. They found a table and sat down.

"My name's Nell by the way, short for Helen."

The woman smiled but did not give her name.

After they ordered their drinks, Nell riffled in her handbag, then looked directly into the woman's dark eyes. It was strange, she had such a familiar look about her, but Nell could not pinpoint what it was.

"I met the survivor of that terrible crash a year ago. As you may know, he managed to escape the wreckage and somehow get down from the hill. He arrived in the hotel I was working at and – though I've not heard much about him afterwards, apart from the fact he's fully recovered – he gave me something."

They both sat back as their teas and scones arrived. Then she lifted the photo from her lap and handed it to the woman.

"This is what he gave me. He told me I should keep it safe. He said I shouldn't let 'them' see it – whoever 'them' was."

As the stranger took the photo, Nell watched her eyes widen as she stared at the picture, turning it over to read the inscription. Her entire body seemed to tense up. Her mouth opened and she let out a long breath.

"You say this was given to you by the survivor?"

"Yes, he asked me to keep it safe. I presumed it was his, but perhaps it wasn't?"

She shook her head. "It was Pierre's. He told me he always had it in his pocket when he was flying, as a lucky token." Her eyes brimmed with tears. "Though that time he wasn't lucky."

She picked up her scone and bit into it. She was clearly ravenous.

"Here. Let me spread it with butter and jam for you," said Nell, reaching for her plate.

The woman kept gazing at the photo, then the inscription on the back.

"He must have told the other crew members, if anything happened to him, to take my photo."

Nell handed back the scone then poured them both some tea.

"You see, though I was his sweetheart, his family knew nothing about me."

"But would it have mattered if they had? It's war time after all." She sighed. "He had a fiancée back in Quebec."

"Ah," Nell said. "Was she there today?"

"No, there was only an older couple, presumably his parents. We'd only been together for a few months, but we were in love. We planned to marry. He was going to end his engagement after the war and come to live with me in France."

"I'm so sorry," said Nell. "What will you do now?"

She shook her head. "I don't know. I left the family restaurant where I work to come today, and I suppose I should go back, but, since Pierre is here, I…"

She looked up suddenly. "Do you know where the plane crashed?"

"Yes, it's not that far from where I live, but it's a challenging climb."

"Could you take me?"

Nell put down her cup. "Well, yes, I suppose so, but…"

"I could perhaps leave something, a little cross or flowers or something."

She slumped down in her chair and removed a handkerchief from her pocket. She dabbed her eyes, then leant across the table. "My name's Mathilde."

Nell smiled. "You could come home with me now, if you like, and we could try to get to the crash site when I'm not working, if the dry weather holds."

"That would surely be an imposition."

"I presume you've nowhere else to go?"

She shook her head.

"Do you have any luggage with you?"

The woman lifted a small bag at her feet. "This is it, all my possessions."

"I'm sure I could find you some suitable outdoor clothes for the climb. And you're more than welcome to stay. It's just my sister and me at home."

And then, for the first time, Mathilde smiled. And suddenly Nell realised why she had such a familiar look about her. She looked just like Effie did when she was younger.

Chapter 19

April 1917

Nell woke up with a jolt. What a horrible dream that was. Her father was beating her mother with the school tawse, and even though she was only a child, Nell kept trying to intervene, but Pa continued shouting at her to go away. He stood there, his short, squat frame hunched over her mother, his face contorted with anger, his long nose screwed up as he glowered at her in fury. She shook her head to try to erase the memory, but it had been so vivid. She could see her father's enraged face and his lank ginger hair. Her mother was fighting back, struggling to her feet, her beautiful dark hair flying around her head as she swung back at him, while Nell and Effie cowered down in a corner.

She shook herself and got out of bed, then went downstairs. She knew her parents had latterly had a rather acrimonious relationship, but she'd never seen Pa actually hit her mother. He had beaten Effie once when she lied about something – something so inconsequential – and there was that time he'd lashed out with the tawse at Nell herself, but that was all she remembered. She took a drink of water and gulped it down. It was still strange to think it was seven years since Ma had died.

She stood downstairs at the garage doors and looked out into the courtyard, where two of the chauffeuses were cleaning the ambulance wagons in preparation for the next trip to Creil. The pale cloths were stained red from all the blood.

Effie told her she had once overheard Ma shouting at Pa that if he ever hit her, she would leave him; and though they continued to argue, soon his voice had become conciliatory, and when the bedroom door opened, they were smiling at each other. Her mother was a passionate character, there was no doubt about it, while Pa was a laconic, silent man… unless riled.

"Hélène, have you heard about the picnic?"

She looked over to where Paul was crossing the courtyard towards his herb garden.

"No. When?"

"This weekend, for Easter. To try to bring a little joy to all the patients – and the staff."

"How lovely," she said, smiling at her friend. Their relationship had settled down again now he had accepted that she was not and never would be in love with him. Now, she was always teasing him about his new love.

"How's the baker's daughter doing, Paul?"

He beamed. "She is well, thank you."

"It's funny how it's always Monique who delivers the bread now, isn't it?" She winked. "Never her father."

He laughed. "I'm off to get some garden thyme to add to the pâté I'm making for it. It should be good with bread and cheese. I'm trying to get some more cheeses from the dairy."

"Lovely." Nell looked up at the sky. "It will be wonderful if the weather holds, won't it? Such a boost for morale."

"Yes. Your friend Bella said she wanted to have some races." He shrugged. "Is that traditional at picnics in Scotland?"

"Sometimes we do wheelbarrow races, sack races or tugs of war. But it'll depend how many of the patients are able."

"They're saying a lot of them are fit enough now to go back to the Front, have you heard?"

Nell nodded. "Yes, there are quite a few who have recovered enough at last – well, certainly physically. I'm not sure they ever will be prepared mentally. So maybe some fun races or games will take their minds off the prospect."

Paul smiled. "I'll do what I can to make the picnic special." He headed off towards the herb garden, waving at her. "See you later, Hélène. Take care on the roads."

Nell beamed as she watched him limp off. His gait was so much better now, and he seldom used a stick. Every time he saw her taking the ambulance out, he shouted to her from the kitchen window to take care. It always made her smile. She was so delighted he and Monique seemed to be such good friends; in fact, she was now convinced it was more than just friendship. She went back inside, where she splashed her face with water, then headed to the main hall in the abbey to receive her orders for the day.

* * *

One of the men who was soon to be returned to the front was Douglas Harrison. Nell had realised who he was soon after his bandages had been removed and she saw his face fully. That was when she understood how he could be attractive to some women, even her younger sister. He had classic features and deep-set blue eyes that bored into you. She'd not spoken to him very much since that first day, when she'd brought him upstairs on the stretcher. He'd been too ill to speak at first. Then he had been so traumatised, and his injuries had been so severe, he could neither see nor move. Over the long weeks, he'd begun to talk to her about home, and she felt obliged to speak kindly to him, even though she had doubts about his character. She could not exactly pin down why; even though he was ill, there was an arrogant air about him. He was rather too full of himself for Nell's liking.

Then, just a few days before, he'd suddenly walked without sticks into the kitchen where Nell was chatting to Paul and asked for a drink.

"Goodness, you're looking well, Douglas," Nell said.

He beamed. "Thanks. I can see much better now. That ointment has taken effect at last, and my limp's almost gone too. I'm a proper man again," he said, laughing.

Paul stared at him, stony-faced, saying nothing.

"So, what does a gentleman have to do to get a drink around here?" he said, winking at Nell. Of course he emphasised that he was a gentleman, an officer, not merely a humble soldier and certainly not a lowly chef.

She could feel Paul tense beside her.

"What do you want? Cup of tea?"

"If that's all there is, then," he shrugged, "yes. That wine we're given at dinner is rough as anything. I thought there'd at least be brandy for the officers."

Nell burst out laughing. "You're lucky to have any alcohol at all, Douglas. It's just because you're in France that you get wine every day. This isn't a hotel, you know."

"Nothing like the Glen Clova Hotel, is it, Nell?" he said, coming close.

Paul shuffled away, muttering that he had to see to his potatoes.

"Did you used to go there when you were teaching at the school?"

"Yes, though I never told your father I was going. He didn't seem to approve. Probably worried I'd breathe alcohol over the children the next day."

While Nell prepared his tea, Douglas talked more about Clova, glancing towards Paul who was crashing pans around on the cooker. The one thing they never discussed was Effie; Douglas had not mentioned her name once, and Nell was certainly not going to bring the subject up.

"So I hear there's to be an Easter picnic, Nell?"

"Yes, Paul's busy preparing some delicious food for it, aren't you, Chef?"

Paul turned to nod at her, avoiding Douglas's gaze, then continued stirring at the stove.

"Will you take me for the wheelbarrow race, Nell?" Douglas asked. "I think my arms are strong enough and you can hold my rather weak legs."

"Well, let's see who's going to be there and who's able to race, shall we?"

He downed his tea just as Matron was passing the door. "What are you doing in here, Lieutenant Harrison? Out! Back to the ward. This is not a restaurant, you know."

Douglas winked at Nell and sauntered off after Matron.

Paul left the stove and came towards Nell. "Steer clear of him, Hélène. He is not a pleasant man." His expression was grave.

"He's just a bit full of himself – nothing I can't handle."

"I tell you, Hélène, he is dangerous. I feel it in my bones. Please take care."

Chapter 20

August 1943

The bus jolted along the Clova road, and Nell was pleased all the clouds had gone and the sky was clear so Mathilde could see the hills in all their glory. As they came to the fork in the road, Nell pointed out the stone bridge at Gella and the river below, which sparkled in the afternoon sunshine.

"That's where the kids around here fish for trout. The river's full of them." She explained that the glen was wider there than further upstream.

Mathilde was peering up at the hills where the heather still covered the moorland.

"The purple colour – what is that?"

"Heather," Nell said. "Oh," she cried, leaning over her companion towards the window and pointing down to the river. "That bird there, can you see?"

Mathilde nodded.

"It's a curlew," Nell said, then frowned. "It's not that usual to see them in August, mind you, it must be a late fledgling."

"It's got such a long beak."

Nell nodded, then turned to Mathilde. "I can't think of the French word." She sighed. "Ah, is it *'courlis'*?"

Mathilde shrugged. "I have no idea. I've never seen a bird like that. Can you eat them?"

Nell burst out laughing. "Probably in the past – well, anything was eaten when folk were hungry, which they often were around here."

The bus stopped at Wateresk and the other two passengers got out.

"D'you see that area over there, Mathilde, down by the river? That's where they hold a big picnic every summer. Everyone in the glen comes to it. There's usually races and other activities like tugs of war. Obviously since the war started, it's not been the same. Most families have men away fighting." She sighed. "But they've tried to keep it going, for the children."

She looked around at Mathilde who was turning her head from side to side, looking out as the bus jostled along the potholed road.

"I have never seen hills like these," Mathilde said, looking up the glen. "They are so beautiful. It's all very flat where I come from." Her expression grew bleak. "Is this near where the crash happened?"

Nell shook her head. "That's much higher, more in the mountains, over there." She nodded to the other side of the glen. "We'll get up there at the weekend hopefully, if it stays dry."

The bus turned right over the Southesk river. "That's the church over there." Once they had passed the graveyard, she stood up. "This is where we get off. That's our house there. Come on. Hopefully Effie will have the kettle on."

Mathilde was staring at the large whitewashed building ahead. "That's your house?"

Nell chuckled. "No, that's the hotel. Ours is the smaller building up the back there, the schoolhouse."

"You live in a school?"

Nell nodded. "My sister's the teacher."

She took Mathilde's hand to help her down from the bus and shouted at the driver. "Thanks, Jim. See you next week."

"Bye Miss Anderson," he said as he turned the bus around and headed back down the road.

* * *

"Effie, we've got a visitor," Nell shouted as she opened the door to the schoolhouse.

Effie emerged from her bedroom and came towards them.

"This is Mathilde. She doesn't speak any English."

Effie put out her hand to shake their guest's and forced a smile.

"She'll be staying with us for a few days," said Nell, pulling out a seat for Mathilde. "I'll put the kettle on for tea."

Mathilde asked where the bathroom was, and when she'd left the kitchen, Effie rushed over to her sister. "Who is this young woman, Nell?"

"She's French and was at the cemetery today. She knows no one. I'm going to take her up to Muckle Cairn in a day or two, to see where the crash was."

"Was her husband one of those killed?"

Nell paused, then said, "Yes, he was one of the dead." She'd realised over the years that Effie had become rather prudish, narrow-minded; it was perhaps best to say they'd been married.

Effie was about to ask another question when they heard the bathroom door open. Mathilde had pinned her hair up so her pretty face was more visible. The skin on her arms and neckline had more of an olive hue, but her complexion was sallow. She looked exhausted.

Nell indicated the seat at the table. "We've only got tea, I'm afraid, no coffee. Hope that's all right?"

Mathilde attempted a smile. "Thank you."

"Does she not speak any English?" Effie muttered as she went to fetch the milk from the larder.

Nell ignored her and continued to set the table.

"D'you take milk in your tea, Mathilde?" Effie asked, and Nell smiled hearing her sister speak French again; it had been a while.

"No thanks, just sugar."

"Do you have rationing in France?" Effie pushed the sugar bowl towards their guest, who nodded.

"Coffee, sugar, bread, cheese, meat… a long list. Have you ever had coffee made from chicory?" She screwed up her face.

"That sounds disgusting," Effie said. "What about eggs and milk?"

"We were lucky, even with rationing and the Germans trying

to take all our best food, my uncle has a farm nearby, so we never lacked those things. But if the Germans had found out..." She sighed.

Nell poured the tea. "It must be awful living with soldiers in your streets, the enemy occupying your country. I can't even begin to imagine how that would be."

"Strangely, you get used to it. You have to, there's no choice."

There was silence as the three women sipped their tea, then Nell spoke. "Mathilde, if we can get up the hills in two days' time, perhaps you can have a nice relaxing day settling in tomorrow. You must be tired. Then, depending how you feel, we could maybe see about getting you a job?"

Effie could not conceal her shock. "Will you be staying long?"

"I have no idea," Mathilde said. "You ladies are very kind to take me in, but of course I cannot stay with you for too long. I wouldn't want to be a burden."

"Oh, don't worry about that," Nell said. "I'll sleep with my sister, and you can take my room for now."

She swivelled around to face their guest, her eyes bright.

"Can you cook?"

Mathilde smiled. "My family has run our restaurant for over a hundred years. I learned from a very young age."

Nell clapped her hands. "Excellent. The hotel kitchen's always short-staffed, especially these days. I can ask Mr Noble if he could find a space for you, I'm sure it won't be a problem. He may even have a room round the back you could move into."

Effie was frowning. "Won't your family miss you?"

"It was so difficult for me to actually get away, they won't expect to see me for a while."

"Where in France are you from, Mathilde?" Effie asked.

"It's a village to the south-east of Lille, in northern France."

"I've heard of Lille. Is it quite a big city?"

"Pretty big, though our village is small. Before the war, people used to come from the city – and beyond – to dine at our restaurant, it was so famous. Not expensive, just good food."

"Is it near Paris? Nell was near there during the last war, weren't you, Nell?"

She nodded. "Yes, nearly four years in Royaumont Abbey to the north-east of Paris."

"Lille is further east than that. In fact, it's so near the Belgian border, the Germans have incorporated us into the Belgian authorities for their administration." She pursed her lips. "Though it doesn't really matter; both France and Belgium are not our own countries anymore."

"Belgium," Effie said. "You live near there?"

"She just said that," Nell quipped.

"Yes, do you know anyone from Belgium?" Mathilde asked.

Nell shook her head.

Effie looked away. "I used to, a long time ago."

Chapter 21

August 1943

"Sorry the boots are a bit big. I hope you don't get blisters."

"It's fine, Hélène. The thick socks are helping." She looked up towards the north. "Is that fog or are those clouds up ahead?"

Nell shrugged. "It's hard to tell until you get there. We'll get a better idea once we're up at the loch."

The two women were walking up from Wheen farm on a path that wound its way up the slopes.

"This first part is actually the steepest. Do you want to stop for a drink?"

Mathilde nodded. She had been puffing for the last few minutes, and Nell was worried about her. Even though she must be some fifteen years older, Nell was used to the hills. Also, she cycled miles up and down the glen on her postal rounds.

They sat down on a rock and gulped from their flasks. "The water tastes so good here. At home it's better to drink wine." She smiled. "Look at that view down the river, you are so lucky to live here."

"Well, it is rather lovely when it's dry, but when it pours, as it often does, or floods, or when we're snowed in – then it's a different matter entirely."

"Did I tell you how Pierre and I met?"

"No." Nell stood up. "Shall we keep on going, if you've got your breath back? I don't want us doing the walk in the rain – or mist."

They started to walk uphill again.

"Pierre had been on a bombing mission over Germany and they were shot down. He was the only survivor." She sighed. "So different from this crash up here, though there was also one survivor. Does anyone know what happened to him?"

Nell shook her head. "Dr Geddes said he left the hospital a

couple of weeks after the crash and presumed he was back to normal flying duties. It must be so awful to have to just carry on like that."

Mathilde nodded. "Pierre was not badly wounded, and it was night when they crashed, so he just kept walking in a westerly direction, always under cover of darkness. Eventually he came to our village. He hid in my uncle's barn. Then when I went there from the restaurant to collect the eggs, I found him. He was sound asleep in a pile of hay. I'd noticed something different from usual, so I'd gone over to inspect. He was terrified I was German – he had lost all sense of time and direction – but when I spoke French, he was so relieved."

"How on earth did you manage to hide him? Presumably it wasn't for long?"

"Amazingly, it was for three months. That was the soonest we could get transport across to England sorted. The *Réseau Comète* had just been set up in our area, but there were so many men they were helping escape from the Germans. Luckily it was summer, and it wasn't too cold. He was able to stay out of sight in the barn. The couple of times the Germans searched, we took him down into the wine cellars."

"Not a bad place to be," Nell said, smiling. She looked ahead; they were nearly at Loch Wharral. They'd have another break there, but not for long. The weather was changing; she could feel a nip in the air and the mist was descending.

"And during that time, though it was really scary, we soon fell in love. I'd often creep out of the house and spend the night in the barn with him. It was the most wonderful three months, and yet…" She sighed. "It was so dangerous. We were always on the lookout for the soldiers. When I was working in the restaurant, we often had to take German customers, the officers of course, and I wanted to spit in their faces or poison their food. But we all just had to carry on as if everything was normal. It was funny to think that there they were, stuffing themselves with our delicious food, and just downstairs in the cellar or across the courtyard in the barn was their enemy. Of course we too were their enemies, but we were useful to them: we fed them, and fed them well."

"When was the last time you saw Pierre?"

"The night my uncle managed to get transport for him over to England. The soldiers were usually sent by the Réseau through France to Spain, but it was decided he was better going to England. It had taken my uncle and the *Réseau* operators all that time to arrange the passage, but it helped that my uncle knew the fishermen along the coast." She smiled. "So he made it. He was back to flying duties all too quickly and up to Scotland. And then there was the crash…" She bowed her head, then looked up. "Is that a lake ahead?"

"Yes, it's called Loch Wharral. We can have a quick drink here, but then we have to get moving across the ridge."

They sat down by the loch and looked over the water towards the crags at the far shore, which were still just visible in the mist.

"Can you fish here?"

"Yes, easily. There's fish aplenty and little competition for them: it's too high for most people." A noise made Nell look off towards Ben Tirran to their right. "Oh, can you see the grouse?" She pointed to where some birds were taking off and flying up above the heather. "There are so many of them up here."

"And they're shot to be eaten?"

"Yes," said Nell, grinning. "You might see some in the hotel soon, the season started a few days ago."

They continued on up the hill, then over the bleak ridge as the mist began to settle. It was difficult to see anything more than a few feet ahead. They were now silent, Mathilde walking close behind Nell so she did not lose sight of her.

"Soon we'll be heading down the slope and then up at the other side. If I'd not done this walk before, it'd be really difficult to find in the fog."

Scrambling down the slope, they reached the burn. Nell pointed towards the top. "That's where the wreckage is. We don't have long to go, nearly there."

And as they walked on up in the stillness of the derelict landscape, the ground soon levelled off. Suddenly, in the midst of the bleak and desolate landscape, they saw metal. Lots of it.

* * *

Even through the fine mist, it was easy to see the wreckage. They could make out huge pieces of engine, propeller, fuselage and tail fin.

"How high are we, Nell?"

"Over two and a half thousand feet…" Nell stopped and counted on her fingers. "About 800 metres?"

Mathilde let out a long breath. "So high, surely there was little chance of survival. But why didn't they all walk away like that one man?"

"I think it was because he was in the tail of the plane. It must have hit the ground nose first. I think there was mist up here that day. Some folk say the pilot was attempting a controlled crash landing."

Mathilde began to walk around the area covered by all the debris. Nell stood quite still, watching her. It was clearly causing her such pain, so Nell said nothing. Mist and sadness filled the silence. She stood by one of the engines, staring across the bare moorland as the mist swirled around. How could the survivor have found his way down? He must have had a compass and perhaps knew he should head south-west, away from the mountains, towards the glen. He must also have taken the photo from Pierre's pocket, as he had presumably promised him.

She turned to watch Mathilde pick up a piece of the metal fuselage. "Look how flimsy it is, Nell. How could all this thin metal have carried those five brave men?" She sighed, then replaced the fragment on the grass.

"I'm sure you could take a small piece, if you wanted," Nell said, tentatively.

Mathilde shook her head. "It's where Pierre died. The ground is sacred, perhaps even more than the graveyard where he's buried." She wandered around the wreckage again, then opened her backpack. She had spent the day before up in the woods behind the house gathering twigs and slender branches, and she'd fashioned a wooden cross, tied together with twine.

Nell watched as she came towards the engine and placed the cross into an aluminium ring, pushing it down to make it stay upright. Mathilde bowed her head and shut her eyes. As Mathilde's shoulders began to shake with silent sobs, Nell turned her head away and looked towards the hills to the west where a covey of grouse was flying low across the heather, slowly gaining height before disappearing into the mist.

Chapter 22

April 1917

The morning of the Easter picnic was overcast but warm. Nell had been out till early morning in the ambulance collecting the injured from Creil, but had managed a couple of hours' sleep. It had been another harrowing trip, one of the soldiers so badly injured she didn't think he would survive the drive back to Royaumont. But she'd stayed with the nurses for a while after helping them get the stretcher upstairs to the operating theatres, and she was pleased the initial assessment had been slightly less pessimistic. She hoped to see Dr Nicholl, who'd operated, to ask how it had gone.

"What time are we all meant to be at the picnic, Nell?" Bella boomed at her from the courtyard when she went downstairs to wash.

Nell wiped her face and went over to Bella.

"About midday I think. I was just going to go to the kitchen to see if Paul needs a hand."

"I'll see if the orderlies need help setting out chairs or rugs or whatever we're meant to sit on."

"You've got all the races organised?"

Bella nodded. "Yes, and hopefully those unable to walk will join in in their wheelchairs." She looked up. "Thank God it's not raining."

Bella pointed to the towel in her hands. "You know towels are now washed once a fortnight, Nell?"

"Yes, and sheets. I just got them fresh yesterday, that's why this towel smells so good." She brought it to her nose and inhaled. "I hate getting to the last day, it's so grubby."

Nell said goodbye to Bella, then got dressed and headed for the kitchen.

Paul was standing with his back to the door, looking at the long table which was laden with food.

"That all looks fantastic, Paul. Well done!" Nell said, coming to stand beside him.

He turned and smiled, his dimples appearing in his pale cheeks. Though he'd put on some weight since he had first come to Royaumont, his face still had a sallow hue. He'd told Nell he used to be brown as a nut all summer when he lived in Provence and spent every day outside in the sun.

"Can you help me cover the food?" He handed her some cloths. "And by the way, it wasn't just me. It was the whole team." He pointed towards the sink where a man and a woman were washing dishes and shouted, "You two did a brilliant job!"

They turned around and smiled back at their boss.

"Hélène," Paul said, looking directly at his friend. "I'll say this right now. I am not going to go in for any of the races, even ones I could do, like your very strange egg and spoon race."

"Why not? You can walk fine without your stick, can't you?" She pointed to the stick at the door.

"Of course I can, but I always feel safer knowing it's there, just in case."

"But everyone will…"

"I am not doing it, Hélène. But I shall enjoy seeing you take part."

"Well, let's see who's able to do what, shall we?" She looked at the clock. "When d'you need me back to help take the food out?"

"In an hour or so?"

She nodded. "No problem. I'm off to see Dr Nicholl. She operated on a really sick man last night. I'm really hoping he pulled through."

Paul's expression dimmed. "I saw the night orderlies carry a body downstairs when I came in early this morning. It was dark of course, but I could see as they passed through the moonlit cloisters that the sheet was fully over his head. He must have died in the night."

Nell sighed.

"Then Dr Nicholl ran after them and placed a sheet of paper on top of the body before walking back upstairs."

Nell nodded. So he had definitely died. The document would contain the name and age of the patient and the names of the witnesses there when he had died – usually the surgeon, nurses and often an orderly.

Even with the picnic to look forward to, there was always deep sadness at Royaumont.

* * *

"Paul," Nell said, ramming a piece of bread and pâté into her mouth, "this is really delicious."

She covered her mouth. "Sorry, I shouldn't speak with my mouth full, but it's so good."

Paul smiled as he walked past, carrying more food over to the table set up at the edge of the woods where everyone was gathered for the picnic. Some of the staff sat on rugs, others sat on chairs beside the patients who were either in wheelchairs or in beds that had been wheeled outside.

Everyone said how lucky they were with the weather; though it was still cloudy, it was dry and not cold. There had been no alternative plan in case it rained. Nell watched Paul put the food down on the table, then pick up his stick. He always found it more difficult to walk on grass.

"Right, everyone, time for the races to begin," boomed Bella, and those who could stood up. "It's the wheelbarrow race first. Pick your partners and assemble at the far end please!"

Nell was heading over to one of the French patients who was about to be released and sent back to the Front, when she felt a firm hand on her shoulder.

"Miss Anderson, please would you do me the honour of being

my partner in this race?" It was as if they were at a formal dance, not a hospital picnic in the middle of a war.

Nell turned around and saw it was Douglas Harrison, who she'd been trying to avoid. She didn't feel anything sinister about him, as Paul did, but she just couldn't take to his arrogant ways. She felt it put her fellow Scots in a bad light somehow.

"Well, Douglas, I was going to take Monsieur Mouliet over there, sorry." But as she pointed towards the patient, an orderly was already pulling him up from his seat and taking him over to the start line.

"Looks like you have no choice now, Nell," he said, beaming. The patients were always meant to address the staff by their surname, but he hardly ever did that with her. Nell found it rather too cosy for her liking.

She shrugged. "All right. Are your arms up to it?"

"There's never been anything wrong with my arms, Nell Anderson."

They walked towards the start line, and he crouched down. "Take my legs, let's do a practice walk." They staggered around behind the line before returning as Bella shouted at everyone to get ready.

She counted the racers down, then off they all went at the starter's whistle. Some couples collapsed at the start, others midway, but Nell and Douglas soon pulled into second place, behind one of the orderlies and a large Frenchman with enormous arms. Even through his jacket, you could see his muscles bulge.

The two couples were neck and neck, heading at some speed for the finishing line. Douglas was yelling at Nell to hurry up, that they could win.

"Faster, Faster!" he shouted.

But Nell made the mistake of looking around at the spectators who were laughing and clapping as they cheered them on, and she suddenly got a fit of the giggles. A few yards before the finish, she dropped his legs and bent over, laughing. She straightened up and tried to control herself.

"Sorry Douglas, are you all right?" she asked, pulling him up as they shuffled over the line.

His face was contorted into a scowl. "Why the hell did you drop me?"

"I just couldn't carry your legs anymore, I got the giggles." His face was thunder. "I'm so sorry."

He got to his feet. "We were so near to winning and now they've won instead!"

"Douglas, it's only a bit of fun," she said as he turned away and stormed across to where the drinks were laid out. She watched as he downed a tumbler of wine and screwed up his eyes as he always did, since the wine, in his words, was no better than dog piss.

An hour later, after all the races had been won and the prize-giving was over, Nell was tidying everything up with the other chauffeuses and the orderlies, nurses and doctors. She had just headed towards the woods to pick up a bit of paper she'd seen fly away in the wind when she became aware someone was right beside her. She turned to see Douglas.

"Nell, I must apologise for my behaviour earlier. It was most ungentlemanly. Will you forgive me?"

When he smiled, he really was quite handsome. She could almost see what her sister had seen in him.

"It's fine," she said, smiling back. "Please don't even think about it."

"Nell, I don't know if you remember, but I'm a bit of a geology buff. When I was walking in the woods the other day I saw something interesting. Can I show you?"

"I don't really have time, I have to help the others clear up."

"It won't take long."

Nell sighed. He really did seem sorry. Perhaps she ought to do this for him, by way of accepting his apology. "All right, but I've not got long," she said as he led the way into the woods.

They soon came to a clearing where a couple of large boulders stood.

"Do you see these, Nell? These are sandstone, formed by grains of quartz cemented together millions of years ago. I find them so beautiful."

Nell nodded. "They really are," she said, looking around at the circle of dark trees.

Douglas was gazing directly at her, not at the rocks. It was unsettling.

"Well, I'd better be getting back," she said, starting to walk to the entrance of the clearing.

But he grabbed her hand. "Come on, Nell, let me give you a kiss."

She sprang back and tried to shake his hand away, but his grip was strong. "Don't be ridiculous, Douglas, we both have to get back. Let me go," she hissed as he moved in close.

He was pushing her towards the trunk of one of the trees, and as she struggled to release his grasp, she stumbled on some tree roots, but he held on fast. As he leant in towards her to try to kiss her, she twisted her head around and he let go with one of his hands to place it on her shoulder, finding the edge of her shirt. He began to yank it upwards, and she heard the top button pop loose; he was clearly about to rip it off her. She suddenly understood what was happening and tried to shift her legs so she could kick him, but he had her pinned against the tree. All of a sudden, there was a cry from the woods.

"Let her go! Now!"

They both turned around to see Paul limping towards them, his stick in the air. Nell had never seen him move so fast. Douglas let Nell go, and as she pulled her shirt back down, she could see Paul's face was purple with rage. Douglas raised his hands. "We were just having a bit of fun, she prefers able-bodied men to…"

And that was when Paul swung his stick and hit Douglas with a thwack across his back. As Douglas slumped to the ground,

Paul reached out his hand to Nell. "Come, Hélène, I shall escort you back, we will leave this idiot here."

Nell was too stunned to speak, but at the edge of the clearing, they both turned around to see Douglas stagger to his feet. "She was up for it, you know, she's a game girl!" he yelled after them, before rubbing his back and beginning to follow.

Paul swung around. "How dare he try to smear your reputation, Hélène, I'm going to…"

Nell grabbed his arm. "Leave him, he's not worth a fight, Paul." And as Paul turned back around, she whispered, "Thank you, you were right about him." She squeezed his hand, then straightened up her shirt and they walked back, arm in arm, out of the woods.

Chapter 23

September 1943

Mrs Bell pushed the pile of letters and parcels across the post office desk to Nell without a word. Then she reached her hand inside the pocket of her cardigan and brought out a telegram.

"This is for the manse, Helen," she said gravely.

Nell took it from her. "Oh no." She took a deep breath, then exhaled slowly.

"I'll see you later," she said, looking up at the post mistress, whose eyes were filled with tears.

She swung her bag over her shoulders and headed straight over the road to the manse; there was no point in delaying this. She left her bike at the gate and stepped along the path to the front door, then tapped on the knocker.

Mrs Johnson came to the door, wiping her hands on her apron and smiling. "Hello, Helen, how are…"

And then she saw Nell's face and looked down at what was in her hand. Her eyes opened wide.

"William!" she shrieked. "Come now!"

Nell stood on the doorstep, the telegram outstretched, while the minister rushed out from his study and stopped to take in the scene. As he stood in the hall, Nell could see his face drain of colour. Then he walked towards his wife and patted her gently on the shoulder. She cowered beside him, hands over ears, as if making herself small would mean the words she'd most dreaded hearing simply would not be uttered.

"I see you have a telegram for me, Helen. Thank you," he said, stretching out his hand. And then, in a movement so different from his usual measured actions, he tore into it urgently, letting the envelope drop to the floor. Nell wanted to leave, but she was somehow rooted to the spot as he began reading out loud.

"Rev Johnson, Regret to inform you…"

She spun around and left, taking in gulps of fresh air once outside. As she got to the gate, she could hear the noise of a woman wailing through the open door. Nell looked up to the sky and cursed the fact it was a beautiful, sunny day; it should be gloomy and grey. And then she heard the low, agonising moan from the voice of a man she had only ever known as composed and restrained.

By the time she had done all her deliveries that afternoon, the news had spread.

"Did you hear what was in the telegram, Helen?" Mrs Bell asked. "It was Jimmy Johnson, killed in an aeroplane crash somewhere over Germany. There were no survivors." She shook her head. "Mrs Johnson's taking it really badly. Well, of course she is, but so bad the minister came to find Mrs Tweedie to sit with her while he phoned family with the news. He was worried she'd hurt herself."

Nell shuddered. "It was Mrs Johnson's greatest fear. Her other two lads both prisoners of war and now Jimmy dead. How old was he?"

"Mrs Tweedie thought only twenty-two – so young, such a waste."

"What a horrible time for them."

Mrs Bell nodded.

"Is there anything else we can do for them, d'you think?"

"Everyone in the glen will make food and leave it on their doorstep, but no one will want to intrude on their grief."

"I'll get Mathilde to make a pie or something like that, she's good at pastry."

She looked back at Mrs Bell. "Is there anything else you need me to do here?"

The woman shook her head and raised her hand in a goodbye.

Nell cycled home. As she passed the manse, she glanced over and saw all the curtains were shut. She did not want to meet anyone; she wasn't sure she could speak about it yet. Thankfully she made it to her door without seeing a single soul.

* * *

A week later, Nell sat at the table, pushing away a clean plate. "That was delicious, Mathilde. I don't know how you can make something so good from so little." She grinned. "If it weren't bad manners, I'd lick my plate."

"It's true," said Effie. "What a good pie that was. Your pastry is so light. How do you do that without butter?"

Mathilde beamed. "Lots of practice at the family restaurant during rationing. A splash of vinegar does wonders. I'm so glad you enjoyed it."

Over the past few weeks, the sisters had tried to find out more about Mathilde's family, but she was reticent; perhaps it might make her too sad if she spoke about them. The only person she seemed to want to talk about was her uncle, who continued to run the family restaurant. She shut down when there were any questions about her parents or siblings. Nell wondered if perhaps they were all dead or she had brothers away fighting. Or maybe she missed her mother and father so much, she could not speak about them for fear of breaking down.

"Please let me clear up and wash the dishes," said Mathilde as Nell got out of her seat.

"No, we should do it, Mathilde, you cooked for us."

"And you have let me stay in your house for nearly six weeks now, I'm so grateful." She raised her hand to indicate that the sisters should remain in their seats. "I was just thinking, if it hadn't been for the photo that airman gave you after the crash, Nell, I'd never have come here, to a place I feel so at home."

The sisters smiled.

"Mathilde was in the classroom today, teaching the children the days of the week in French and how to say 'My name is …

Angus or Mollie'," Effie told Nell. She shouted over to Mathilde at the sink. "They seemed to really enjoy it, didn't they?"

"Yes, but they also loved it when you played the piano. You are so talented."

"What did you play, Effie?"

"I was just playing 'Frère Jacques' and 'Au Clair de la Lune', nothing hard at all."

"I tried to learn the piano," said Mathilde, "and though I can read a little music, I can't do anything without a music sheet in front of me. You just do it from memory. That's a talent, surely."

Nell smiled at Effie. "It's true, you don't play the piano enough." She turned to Mathilde. "You should hear her playing Debussy or Mendelssohn. Oh, and Chopin, all by heart; she is so good."

"Yes, well," said Effie, getting to her feet, "it's not that hard really. Now, Mathilde, let me dry the dishes," she said, grabbing the dishcloth from the range.

Nell shook her head. "Always so modest, Effie. You should recognise your talent."

Effie remained silent.

"We're due to go to the hotel in half an hour, Mathilde," said Nell. "Mr Noble is hoping to be free then and we'll discuss the possibility of you working in the kitchen. He said it might just be breakfast duties, but at least that's something."

"I don't mind cleaning the rooms too. Just to have some sort of work would be good after all this time."

Nell went to switch on the wireless and sat beside it while the other two chatted at the sink. Soon she leapt to her feet. "Italy's surrendered to the Allies! Come and listen," she yelled to Effie and Mathilde.

As they leant towards the radio, Nell translated for Mathilde. At the end of the bulletin, they clapped their hands.

"Could that mean the Germans might leave France soon too?" Mathilde's eyes were wet with tears.

"They've got to get out of Italy first. The Allies still have to push them north, out of the rest of Italy; they're still just in the very south."

"But it's a really good sign," Effie said, patting Mathilde's hand. "Hopefully things are going to turn our way at last."

* * *

"Mathilde, this is Mr Noble," Nell said, introducing them.

"Come and sit down. Let's get down to detail."

Mathilde had learned some English in the past few weeks, but Nell said she'd help to translate.

After ten minutes, the terms had been settled. Mathilde was to work every morning on the breakfast shift, then help Mrs Mackie in the evenings when required. She could also help Nell in the bar if it was busy. In return, she would have food provided and a room at the back of the hotel.

"It's really small, but it's quiet round the back; you won't hear the noise from the bar or anything," Mr Noble said as he got to his feet.

Mathilde went off with Mr Noble to see the room, and Nell went to the bar to start her shift.

"Thanks for standing in for me," she said to the woman at the bar who sometimes helped serve food in the dining room. "I couldn't get away before now."

She nodded and headed off. Nell went behind the bar; thankfully it was clean and tidy. She looked around at the customers. There was the usual table of gamekeepers from the estate and a couple of older farmers, but in the far corner was a young man she didn't recognise, sitting by himself.

He had a half pint of beer in front of him and held a newspaper in both hands. He put it down on the table to lift up his drink, then looked over at Nell and smiled. It was such a charming smile, Nell thought, turning away. Then Nell gasped: good God, the man looked exactly like Douglas Harrison.

Chapter 24

July 1917

For once, the half doors in her ambulance cab were a godsend. It was such a hot summer and there seemed to be so little fresh air, it was stifling. Even once they had loaded the injured into the back and she drove them carefully along the road, the breeze through the side doors gave little respite.

Also, the smells were so much worse in the heat. The nauseating stench of gangrene and other infections seemed to hang in the warm air. Thank God it was a little cooler inside Royaumont. The freezing cold conditions the staff complained about in the long, hard winters would have been welcome in the summer.

Nell was walking back across the courtyard after her last shift when she heard Paul call to her.

"Hélène, I've just made some soup. D'you want any?"

She smiled. How did Paul always know when she needed something to eat?

"Isn't it too hot for soup, Paul?" She grinned.

"Never too hot for Provençal vegetable soup with pistou. My basil's really good right now." He waved a bunch of herbs at her.

"Give me five minutes and I'll come over."

Soon she was sitting down in front of an empty bowl in the kitchen.

"I started to make my pâté this morning and thought again of the Easter picnic and what happened after, Hélène."

Nell sighed. She knew what he was going to say.

"I still think you should have reported him. I would have, if you'd not insisted you didn't want to."

"Douglas Harrison is a wicked waste of space, Paul, but he's back at the Front. That's punishment enough, surely?"

He raised his shoulders.

"He might even be dead, for all we know."

"I hope he is."

Nell shook her head. "Maybe, Paul, I don't know. I just feel he's not even worth talking about. He's a sad, arrogant and probably very lonely man. And we'll never see him again or hear anything about him."

"But he might try it again, with someone less able to defend herself than you."

"Paul, we've talked about this too much. I want to forget it." She pointed to a large pan on the stove. "Now, am I ever going to get my soup?" She winked and grabbed a spoon from the drawer.

* * *

The post had just arrived, and Nell had received a letter addressed in handwriting she didn't recognise. She ripped it open and scanned down to the end. It was from Aunt Winnie.

My dear Helen,

Your father gave me your address and I do hope you don't mind my writing to you. He tells me regularly about your work, and I have to say, I am so impressed and proud I have a niece doing such important work in France.

I don't know what you hear from your sister, but, as well as saying how much I admire you for your extraordinary contribution to the war, I also wanted to ask you something about her. You probably heard from Euphemia that her last few months at the farm here in Glen Prosen were a little challenging.

What on earth was she talking about? Effie had mentioned it wasn't all fun and games during her time there, but it was wartime; what had her aunt expected?

Since she returned to Clova nearly two years ago, she has not answered any of my letters. I hear what she is doing from your father, but as you know, he is a man of few words and so I get no detail. I write every two to three months, but never get any reply.

They invited me to stay with them over in Clova two Christmases ago, but the snow was so bad, I didn't even get the letter until early January. Both glens were snowed in for weeks.

Nell remembered when Effie had told her their father wanted to invite their aunt and at the time she had wondered why Effie was so against it.

If you have any insight, dear Helen, about why your sister is ignoring me, I should be only too glad to hear. I would so love to hear from her, and hope she is well. Goodness knows how long this dreadful war is going to last. I am lucky that, at the moment, I have your cousin Allan here to help run the farm, but there are rumblings amongst the farming community that even sons who are keeping the farms going are to be conscripted soon. They're that desperate now. That would be the most awful decision, but as usual, we women are helpless, we have no agency. We still cannot even vote, though hopefully those stalwarts protesting about women's suffrage all over the country might do some good. But nothing is going to happen any time soon.

I will leave you now, but do know I think of you often and admire what you and your fellow women are doing over there for the war.
  With love
  Aunt Winifred

Nell re-read the letter and was about to write to Effie when she heard the alarm bell down below. She flung her writing things back in the drawer and sped off towards the ambulance and another load of poor, injured men.

Chapter 25

October 1943

When she arrived at the hotel for her bar shift, Mr Noble told Nell that Mathilde was still in the kitchen with Mrs Mackie. She popped her head round the door and saw the old cook laughing beside Mathilde, who had a huge grin on her tear-stained face. The two of them were chopping onions.

"Are you all right, Mathilde? What are you two laughing about?"

"It's the onions, Nell," said Mathilde. "We can't really speak to each other as my English is still so poor, but we're teaching each other to do different tasks in the kitchen. But now of course the onions are making us cry."

"Helen, you should have seen her peel a turnip. She'd never done one! She says they're only ever fed to animals in France. Well, probably not now, with the war on, but she said it was impossible to peel. She hacked half the flesh off!"

Mathilde continued to chop the onion with dexterity and finesse.

"But would you look at the way she does an onion, such skill that girl's got. And she's so fast. Maybe it's my arthritic fingers, but I certainly can't chop like that. I've never seen anyone work so quickly on vegetables." She burst out laughing again. "Well, apart from turnips."

Mathilde finished the chopping and tidied everything away from the counter. "What can I do now, Mrs Mackie?"

"Your English is coming along fine," Nell said, clapping her hands. She'd had very little time to teach her, but Effie said she would give her some lessons in the Tattie holidays, which had just started.

"You're looking much better, Mathilde. You're settling in well."

"It could be something to do with the attention she's been getting from that young man," said Mrs Mackie, winking.

Mathilde frowned, and as Nell translated, she noticed a pink hue flush across the French woman's cheeks.

"Not at all," she said, heading towards the larder with the prepared vegetables.

"Is that the single man I've seen in the bar a couple of times, Mrs Mackie?" Nell leant in to whisper to the cook.

She nodded and they both looked towards Mathilde as she came back through the door.

"Right, I'll be off home now," said the cook. "Thanks, Mathilde, you're such a good worker! Remember to soak the breakfast porridge please – and I'll see you about nine."

She turned to Nell while Mathilde went back to the larder for the oatmeal. "I don't know why, but she reminds me a little of your grandfather, Monsieur Fournier. It must be her cooking skills." She grabbed her coat at the door and waved goodbye. "See you tomorrow."

* * *

"Were you not meant to be going on an outing this week, Effie? The priory near Forfar or somewhere like that?"

Effie's face clouded over. "I decided against the trip. I can feel a cold coming on." She sniffed noisily.

"You seem perfectly well to me," Nell said, then saw her sister's lips purse together. She knew not to continue with a conversation when she was like that.

She delved into her jacket pocket and brought out a letter. "Effie, since you make such a song and dance about who's first to read letters addressed to the Misses Anderson, I decided not to open this one. It's for both of us. Here you go," she said, flinging the letter over to Effie.

Effie's eyes narrowed as she peered at the letter. "Whose handwriting d'you think it is? It looks like an old person's?"

"That's what I thought."

Effie removed the letter from its envelope and looked down to the foot. "Oh, it's from Aunt Winnie." Nell watched her quickly scan the contents before beginning to read out loud.

Dear Helen and Euphemia,

I am writing to tell you I shall be coming to Clova next week. Euphemia, you will remember my devoted housekeeper Betty? Very sadly, she died last Friday, and her funeral service will be at Clova kirk. I think you knew her family are from up the glen, towards Doll.

I shall be arriving at the schoolhouse next Monday to stay with you for two nights and look forward very much to seeing you both again.

Your loving Aunt Winifred

"She doesn't even ask if she can stay. She just assumes she's welcome!" Effie was scowling.

"Well of course she can stay. She can have my room; I'll share with you."

"I'm sure she can afford to stay at the hotel. She's never been short of money."

"But Effie, she's our aunt, our father's sister. And we've not seen her for years. Remember she was too ill to come to Pa's funeral? Also, you stayed with her for almost a year back in the last war."

"You can look after her, then. I will be back teaching next week. I'll be far too busy."

Effie stood up and began to thump dishes around to set the table for supper.

"Well, I'm looking forward to seeing her. What age must she be now? Late seventies?"

Effie shrugged and continued to busy herself with tea.

"I'll ask at the hotel if they've been asked to do the wake. I imagine so, as it'd be too far for folk to go to the family house if they're from along at Glen Doll."

Nell stood up and looked at the letter. The handwriting was spidery. "It's interesting how old people's writing becomes so bad. It must be her eyesight." She put it back in the envelope. "Oh, she hasn't mentioned if our cousins will be coming, has she? Presumably not, but it'll be good to hear all about them, won't it?"

Effie remained silent and Nell shook her head, smiling. Honestly, her sister was so sulky at times. She had no idea, though, what this was all about.

Chapter 26

October 1943

"It's so good to see you again," Aunt Winnie said, easing herself carefully into an armchair at the schoolhouse.

"How are you?" Nell hung up her aunt's hat and coat, then came to sit down opposite her by the fire. She looked much frailer than the last time she had seen her. Her hair was quite untidy, wispy strands falling down over her face; Nell was sure she'd always had her hair pulled back neatly into a tight bun.

"I'm doing rather well today, Helen, I must say. Though some days I am a little, how does Allan put it… forgetful." She shrugged and looked around the room. "Where is Euphemia?"

"Oh, she'll be here later, she's doing some preparation in the classroom for tomorrow's lessons. She can't manage to go to the funeral tomorrow; she has to teach, of course. But I'll accompany you. I've got someone to cover my post rounds."

Nell didn't like to say her sister had made it clear she did not want to see their aunt at all, and Nell had to persuade her to join them for supper. She had refused to explain why she was reluctant.

"It's such a long time since we saw you. Was it the Glen Prosen picnic the year before Pa died?"

Winifred screwed up her eyes. "Was my brother there?"

"Yes, he and I drove round to Prosen in his car."

"Yes, I think I can remember that. And was your sister there?"

Nell shook her head. "Effie's friend Bessie's mother had just died. She wanted to stay with her."

"Ah, I see. And when did my brother die? Was it last year?"

"No, it was about four years ago. You had pneumonia and were in hospital."

"Pneumonia? Well, well. And me as strong as an ox, too." She shook her head.

The door swung open, and Effie came in and stood, unmoving, on the mat. Nell watched her sister take a deep breath. Then she smiled and ran to embrace her aunt. When she stepped back, she had tears in her eyes.

"How lovely to see you, dear Euphemia, and looking so well. It's been far too long, child. Far too long!" Aunt Winnie was flushed. She was clearly not expecting a hug.

"I know, I'm sorry, I just couldn't…" Effie was snivelling.

Nell was looking on, eyes wide. Then, to fill the silence she said, "I'll go and put the kettle on and make some tea. Why don't we sit over at the table. I've made treacle scones." She went to fill the kettle and glanced over to her sister and aunt. They were both still silent. "Come on over, there's so much news to catch up on."

As Effie gave Aunt Winnie her arm to take her to the table, they began to speak.

"I was sorry to hear about Betty. She was so kind to me."

"She was indeed a kindly woman. She had a heart of gold underneath that brusque exterior. I will miss her very much."

Nell placed the teapot on the table and pointed to the plate of buttered scones. "Help yourselves. I've got to pop over to the hotel for a quick shift at the bar and to see if everything's ready for the wake tomorrow. But I'll be back for supper. Mathilde's made us some soup."

"Who?"

Effie poured the tea. "I'll explain who she is in a minute, Aunt Winnie. First tell me about everyone over at Prosen. How is Allan?"

Nell grabbed her coat and shut the door quietly behind her. On the way past the window, she looked in and saw Effie and her aunt holding hands over the table. Effie looked like she was crying. What on earth was going on?

* * *

The next day was typical funeral weather: grey and wet. Nell put up the umbrella and held it over her aunt's head. She cowered underneath too, and as they strolled over the road towards the church, she thought back to the strange evening they'd had at the schoolhouse: by the time Nell had returned from her shift at the hotel, Effie and her aunt had had their supper, and Aunt Winnie was in the bathroom getting ready for bed.

"It's only seven o'clock, Effie. Is she actually going to sleep now?"

"She said it was a tiring journey."

"It's only fifteen miles by car – hardly like a trip to Dundee or Perth."

"Well, she's old now and that's what she wanted to do."

"I thought you might have persuaded her to stay up a bit later. You knew I'd be back about now."

Effie shrugged and went to the stove. "Shall I ladle out your soup, Nell?"

She nodded and sat down. "So what were you and Aunt Winnie talking about? You seemed deep in conversation when I left."

"Oh, just news of the village and everyone I got to know there."

She placed Nell's soup on the table, then headed for the door.

"Where are you going now?"

"Off to practise the piano, I'm doing some more songs with the children tomorrow." She grabbed her coat from the hook. "See you later," she said, slamming the door behind her.

Later, in the bedroom, Effie clearly feigned sleep when Nell had come to bed after her, having stayed up listening to the wireless.

The next morning, as she sat with her aunt, who'd worn a forlorn expression all morning, she continued wondering why Effie was being so odd. Then she thought back to that letter from Aunt Winnie while she was at Royaumont. Nell had written soon after to her sister, asking why she hadn't replied to any letters, and Effie's return letter had referred to it in a short PS. Thank you, Nell, for telling me about our aunt. I shall respond when I have time. And nothing else was ever mentioned as the absurdity of war took over each sister's life.

They passed the hotel and saw a huddle of people wearing black, sheltering under the awning at the front.

"There's some folk waiting over there; they'll be coming to the funeral too, Aunt Winnie," said Nell, pointing.

"I don't imagine there will be many able to come from Glen Prosen, unless they get a lift. It's not the sort of day for walking the Minister's Path."

"No, it couldn't be worse weather for a walk – or a funeral," Nell said, huddling in closer under the umbrella.

They took their seats near the front of the church and Nell looked around. She recognised some of the people from Glen Doll from her postal rounds, but none of the others. She presumed they would all be from Prosen. Aunt Winnie did not look around at all but kept staring ahead. Morning light usually poured through the stained-glass window at the front, but today it was just dull and gloomy.

Soon the organist stopped playing medleys and began to play a solemn piece which Nell recognised but could not identify; Effie was the one who knew all the hymns. Everyone got to their feet and looked around as the minister walked in, in his flowing robes, with the coffin borne high behind him.

Once the casket was placed on the bier and the coffin-bearers were seated, the minister went to stand before it. He lifted his head to address the congregation of mourners, and as he said the words "Let us pray", Nell stared: she knew Mr Johnson was on compassionate leave and would not be taking services for a while, but now she realised this minister was familiar. He was the young man she'd seen in the bar, the man who Mrs Mackie had said was keen on Mathilde, the man who looked just like Douglas Harrison did all those years ago.

Chapter 27

October 1943

Nell eased her aunt onto a chair at a table of Glen Prosen mourners and headed off to the kitchen. She'd offered to help serve them tea and sandwiches.

Mathilde was arranging sandwiches on the plates, and Mrs Mackie was in the corner filling teapots.

"Right, I'm here. What can I do?"

"Check the sausage rolls in the oven, would you, Helen?" The cook looked up at the clock. "They should be ready any minute."

As Nell opened the oven door, the most glorious smell emerged. She brought out a tray of crusty, golden sausage rolls. "Where are these to go?"

"On that ashet over there, Helen, and if you could take them round the tables while they're still hot, please."

Nell lifted the tray to the counter beside Mathilde and leant in close. "Mathilde, I didn't know that young man I've seen in the bar was a minister. I presume you did?"

She nodded, and though her head was bent over the plates, Nell could see her cheeks were flushed.

"Will he be here at the wake?"

Mathilde looked up. "No, he has to go to Kirriemuir straight after the service, some Presbytery meeting."

"What's his name?"

"Nell! You need to get those sausage rolls out to the guests while they're hot," Mrs Mackie yelled from the corner.

"All right, I'm on my way," she said, picking up the tray.

After she'd helped serve, then tidy up, Nell sat down beside her aunt, who was nestling a sherry glass between her hands. Everyone else had left to return home to Glen Prosen or back to Glen Doll.

"Were you pleased with the way the service and wake went, Aunt Winnie?"

Her aunt turned to her, her grey eyes rheumy, her complexion wan.

She sighed. "It all went fine, Helen, just fine. Betty's family seemed pleased at the spread here. They kept thanking me for my generosity, but it was a pleasure to give her a good send-off. It was Betty's kindness and thoughtfulness that kept me going all those years." She shrugged. "So many years living with us at the farm, I can't even tell you how many."

Nell patted her liver-spotted hand. "You were a good employer to her, Aunt Winnie."

"She was more a friend than an employee." She sipped her sherry and turned to gaze out the window, towards the church. "I still find it strange that in this day and age women can't go to the graveside for the burial. I would like to have been there."

"There's nothing to say women can't be there, it's just some miserable, old tradition. I presume the men imagine women can't bear to watch the coffin being lowered into the ground." Nell frowned. "Were you not at Uncle Robert's burial either?"

She shook her head. "And do you know, Helen, I've regretted it ever since. My three sons were only teenagers, yet they were all there. It really is a ludicrous custom." She scowled. "I should have just defied tradition and gone with all the men to the graveyard today."

"You can go over tomorrow morning before you leave if you want. You could take some flowers? We've still got some nice orange chrysanthemums round the back of the house."

Aunt Winifred nodded then looked at her watch. "Will Euphemia still be playing the piano?"

"Well, I'm not sure about the piano, but she should be home from school in an hour or so."

"Ah of course, she's still at school. Such a pretty young thing she is."

Nell frowned and helped her aunt to her feet. "She's the teacher now, remember Aunt Winnie?"

The older woman turned to look at her niece. "Of course, silly me. Allan does say I'm getting a little absent-minded at times."

They walked into the corridor together, then Nell ran ahead to pop her head round the kitchen door to say goodbye to Mathilde and Mrs Mackie. After, she took Aunt Winnie by the arm and they ambled across to the schoolhouse.

"I presume you've had enough tea, Aunt Winnie? Can I get you anything else?" Nell helped her into the armchair and knelt down to stoke up the fire. Effie had promised to pop in at lunch break to get the fire going. Her aunt was silent all the while, sighing gently to herself, but then, once Nell had put the poker back on its stand, she grabbed Nell's hand.

"Nell, I didn't want to give away the baby, I knew it would be best far away from us, but she didn't want that and, well, it was hardly surprising, was it? And then, you know what happened…"

"What? Whose baby?"

Her aunt bit her lip. "Euphemia's baby… and then what happened was all so sad, and she never really forgave me and…"

She looked directly into Nell's eyes. "But I think she's forgiven me now."

As if a switch had been flicked, her aunt shut her eyes and leant back in her chair before promptly falling asleep. Nell stood up and staggered over to the table, where she sat watching the door for her sister to arrive home from school.

* * *

Supper that evening was rather strained. Nell wanted to get Effie on her own but could not. When her aunt woke up, she seemed brighter and more alert and wanted to talk about the funeral service and the people at the wake.

Early the following morning, Nell had gone round the back of the schoolhouse to cut the flowers for their aunt to take to the graveside. Then she had to leave for the post office. She left the flowers on the kitchen table with a note wishing Aunt Winnie a good journey home. Thankfully the rain had stopped, and it was warm again, so when she arrived home after her round, she flung off her jacket and went to put the kettle on. There was no sign of Effie, but Nell knew her classes were over as she'd passed some of the children walking home along the road after her last delivery down at Clachnabrain.

As she drank her tea, she began to hear mellifluous notes from the piano. Even through the thick, stone walls, she could hear when Effie played. This sounded like a Mendelssohn piece. It started off softly, almost melancholic, then became louder, and by the final crescendo was truly triumphant.

She headed next door and walked into the classroom where, at the far end, Effie sat, head arched backwards, playing one of her favourite rondos.

Nell waited till she had finished, then moved towards the piano, clapping. "That was beautiful, Effie. I love that piece."

Effie swivelled around. "What are you doing here?"

"Nice to see you too. I live next door," she said, raising an eyebrow. "Come and have a cup of tea, there's something we need to talk about."

Effie got up and followed her sister silently next door. At the table, Nell asked if she'd enjoyed their aunt's visit.

"Well, yes, it was good to see her after so long. Though she is rather frail, isn't she?"

"Definitely, but she's still feisty. I think she'd have been a suffragette in her day, if she'd been allowed."

Effie smiled.

"Effie, I want to ask you about something she said to me."

Effie's lips pursed together.

"She talked of you having a baby. And you not wanting to give it away…" Nell looked at her sister, whose eyes were downcast. "Well?"

There was silence and then an outburst. "Honestly, Nell, do you believe anything she says? Her mind's so wandered." Effie looked up and glared at Nell. "You know she's got dementia, old age memory loss; some people even call it madness. She says some very strange things, she's becoming senile. Sadly I don't think her mind will ever get any better. Now I think about it, I reckon Betty covered up a lot and…"

"Effie, you haven't really answered my question. Why was she talking about a baby?"

"I have no idea, Nell," she seethed. "And now, I must go and continue with tomorrow's class preparations next door." She went out, slamming the door behind her.

PART 4

Effie

Chapter 28

March 1915

"When's lambing due to begin, Aunt Winnie?"

Effie stood by the window gazing out at the sheep in the fields at the back of the farm.

"Any time now. We're always later starting here in the glens, but it's usually the first week of April or so." She looked up from her knitting. "But little ones come when they are ready. You'll soon know all about this."

Effie sighed and eased herself back into the armchair. She picked up her needles and white wool and began knitting again.

"How are you getting on with the bootees?"

"I'm still not great at knitting, Aunt Winnie, but you've taught me such a lot. I don't remember ever seeing Ma knit."

"She had other talents," her aunt said, peering over at Effie's knitting. "Those are looking fine. The baby will be very well dressed."

She smiled. "Whenever I think of lambing, I think of the Service of the Lambs at Clova kirk. D'you remember that?"

"Yes, it's such a lovely service, every year at the end of May, to celebrate all the lambs having been born in the glens. We used to love it as children."

Aunt Winifred picked up another ball of wool from the basket. "It was the last time I saw your mother."

Effie laid her needles down on her massive belly. "When was that?"

"Your mother died in 1910, didn't she?"

Effie nodded. "Yes, in September."

"So it would have been in the May of that year. Can you remember us coming over from Prosen?"

Effie shrugged. "I don't think so, but I would only have been about twelve at the time."

"Ah, no, I'm remembering now, it was only your sister there. You were in bed with a sore throat or something."

"I sort of remember that."

"We didn't stay with you anyway. We just came for the day, the boys and I all crammed into the small trap behind the pony."

"Did you see Ma at the church? Or later?"

Aunt Winifred glanced up from her knitting. "I saw her afterwards too. But she wasn't happy I'd seen her then." She returned her gaze to her row of purls.

Effie frowned.

"We were all going to have lunch at the hotel after, you won't remember that either? I can still recall the delicious steak pie and treacle pudding. I raved about the pudding so much when I got home; Betty tried to recreate it, but she never could. She put the treacle at the bottom of the basin, even though I told her the hotel's pudding had it mixed through the sponge."

"Was my grandfather still cooking at the hotel then?"

"No, he'd died a couple of years before, but there was a French man helping the locals run the kitchen."

Effie was still frowning. "What did you mean, Ma didn't want you to see her?"

"Manon was a very attractive woman; I'm sure you must remember that about your mother. Before they married, your father told me she'd got her colouring and black hair from her Provençal mother, not her pale, blond-haired father who was from northern France." She pointed at Effie's thick dark hair. "Your hair is so like hers. Nell's isn't quite as thick, I seem to remember. Anyway, she wasn't at all vain, just lovely in a natural way. Perhaps it was a French characteristic, but I always thought men were unwittingly attracted to her."

"Really?"

Aunt Winifred nodded. "Not that she ever seemed to want

attention. She just had some kind of allure. I remember asking my Robert when she first married your father what it was about her, and he said she exuded a kind of charisma that no Scottish women he'd ever met had." She chuckled. "It was so true."

"But what's that got to do with you saying she didn't want you to see her later that day?"

Her aunt leant towards her niece. "We'd all finished lunch, and I had to go round to the stables to tell the stable lad we'd soon be ready to return to Prosen, to bring the pony and trap round to the front. Your mother had left the table some ten minutes before." She nodded. "Yes, now it makes sense. Of course you were ill that day and in bed over at the schoolhouse, and she said she was going to check on you. So I went out the back towards the stables, and there she was – with a man. Not your father. And they were…"

The doorbell rang loudly. Aunt Winifred looked up at the clock. "Dear Lord, that must be Mrs Lowden. She said she'd call after lunch. Off you go, my dear. Betty'll come and find you once she's gone."

Effie pushed herself off the chair and hobbled towards the door. Whenever there was a visitor, she had to go to the kitchen or over to the Belgians' cottage till the visit was over. Her aunt had managed to keep her pregnancy a secret thus far and was intent on continuing till after the baby was born.

She headed to the kitchen and looked out to the courtyard, where she saw Gabrielle running home from school. Effie went out the back door towards their cottage to 'hide from the neighbours', as Madame Dubois used to say, laughing. The first time she'd said it, Effie had been offended, but now it was their little joke. She knocked on the door and pushed it open and, as usual, even though it was mild outside, the chill of the damp interior hit her.

* * *

"Euphemia, I know you told me before, but remind me where your mother's parents were from in France?" Madame Dubois had just lain the baby in the crib by the fire for his nap. She sat down at the table.

"Well, Ma's mother was from Provence – a small town called Maussanne – and her father was from somewhere in the northeast of France, very near the Belgian border. I'm not sure about the name of the town."

"So that's why, though your French is perfect, your accent has a southern lilt to it. I presume you've taken on your mother's and grandmother's accents." Madame Dubois smiled and picked up a sock and her darning needle.

"I suppose so. We never met my grandmother; we only knew our grandfather because he cooked at the hotel just over the road from the schoolhouse. He was a lovely man." Effie smiled. "My sister and I always spoke French with Ma, though I remember Pa not being happy when the three of us were speaking together. He was quite good at French too, but not as fluent as Nell and me."

"He probably guessed you were talking about him," Madame Dubois said, winking.

Effie pulled her shawl around her shoulders. "Has Allan not managed to fix that window yet? It's still a bit chilly in here."

"He's already done it – look, it's sealed. But my husband thinks there's something in the foundations or the walls, some kind of rot or humidity perhaps."

"Euphemia!" Gabrielle rushed in with the laundry from the line outside the window. "Have you seen my picture? I did it today, it's Easter." She pointed to a piece of paper at the far end of the table.

Effie lifted the picture up. "Gabrielle, that is very good, you've got such a talent. I love the lambs and the daffodils. It's really well drawn."

"Mr Forbes said I could bring it home for Maman as it was so good."

Ever since Effie had been banned from leaving the farm, she'd relied on Gabrielle telling her all about school. When she'd asked her aunt what she would tell everyone, she said that if anyone asked where her niece was, they'd be told she was indisposed. If they probed further, all she had to say were the words 'women's troubles' and everyone looked away.

Gabrielle was too young to realise Effie was pregnant, and her teenage brother was always up on the hills with their father helping with the sheep when Effie visited. The girl took the picture from Effie and headed through to the one tiny bedroom where they all slept.

"How old is the baby now, Madame Dubois?"

"He's eleven months, so I'd usually stop feeding him myself soon as his weaning's going well, but your aunt wants me carry on so I can feed your baby too."

Effie sighed. "But I don't see how that's going to work. All your family would then know about it. Gabrielle would surely tell Mr Forbes and the other children and…"

Madame Dubois stretched out her hand to take Effie's. "We will work something out, don't worry." She leant in to whisper. "Gabrielle has no idea how babies happen so she will just think it's mine."

Effie frowned. "But it will be like yours, won't it?"

"Until your aunt has found a family for the baby, yes. But don't worry, Euphemia, it will be just fine. And after it's born, you can find a new life back in your glen."

Effie nodded, disconsolate. She did not know what to think. Until the baby was born, she simply had to trust in her aunt's judgement.

There was a sharp tap on the door and the women both looked around. Gabrielle ran to open it, and there stood Betty, a bulging cloth in one hand.

"Mrs Lowden's just gone. Your aunt said you're to come back to the house." She placed the cloth on the table and unravelled it to reveal six soda scones. A warm floury smell filled the air as she placed them on the table. "I made an extra batch for you to have," she said, her face inscrutable as usual. "Come away over, Euphemia. Let's get you back into the warm."

Chapter 29

September 1943

Effie sighed with relief as she posted the letter to Douglas Harrison to say she was indisposed and could not make their rendezvous in Forfar the following week. She had lost sleep worrying about the meeting, which had all been arranged. She was to get the bus to Forfar, where he would meet her in his car and drive her to his house. After lunch, prepared by his housekeeper, they would visit the priory. It had all sounded so plausible. But then, wide awake at three in the morning, she realised she simply could not do it. She should not even have replied to his letters, even though she had sent only one reply.

Did she really want to revisit the feelings she'd had for him when she was so young? It had taken her so long to get over him – years, after all that had happened. And when she thought about it later, as a more mature woman, she realised his feelings could not have been the same as hers. She had been obsessed by him; she truly thought she was in love. But on reflection, she had to admit that perhaps he had felt very little for her in those days. And since his wife was now dead, was he simply after some female company?

She had asked him in her letter about children, but he had not answered her question. That made her think that perhaps he did not have any – though why did he not answer her precisely with a yes or no?

But now that she had posted the letter to him, that would hopefully be the end of his correspondence with her. She felt so much better.

All she had to do now was think up an excuse to tell Nell. As she walked back down the road from the post box, her eyes began to tear up and she started sniffing. Irritated, she wiped her nose.

She looked around at the trees and shrubs, then suddenly smiled. Hay fever – of course. It was that time of year when the ragweed pollen always bothered her. Nell's hay fever came in the spring, but hers in the late summer and early autumn. Excellent: she would tell Nell she had a bad cold coming on, while she sniffed away to her sister's annoyance.

* * *

"Mathilde, are you sure you really want to go and live in the hotel? You're welcome to stay here if you want," Effie said, setting the table for the three of them on their visitor's last night.

"I've stayed long enough with you. You've both been so kind, I'm very grateful. But I really am excited about working in a restaurant kitchen again, especially one where your grandfather cooked."

"I suppose it will be nice to have your own room and your own peace and quiet. We sisters can be rather noisy, in our own ways." Effie smiled. "I wonder if our grandfather came from anywhere near where you're from, Mathilde. We know he was from northern France, but that's all. It may even have been near Lille, where your family restaurant is."

"Or it could have been further west, nearer Creil where Nell spent all those years driving the ambulances. She was so brave."

Ah yes, good old Nell. She and Mathilde had spent an entire evening talking about nothing but her time at Royaumont Abbey. Mathilde was fascinated by her work there and the fact that, though it was funded by the French Red Cross, it was run by Scottish women. Effie had had to feign interest. Well, she too had worked hard in the war. Had anyone asked her about her sudden immersion into teaching when she was just shy of eighteen? And as for her time before that over in Glen Prosen – that certainly had its challenges too.

Effie looked at Mathilde's back. She seemed to be so at home in their kitchen, peeling, chopping, cooking, making things taste good with very little. It must have been wonderful to have been brought up in a family of cooks.

"Mathilde, I know your uncle owned the restaurant and some of your cousins worked in the kitchen and waited at tables, but did your mother work there too?"

Without turning around, she sighed. "Yes, sometimes."

"Does she still work there?"

"I don't know. I don't know what's happened to her." The sisters heard her sniffing. "She also used to help in the local school. She was always full of energy, but before I left she had become so fatigued."

She turned around. Her eyes were filled with tears. "In fact, I was worried about her health, but she insisted I come over... for Pierre. She always said I should follow my heart, even though it might end in tragedy. Does that sound strange?"

"Don't carry on if you don't want to, Mathilde," said Effie, getting up and placing a hand on her shoulder.

"No, it's fine." She shook her head. "Sorry, it's just that not hearing from her – or any of them – is so hard."

"Of course it is," said Nell as Mathilde turned back to continue at the sink.

The sisters glanced at each other.

"I bet she's a good cook too?" Nell asked, gently.

"Yes, she really is." Mathilde's back was still turned around.

Effie decided to stop asking about her mother. She and Nell had asked about her parents when she'd first arrived, and they both got the impression she didn't want to discuss them. As Effie went off to the bathroom to wash her hands, she decided to leave the matter for good now. She clearly missed her mother so much; it was too painful to talk about.

Since it was Mathilde's last evening at the schoolhouse, the sisters had agreed not to discuss the minister's son's death at supper. Jimmy Johnson's death the previous week had taken up so many of their conversations at home, and indeed throughout the entire village. Now it was time to leave the Johnsons to their grief. Effie had seen the minister in the garden the day before and had watched him turn around and trudge back, head low, into the house, where the curtains remained closed. Everyone in the glen knew that his wife had taken to her bed and that Mrs Tweedie now stayed with them to care for her full time while the minister tried to carry on with some parish duties.

So when Nell arrived home, the sisters discussed anything other than sadness. Nell talked about her recent walks up into the hills, the game birds she had seen, the berries she had found; and Effie talked about her favourite piano pieces, promising she would play Mendelssohn's Rondo Capriccioso for Mathilde soon.

As they were finishing the delicious supper and Mathilde was trying some sentences in English, she asked about their mother.

"Did you always speak in French with her?"

"Yes, we did if it was just the three of us. But when it was the four of us, Pa insisted we speak English."

"Was he fluent too?"

"I suppose he was, but he seemed to begrudge the three of us speaking French together. D'you remember Effie?"

Effie shrugged. "Not really." She looked at Mathilde. "I was only twelve when Ma died. Not a good age. I kind of resented Pa for a while."

"But then we ended up just wanting to please him, didn't we?"

Effie scowled. "Well, I had to try to please him. Since you were always his favourite, you never had to try."

Nell turned to Mathilde. "Families are always the same, aren't they? Bickering about silly things, but we all love each other really." She beamed.

"You might have questioned that if you were the one to get the tawse from Pa when you were fourteen. I was almost a woman, and he continued to treat me like a child."

"The tawse?" Mathilde frowned.

"It's a belt they hit children with at school, as punishment. Our father liked to use it in the classroom."

"And occasionally at home," Effie said, pursing her lips together.

"Anyway, Mathilde," Nell said, "that was lovely, thanks so much." She reached out to take her hand. "We'll miss you."

"I'll only be just over the road," Mathilde said, laughing.

"I know, but it's not quite the same."

"Mathilde," said Effie, her scowl receding, "as well as having you stay with us, I've so enjoyed speaking French again. It's so funny, I've started dreaming in French again. I haven't done that for years."

Chapter 30

April 1915

Effie awoke sweating. She sat up and shook her head to try to rid herself of the memory of the horrible dream. She had been running away from someone, up in the hills. She kept looking around and there was a figure there, catching her up. He was too far away to recognise but she felt threatened and scared. Her stomach was huge so she could not run far, and the person was getting nearer.

Then, by a small loch, she saw a woman sitting on the grass, smiling at her. She beckoned her over and spoke to her in French, and she realised it was her mother. She felt safe with her and stayed to talk for a while, eating a delicious picnic spread out on a rug. Then the woman disappeared, and the man chasing her came over the brow of the hill, and she had to start running again. When she finally turned around, she realised it was Douglas Harrison, a sinister expression on his handsome face. She continued trying to run away from him; he was almost upon her when she woke up.

She downed the cup of water by her bed, got up and walked over to the window. She felt stifled, upset. It had been such a scary dream, yet the part with her mother had been magical: she'd felt so safe, protected. She remembered someone – was it Bessie? – had told her that dreams were unconscious desires being played out in your head. Well, if that was true, what on earth did her dream mean? It had all been so vivid. Of course she felt safe with her mother, but why was she running away, terrified, from Douglas Harrison? Had he really been so evil? Surely what happened with him was also her fault.

She flung open the curtains and looked out to a beautiful spring day. She could see the newborn lambs in the field below her, close by their mothers. The sun glinted on the water in the burn at the foot of the field. The sun was higher than usual when she woke up; it must be late. She checked the time and saw it was after eight. Dear Lord, how had she slept so late?

She dressed as quickly as she could, then went downstairs to the kitchen, where Betty was washing up at the sink.

"Betty, I'm sorry, you should have wakened me. Have I missed breakfast?"

The woman pointed to the bowl and mug on the table. "I left you some porridge. Sit down."

Effie now knew that though the housekeeper's expression was always stern, usually surly, she meant well.

"Thank you," Effie said, spooning the porridge into her bowl. "The tea's stewed but it'll have to do," she said, pouring from the large teapot into her cup.

"When did Aunt Winnie go out?"

"Really early. The last of the ewes were lambing in the night. She took over from Allan." She looked up at the clock. "She should be back soon; she said to tell you she'd be free for lunch today as the shepherds are coming over to help this morning."

Effie nodded. Her aunt had been so busy with lambing that the two of them had had no time alone since the day they'd been knitting the bootees together. She lifted her cup and sipped the peat brown, cold liquid, forcing a smile of thanks to Betty, who then headed back to the sink.

* * *

"Aunt Winnie, do you ever have dreams where you're running away from someone?"

"I've not for a while, but I do remember they're usually more nightmare than dream. Why?" Her aunt looked over the table at Effie.

"I had a horrible one last night, running away from someone, but then Ma was there too for a while, and everything was better while I was with her."

Aunt Winifred put down her soup spoon. "Of course everything was better when you were with your mother, you were too young to lose her." She shook her head. "Such a tragedy."

"Did anyone from here go to her funeral?"

"No, I don't think so. Well, apart from your father." She tilted her head. "Though when I think about it, perhaps he didn't go to France, did he?"

"I don't remember him being away for a long time, so maybe he couldn't go either. I know I was only a child, but surely I would have remembered that. But then how did they take the... the body over to France?"

Aunt Winifred shook her head. "I have no idea what happened, my dear. I'm sorry."

Betty came in with the stew and Effie sighed. "I'm not feeling terribly hungry, Aunt Winnie. Sorry, I got up so late this morning."

"I heard," she said, smiling. "Just eat a little, you need to keep your strength up. The baby'll be coming any day now, Euphemia." She tucked in as she always did, with gusto.

Effie managed a couple of forkfuls, then laid down her cutlery. "Aunt Winnie, it's ages since we've been alone." If her aunt did have time during lambing to have a meal with Effie, Allan was usually there too. "I was wondering if you could continue telling me about the last time you saw Ma?"

Aunt Winifred scraped her plate clean, then placed her fork and knife together in the middle. "Where was I?"

"You said you saw Ma with someone…"

"Ah yes. And they were…" She stopped and leant in towards Effie. "Euphemia, I am only telling you this so that you can perhaps understand a little why I said your mother and I did not always see eye to eye."

Effie nodded.

"They were in a deep embrace."

Effie gasped. "Who was it?"

"He was a fairly new chef at the hotel. He too was French, though not a relative of your mother's."

"But Aunt Winnie, you know French people kiss each other all the time. When we shake hands, they kiss cheeks."

"This was not a casual greeting, this was a full embrace, as if between two lovers, Effie." She sighed. "I'm sorry to tell you about it, but I wanted you to understand."

"What did you do?"

"I was utterly speechless for a few seconds, then I coughed loudly. And as they broke apart, the young man – I seem to recall he looked in his late twenties – sprinted back into the kitchen through the back door. And your mother rushed towards me."

"What did Ma say?" Effie's eyes were wide.

"She grabbed my hand and told me she was merely saying goodbye to her colleague, that he was leaving very soon for France and to please not say a thing to my brother. She looked forlorn, desperate. I promised I would not and presumed the matter was finished. But then a few days later, I was passing along Bank Street in Kirriemuir in the wagonette, and who should I see walking along the street, arm in arm, but your mother and that man. Again, they looked very intimate."

"But again, perhaps it was a farewell meeting?"

Aunt Winifred shook her head. "The look between them was not simply friendship. This was something deeper than that, child. You can see why I only felt I could tell you this now. Your father does not know of course, and then quite soon afterwards we had the tragic news of Manon's death, and so I forgot about it… until recently when we were discussing the Service of the Lambs."

"Thank you for sharing this with me. I won't tell Pa, obviously. And in fact I don't think I'll tell Nell either. What would be the point? Although that's yet another secret I'll be keeping from her…" Effie winced.

"What is it?"

She placed her hand low on her belly. "I've got a pain, I must have eaten too much stew." Her face grew pale as she held onto the table edge.

"I don't think it's the food, Effie. Upstairs, let's get you into bed right now," she said, taking her arm. "Betty! Come now!" she yelled at the door. When the housekeeper appeared, she instructed her to get Allan in from the lambing shed and to run and fetch the midwife. "At once!"

Chapter 31

October 1943

"So why on earth was Aunt Winnie talking about a baby, Effie?" Nell flung open the classroom door and shouted at her sister, who sat snivelling at her desk in front of the empty room. Nell had followed her sister after she'd run out of the schoolhouse, slamming the door.

Nell strode over to the piano to grab the only other adult chair in the room and sat at the opposite side of the desk. "Tell me now. What's this all about?"

Effie's head was bowed low. "Let's go back next door. I'll tell you while we sit by the fire so I don't have to look at you," she muttered.

"All right."

Once Nell had stoked up the fire and they were seated side by side, Effie began telling Nell about how she had worried she was expecting a child in those first few weeks at Aunt Winnie's.

"Did you feel sick? How did you know?"

"Feeling queasy, missing my monthlies, and then I started to get fat."

Nell let out a long breath. "Carry on."

"Aunt Winnie is – well, more likely was, given her dementia – a shrewd woman, very wise. She had guessed for a while, then eventually got it out of me."

"When was that?"

"Before Christmas."

"So, December 1914. What did you decide to do?"

Effie turned to her sister. "What d'you mean, what did I decide? The decision was never mine, this was nothing to do with me! Obviously I had no choice but to have the baby. Aunt Winnie was setting up a family to adopt, somewhere far enough away, in

Dundee. So then…"

"Hang on, Effie, it clearly did have something to do with you." Nell's face was bright red. "These things don't just happen!" She stood up and stomped over to the sink where she poured two glasses of water. "Here," she said, thrusting one at her sister.

"Well, in my innocence, my insane naivety, I can honestly say I had no idea what he was doing."

Nell's shoulders slumped. "You truly had no clue what was happening?"

Effie began whimpering again. She shook her head.

"And before we go any further, I presume the 'he' in question was Douglas Harrison?"

Effie nodded and bent her head down as her tears flowed.

Nell leapt to her feet. "That man's a bloody pervert, taking advantage of a young innocent. God, I hate him. He…" Nell clamped her mouth shut before she blurted out about her own experience. She let out a long sigh and indicated to her sister to continue, then sat down again.

"Aunt Winnie managed to keep it a secret from everyone in the village. Only Betty and the Belgian mother knew. And then the baby was born." Effie's eyes were now streaming. "And she was beautiful, and…"

Nell grasped her sister's hand. "A girl," she said, blinking away tears.

"She had a gorgeous head of black hair. And…"

There was a loud knock at the door.

"Dear God, who's that?" Nell muttered as she got to her feet, wiping her tears. She raised her head high, then went to open the door. It was Mathilde.

"I'm sorry to interrupt, but I have a favour to ask." She swept her wavy dark hair from her face.

"Of course, come in, Mathilde." Nell ushered her in and pointed to the table for her to sit down. Effie turned around and, having also wiped her tears away, came to join them.

"Sorry, is this not a good time, Mesdemoiselles?" Mathilde was frowning as she took in their expressions.

"No, it's fine," said Effie, forcing a smile.

"Well, if you're sure. I wanted to ask if I could bring a man to meet you, a special friend. Perhaps for a cup of tea. I'd like you to meet him."

Both sisters beamed. "Is it the man from the hotel?" Effie asked. She nodded.

"Mathilde, he's a minister, isn't he?" Nell asked. "Someone looking very like him took the funeral I was at yesterday."

Effie turned to look at Nell. "What?" she said.

"Yes," said Mathilde, laughing. "His name is Doug and he's a minister, he's funny and handsome and…"

"Wait a minute, Mathilde," Nell said. "What's his second name?"

"Harrison," she said, beaming.

Chapter 32

May 1915

By the time the midwife arrived at the farmhouse, Aunt Winnie had Effie undressed and lying on the bed. Betty was running up and downstairs with boiling water and basins, then sprinting along the corridor to the laundry room for fresh sheets and towels. The labour pains were so frequent Aunt Winnie worried that she might have to deliver the baby herself, but thankfully Mrs Russell arrived just when Effie began to moan that she wanted to push.

"Wait, lass!" she shouted as she came running through the door. "Wait till I get my coat off and wash my hands."

Betty yanked the woman's coat off her and brought the basin of water and soap over.

"Right, I'm just going to have a look and see what's what."

"But I need to push!"

"Wait!"

The midwife quickly examined Effie, then said, "You're right, lass, baby's nearly here."

The next ten minutes were agony and ecstasy as the baby emerged and Effie smiled more than she had ever smiled in her life.

"Can I hold her please?" Effie's arms were outstretched.

In her meticulous planning for this moment, Aunt Winnie had decided this would not be allowed, that the baby would be washed and then would leave Effie at once. But since the original plan could not be in place – there was a delay over the adoption – she shrugged and said, "All right, Euphemia, but just for a short while."

The midwife cleaned up the little girl and handed her over to Effie, whose cheeks were stained with tears. "Look at her hair,

Aunt Winnie! It's the colour of Ma's." She lifted up a tiny hand. "Betty, have you ever seen more beautiful fingers? Those tiny little nails!" She bent over her little head and smiled. "And the smell of her..."

Aunt Winifred and Betty stood side by side, smiling as they watched Effie gaze in wonder at the little girl while the midwife huffed all around them, tidying up. "Would someone give me a hand with these sheets?"

"Sorry," said Betty, whose face betrayed a rare flicker of emotion.

Aunt Winnie sat down on the bed as the baby began to cry. "Now my dear, it'll be time soon to take her over to the cottage." She turned to Betty. "Go and tell Madame Dubois the baby will be over shortly and to stoke up the fire. Make sure they have plenty of kindling."

Effie continued to stroke her baby's soft skin and lifted her up to place a gentle kiss on her cheek. "Oh, the aroma from her head, Aunt Winnie. It's intoxicating. Why didn't you tell me how sweet it would be? Isn't it wonderful?"

Her aunt nodded in agreement.

"What shall I call her?" She looked eagerly at her aunt. "Can I call her Manon, after Ma, Aunt Winnie? Can I?"

Her aunt patted her hand. "Let's just wait for now; there's no rush on anything, certainly not giving her a name." And she turned away so her niece could not see the sadness in her eyes as she began to think about the next step in her plan.

* * *

"It hurts, Aunt Winnie," Effie said, crying as her aunt bound cloth tightly around her breasts. "Surely the milk won't come in if the baby doesn't feed?"

Her aunt shook her head. "Not according to the midwife. You've got to start with these bandages, then you may need to wear cabbage leaves to alleviate any pain."

Effie sighed. "That sounds absolutely disgusting."

"Yes, well, it has to be done, Euphemia; you know that. Here, lift your arms up," Aunt Winifred said as she wound the bandages around tightly.

"It's really sore," Effie said, sniffing. She had cried so much over the past twenty-four hours; she thought she had no tears left.

"The midwife'll be here this evening. She'll see how you're doing and how long you'll need to keep them on for. We've got to do exactly as she says. You can't risk getting an infection. I don't want to call in the doctor; he knows nothing, remember?"

"So why is Mrs Russell trusted not to say anything?"

"Because I am paying her way above her usual fees," her aunt replied. "I've told you this."

"Sorry, I know. You've been so kind and…" Effie looked up. "Can't I see my baby for a short while? Just a few minutes, I wouldn't need to stay long but…"

Her aunt shook her head. "First of all, Euphemia, hard though it is, you must not consider her your baby. Also, as well as everything else, the weather's turned. We don't want you catching a cold, you've got to recover in bed. Then, once you're back to normal, you can return to Clova, and we must never again think of any of this."

"But…"

"No, Euphemia, we have discussed everything. In detail. That's how it's going to be. The baby will stay with Madame Dubois only till the Dundee family have found a wet nurse. Then they can come here and collect her. Though in fact I am wondering whether a less obvious rendezvous would be best…" She went to open the curtains. Outside was grey and wet. "I'll get Betty to stoke up the fire, it's become cold again."

"The baby will be freezing over in the cottage, Aunt Winnie. I don't…"

"Madame Dubois has plenty of kindling. We won't let the baby – or any of them – get cold. Now, lie down and get some rest. I'll see you later, once I've been to the lambing shed. I think Allan said that's all the ewes done now; all the lambs have safely arrived."

"So now they can be with their mothers," mumbled Effie as she slithered back down the bed. "Just like nature intended."

* * *

"You're looking much better, Euphemia," Aunt Winifred said as she brought in a tray to Effie's room.

"Where's Betty? Why are you bringing me my lunch?"

"She had to go over to Clova to see her mother, she's gravely ill. I told her to avoid the schoolhouse, and if she sees your father to pretend all is well over here in Prosen."

"I'll have to write to him soon, though. I usually send him a letter every fortnight. What shall I say?" Effie sniffed as she started to sup her soup.

"Just the usual things. You can talk about the lambing season, how successful it was, how it was all over by the first week of May and that there are now many happy ewes with their lambs back out in the spring sunshine."

Effie put down her spoon. "Those ewes are lucky, they can keep their little ones with them."

"Euphemia, for the last time, stop this!" Aunt Winifred snapped. "Do you realise how lucky you are? Any other girl in your position would have been sent away in disgrace, perhaps never to see her family again. Your shame has been hidden, and you can hold your head high when you return to Clova." She leant towards her niece. "I will not hear such things again."

"Sorry. I am truly grateful, really I am, Aunt Winnie," she said, eyes brimming with tears.

"Good. I have to go out soon to the blacksmith with the new stable boy, but shall I bring you some paper and ink so you can write to your father?"

"Thank you, yes please, Aunt Winnie."

Once her aunt had brought her the pen and paper, Effie slid out of bed. She opened the door and listened. Her aunt was in the bedroom, probably putting on a hat for the outing to the village. She waited until she heard the front door slam, then quickly got dressed. It was a struggle; she had not worn proper clothes for days. This week in bed had been one of the most boring in her life. She kept thinking that while most new mothers spent their time happily dozing and gazing at their new babies, all she could do was lie there, sobbing with the weight of her loss.

She crept downstairs and into the kitchen. With Betty away, this could be the only opportunity. She grabbed her coat from the peg and slid on some boots which were far too big. She opened the door and began to plod across the courtyard to the little cottage, trying to breathe normally. Her heart was beating so fast. She got to the Belgians' cottage door and tapped with a light knock.

Madame Dubois came to the door and stared at Effie.

"What are you doing here? It's not allowed, your aunt said it was forbidden." She was barring the door with both arms, but Effie could hear mewling sounds from behind her.

"Please, can I just see her? I won't do anything else, just let me see her?"

The woman shook her head. "I was told you must never see her. I don't want to risk your aunt throwing us out. I must obey her, I can't…"

Effie slipped underneath her arm and rushed over to the fire, where two babies were sleeping in the crib. One was large and plump and pink-cheeked, the other tiny and mouse-like, her cheeks pale in comparison. Both were swaddled up tight, facing in different directions. Effie's tiny baby snuffled, and her adorable little nose twitched.

Effie reached down to take the newborn into her arms, and Madame Dubois came to stand beside her. She stretched out her hand to Effie's, then withdrew it, shaking her head. "I can't stop you, can I? Go ahead, pick her up. But only for one minute: no longer. Then you must go back to the house and never come here again."

PART 5

Manon

Chapter 33

July 1908

The day of the Wateresk picnic changed everything. Manon's father, Monsieur Fournier, had died just a few weeks before, and though her husband did not approve, she had been helping out at the hotel, just until they got another chef.

"It will almost definitely be a female cook they'll employ this time, not a male chef," James had said one night when she returned from an evening shift.

"Why is that?"

Her husband sighed. "The hotel cannot afford to bring an expensive chef over from France these days. Your father was affordable as he had board and lodgings for his family, but according to the laird, chefs have begun to cost a lot more."

"Yes, well, he'd know all about that, wouldn't he?" she said, pouring the boiling water into the teapot. "Did the girls go down to sleep easily?"

"Helen did, but Euphemia as usual was wanting her mother. Honestly, the girl is ten. You'd think she wouldn't be quite so needy."

"Did you read her a story?"

"Manon, the child is at an age she can read perfectly well herself."

"But she likes it at bedtime and I usually…"

"If you decide to abandon your maternal duties to go and help out in the hotel, then my rules take precedence." He pushed his cup over the table, clearly wanting his tea. "Also, unless they find someone soon, they'll have to ask a woman from the village. I can't have you working in there for much longer. It's unseemly for the dominie's wife to be working in a kitchen."

Manon clattered the teapot down on the table. "Have I

neglected you? Or the girls?" She poured his tea then hers. "And am I still able to help you in the classroom most days? Yes, I am." She forced a smile, hoping the conversation would be over soon. She was tired.

Her husband harrumphed and took a sip of his tea.

* * *

The morning of the picnic she had told her daughters she'd be gone for a few hours down at Wateresk for the annual Kirriemuir church picnic.

"You know I'll be away till later this afternoon, but Pa will be here. If you decide to cycle along to join me, be sure to let him know you're coming. If he's not here, he'll be in the classroom."

"Why's Pa in the classroom?" Nell asked. "It's school holidays."

Her mother smiled. "A good question, darling. He says he's preparing for the new term. But that's four weeks away." She kissed her daughters, then headed to the door. "Oh, don't forget to put on your Sunday hats if you're coming to the picnic. Everyone will be dressed up." She grabbed her jacket, then went over to the hotel to help load the food, crockery and urns into the trap.

Once the pony and trap arrived at Wateresk, she helped unload, then set up the tables and rolled the rugs on the ground. She looked up at the sky, which thankfully was now clear; there had been threatening dark clouds at dawn. Manon pulled some straggly strands of hair back into her bun and looked along the narrow road. A couple of charabancs were approaching slowly, followed by a couple of pony and traps further down the glen, and she could see many Sunday hats bobbing along behind.

While she laid out the cups and saucers and set up the tea urns, she watched the ladies emerge, wearing best frocks belted neatly at the waist or ruffled blouses with long wide skirts; and hats – glorious hats.

"Would you look at the finery on those ladies, Mrs Anderson," said young Josie, who had been roped in to help.

"I know. I just hope they've got boots on and not dainty slippers. The ground's still a bit wet from last night's showers."

The ladies were helped down from their seats and headed over to the picnic area from the roadside, walking gingerly on the clumps of wet grass.

"What's that mat there for?" Josie pointed to a long covering that was being unrolled on the grass at the other side of the tables. A piper was tuning up his bagpipes at the far end.

"That's for the dancing. I remember they had it last year too."

"Doesn't look like much room for dancing."

"You'd be surprised – I seem to recall some twenty or so couples dancing to the piper's tunes. Just you wait and see."

Manon turned around as the driver of a large carriage whoa'd his horse and, once it had stopped, she saw a lady stand up. She had on a large hat with billowing ribbons tied in bows on top, and a fancy striped gown. She watched as a young man rushed around to help her down. She took a gentleman's hand and walked towards the picnic, servants hurrying behind with chairs and parasols.

"Is that the laird's wife from down the glen?"

"Yes, from Cortachy. She's always invited to the Kirrie picnic."

The man who had helped her descend from the carriage came towards them. "Excuse me," he said, "might I prepare a tea for her Ladyship?"

Manon studied him. He was a handsome man – perhaps in his mid-twenties – and had warm dark, almost black eyes.

"Yes of course," she said, stepping aside. She took in his tanned skin, so much darker than most people in the glens.

"Thank you, I won't be long."

"Are you from here?" Manon asked.

He shook his head. "I'm French."

"I thought so," Manon said, clapping her hands and reverting to her own language. "Why are you here?"

"I work for the laird as an assistant cook."

Manon gasped. "Once you've given her Ladyship her tea, come back and chat. It's good to speak to an adult in French."

"Of course. So why are you here?"

"My father was chef at the hotel," Manon said, pointing up the glen. "But he died a couple of months ago, so I've been helping out in the kitchen."

After the games were over, it was time for tea, and Manon took up her place at the table, pouring tea and serving cakes. Her friend from Kirriemuir, Edith Bain, had come in the charabanc as her father was the minister. Manon and Edith had become friends over the past couple of years, getting together at harvest festivals and summer picnics, but they also met up in Kirriemuir when Manon was free from school duties.

"Can I help you, Manon?" Edith asked.

"If you don't mind. Josie's making the tea, so a hand pouring it out would be great, thanks."

Edith went round to the other side of the table. "Have you seen that French man over there, Manon?" She nodded to where the man was helping her Ladyship into her seat after a stroll around the picnic area. "He's really nice, you'd probably enjoy chatting with him."

Manon smiled. "He does seem rather nice." She winked. "If only I was ten years younger."

Her friend chuckled. "And if only you weren't married to the dominie," she whispered. "Right, shall I take the plates of cake around? Would that be easier?"

Manon nodded. "Thanks Edith, what would I do without you?"

She had just finished her final round of tea duties when the man wandered back over.

"My name's Emile, by the way," he said, smiling. "Do you think the hotel would have a spare job in the kitchen?"

"I know they do. I live in the schoolhouse right opposite the hotel. I've had to help out these past few weeks since my father died." She raised a hand. "But you already have a job."

"I wouldn't be too sad to leave it. I've been there for about three years now, so I'm ready for a change."

The piper began to play a tune, and couples rushed towards the long mat. Manon and Emile watched them all form circles for the Eightsome Reel, clapping in time.

When the next tune began, he stretched out his hand. "Could you show me how to dance this one?"

Manon smiled. "I'd be delighted. It's called the Gay Gordons." And as they walked hand in hand to the dancing area, she grinned at her friend Edith, who winked back at her. Manon and Emile spent most of the dance laughing as he tried to avoid stepping on her feet.

The next dance was a Strathspey, and since it was rather slower, Manon glanced up at Emile's face every time she turned back towards him after a twirl. He looked at her continually, and his smile never faded. At the end of the dance, he drew her towards him so that she could feel his breath on her face. "You are very beautiful. I don't…"

"Ma! Ma!" A cry came from the road. Manon jumped apart from Emile as she saw her two daughters cycling one-handed along the road, their other hands clamped onto their heads to keep their straw hats from flying away.

Chapter 34

July 1908

"Pa, you should have seen the tug of war at the picnic. And the dancing – it really was grand!" Effie burbled excitedly as they entered the schoolhouse.

James Anderson got to his feet as his younger daughter rushed towards him.

"Calm down, child," he said, tutting in his schoolmasterly way.

"It was really good to watch, Pa," said Nell. "They had that long mat thing on the grass – they had it at our picnic last year, d'you remember? And they all danced to the piper's tunes."

"I see." Their father smiled. "A fine day for it." He looked over to his wife, who was hanging up her hat. "I presume your tea duties prevented you from dancing, Manon?"

"Of course, James. I was there to work," she said, picking up the kettle.

"But Ma, we saw you dancing," said Effie.

Nell glanced at her father's face. "Well, we didn't actually, Effie. Ma was standing beside the dance floor when we arrived, that was all."

"So, were you dancing, Manon?"

His wife busied herself at the stove, not turning around as she mumbled, "Of course not, not when you weren't there, *chéri*."

"But Ma, I was first there on my bike – I can go faster than Nell now!" said Effie, beaming. "And I saw you finishing up your dance before you saw us arriving."

Nell looked again at her father's face. His lips were pursed; she knew that expression.

"No she wasn't, Effie, we couldn't see from the road and…"

Manon swivelled around. "Yes, I had a dance, James! Does it matter?" She came over with the cups and saucers, clanging everything down on the table. "Go and fetch the milk jug, Euphemia," she said, still not looking at her husband.

"And who, pray, was kind enough to ask you to dance?"

"Just a man from Cortachy, you wouldn't know him."

"Did he have a name?" James raised his eyebrows and attempted a smile.

She shook her head and began to pour the tea.

* * *

"They're interviewing someone for the job in the kitchen today," Manon said the following week. She had just returned from the hotel.

"About time too. And then you can return to your role as wife and mother," her husband said, scowling. He turned the page of the newspaper.

She spread out her hands. "The girls are out playing with their friends. That's normal at their age; mothers are not meant to be playmates."

"You will also be required to assist more in the classroom. We have an extra two pupils next year. We shall be up to fourteen pupils, and I'll need you to help the younger ones with their reading and writing."

"I did that all last year for you too, James, if you recall."

He glowered at her. "I'm sure you never used to answer back quite as much, Manon. I find it disrespectful. And also a bad example to our daughters. They must learn a woman's place."

Manon sighed. "Of course, but I want them to be strong and independent too – well, as much as society allows."

"You are beginning to sound like one of those ghastly suffragettes in London." He pointed to an article in the paper. "They've been chaining themselves to railings again and interrupting men's political meetings as if they merited a voice equal to men!" He shook his head.

"If I lived nearer, I'd want to join them. I'd have nothing to do with the violence of course, but perhaps for the marches."

James swivelled around. "That would not be permitted." His eyes were blazing.

"Your sister wanted to join the march in Dundee. She'd started to make her 'Votes for Women' banner."

"Winifred? Really?"

"Yes, she told me."

"Presumably her husband intervened and forbade it?"

"No, it was in the middle of lambing and she was needed at the farm to feed the shepherds."

There was a knock at the door. Manon went to open it and standing there, smiling his beautiful smile, was Emile.

"Bonjour Madame, I bring news."

James peered over his newspaper. "Who is it, my dear?"

Manon put her finger to her mouth, then turned back round to her husband. "Just Josie from the hotel kitchen telling me I'm not needed any more, they've filled the post."

"Well, thank the Lord for that," he muttered, head back down to his paper.

Manon went outside, closing the door behind her. "Why are you here?" she whispered, moving him along the wall away from the door a little.

"I wanted to tell you I've got the job at the hotel."

"How did you know where I lived?"

"You said something at the picnic about the schoolhouse in Clova village."

She nodded, then could not suppress a grin as she took in his handsome face and deep dark eyes.

"When are you moving into the hotel?"

"Whenever the laird's found someone else, but that shouldn't take long."

"I look forward to seeing you again," she said, slipping back in the door. Fortunately, her husband had his back to the door and could not see her enigmatic smile.

Chapter 35

May 1910

"Manon, I've got to go back to France. I've just had a letter from my brother." He pushed a letter at Manon as she entered his room at the back of the hotel. For the past year, since they had become lovers, she usually hovered around the stables until she could see there was no one passing, then dart into his room.

She read it and sighed. "I'm so sorry, darling. Has your mother ever been unwell before?"

"No, she's always been really well, strong – which is why I've got to go. My brother wouldn't have asked me to return unless she was gravely ill. As soon as I can organise the journey, I'll be leaving."

"When?"

"Hopefully in the next week or so, but I won't tell them here till I know a definite date."

"But then you'll be back?"

"I don't know, I really hope so." He took her in his arms and, as always, she just wanted to lie down with him. "Let's go to bed, Emile, who knows what's around the corner."

"So true. I'll come back for you, like we discussed… I just don't know when that might be." He began to kiss her as she started to shake her hair loose from the bun at the back of her head. As he pushed her gently towards the bed, he said. "You know I love you, Manon. I'll be back."

* * *

Two days later was the Service of the Lambs at Clova kirk, and Manon had spent the morning with Effie, who was in bed with a sore throat.

"Ma, I'm feeling much better now. I'm sure you could join

Aunt Winnie and the boys for lunch at the hotel. I'll be fine here," she said, picking a book from the pile by her bed.

"Are you sure, darling?" She kissed the top of her daughter's head. She had no temperature, just a raw throat. "I'll go and make you a chamomile tea. Keep sipping it and hopefully your throat will be better very soon."

At the lunch, she had sat beside Winifred, who always seemed wary of her. Even after nearly fifteen years of knowing her, there was an uneasiness between them. When James had asked her to marry him, when she was only eighteen years old, his sister clearly had been surprised, not only that her brother was at long last marrying; but mostly about his choice of bride. She'd presumed he would marry a farmer's daughter from the glens, or at least someone with a similar upbringing. Instead he chose this young French beauty, daughter of the hotel chef. It took Winifred a long time to get used to her.

At lunch, Manon tried, as usual, to ask her sister-in-law about the farm and what else she did over in Glen Prosen, but they really had very little in common, apart from James. After she'd finished her pudding, Manon looked up at the clock.

"I'm just going to pop over to check on Euphemia," she said, pushing her chair back. "I'll be back shortly."

Her husband looked up from his pudding plate and nodded. Aunt Winifred was still speaking to the waitress about getting the recipe for the steamed pudding from the kitchen. Manon went out the front door and began to cross towards the schoolhouse when she saw a figure round the back of the hotel. It was Emile.

She glanced around and saw no one was there so rushed towards him.

"Have you made any progress with your plans about the trip back to France?"

He nodded. "Yes, I leave in eight days' time. I'm taking the bus to Kirriemuir, then the train to Dundee, and south to London from there."

"Eight days," she said, shaking her head. "That's not long, we must make the most of it. My husband has a meeting in Dykehead one evening this week. I'll find out when and…"

Emile leant forward to kiss her and she flung her arms around him, fighting back tears. "I'm going to miss you so much, I'm…"

There was a loud cough from behind them. They sprang apart and saw Aunt Winifred standing there, eyes wide. Emile turned around and strode straight back to the kitchen. Manon rushed towards her sister-in-law.

"Winifred," Manon said, face flushed, "I was just saying goodbye to one of the kitchen staff."

"Goodbye?" Winifred raised an eyebrow. "That looked like more than a goodbye, Manon." She stood her ground, expression grim.

"He's… he's leaving very soon. I was just giving him a goodbye hug, you know, like we do in France." She forced a smile. "That's all."

"I see." Winifred clasped her hands together. "Well, that was quite some farewell…"

Manon grabbed Winifred's hands. "Please don't tell James. He wouldn't understand." She let out a long breath. "Please, Winifred, I beg you…"

"Very well, Manon, this is our secret. But you must promise me that it will not happen again. If so, my brother is bound to find out somehow." She narrowed her eyes.

Manon shook her head. "Never again…" She gave Winifred's hands a tight squeeze, then dropped them. "I must run and see Euphemia before you go." She set off towards the schoolhouse, then stopped and turned around. "Thank you, Winifred."

Her sister-in-law watched her sprint over the road, then headed round to the stables.

Chapter 36

September 1910

"You've been quieter than usual over these past few weeks, Manon," James said as they cleared away the children's things in the classroom. "In fact, you hardly speak to me outside the classroom, you only communicate with the girls. I've been observing you over the past few days."

Well, this was quite something: her impassive husband had actually noticed something wasn't right with her. It had been three months since Emile had left.

"I'm fine, James." She bent down to pick something up from the classroom floor. "Here are Phyllis's hair ribbons. Her mum'll be furious she's left them; she won't have any for the weekend."

"Does she not have a younger sister?"

"Yes, but she's not even at school yet so hardly likely to need ribbons like these."

Manon's husband approached her and took her hand. "Is everything all right? You've not been yourself for a while now."

"I told you, I'm fine." She glanced at him, trying not to feel repulsed by the touch of his damp hand. For once he actually did look concerned. "I'm still grieving for my father, I suppose. All those years with him in my life and now…"

"Of course, though such sentiment does not help us, Manon. We must move on. It was quite some time ago. Old people die; that is the way of life."

She sighed. She had wondered, over the past couple of years since she'd met Emile, if she'd ever loved James, and she had come to the conclusion that no, she had not. She had been rather infatuated with him at first, and flattered that an older man – a teacher at that – had asked her father for her hand in marriage.

But truly, he should have married someone more biddable, like one of the village ladies. If she didn't have her wonderful girls for company and comfort, she didn't know what she would do.

"I'm going round to the schoolhouse; I've got supper to prepare."

"Are the girls still out on their bicycles?"

"Yes, I told them there was no rush, it's such a beautiful day."

Manon wandered round the school building to their house, but at the door she stopped and gazed down the glen. The green colours of the grass, the trees and the hills never failed to delight; it was so calming. As she went inside, she thought about her husband's words. It was so strange that he had noticed she'd been quieter. She must try to seem more cheerful, involve him in conversations.

She stepped onto the inside mat and stared down: there was a letter. She turned it over – it was from France. She rushed to the table, grabbed a knife and slit it open.

Chère Manon…

I have thought of little but you since I've been here, and now that we've had my mother's funeral, I am planning my journey back to you and…

There was a noise behind her and the letter was seized from her hand. Her husband stood there, eyes glazed with fury. He had clearly been reading it over her shoulder.

"So this is why you have been quiet? Why is this person writing to you?" He held the letter outstretched with one hand to finish reading it. "Ma chere, I shall come back to Clova and we shall leave together with the girls and…"

Manon leapt towards him and tried to grab the letter from him. But he held on tight. "It's from Emile, that young lad – a mere boy – who worked in the kitchens?" He shook his head. "I cannot believe your depravity – you, a respectable wife and mother." He went over to the fire and crumpled up the letter. He threw it in and, as she rushed to save it, strode out the door.

She managed to rescue some pieces but was still at the hearth, sobbing, when she heard him return. She turned around and saw him standing at the door, tawse in hand. He closed the door behind him.

She opened her mouth to say something as he approached, strap raised. Then the door was flung open and the girls rushed in. They stopped, eyes wide, when they saw the raised tawse.

"Why have you got that in here, Pa?" Nell asked, coming towards him. Effie ran and cowered behind her mother.

"Get out! Now!" he yelled at his daughters. But Nell ignored him and went to stand in front of him. "Ma's coming with us too. Let's go over to the hotel, Ma. We'll let Pa lose his temper alone." She turned to go. Her father swiped at her with the tawse and it caught her on her back. She yelped, and Manon rushed to comfort her.

"Put that thing down!" she yelled as she took her daughter in her arms. James turned around and went outside, slamming the door, leaving his wife and daughters crouching on the floor, arms around each other.

* * *

When the girls were in bed, the door opened and James returned. He had clearly been in the classroom for the past few hours. He sat down at the table, and she went to reheat his supper in silence. She put it in front of him and sat down opposite. She watched him eat, barely moving, then leant across the table. "If you ever hit me or our girls again, I will leave. I will take them away from you. Do you understand?"

He stared at her for a moment, then snickered. "Do you really think you can make threats to me, you shameless Jezebel? I am the one who has authority over our daughters, I think you forget that. I can do whatever I like with them; you cannot. In law, they are wholly mine." He was enunciating each syllable slowly as if speaking to a child. "They will remain here, with their father, in this house."

He pushed the plate across the table towards her. "Come next door with me."

"Why?"

"Get up and come next door. Now!"

She stood up, her eyes wide with fright. He grabbed her hand, his long nails scratching her skin, and she winced. "You're hurting me, James. Please let go."

She struggled to release her hand, but he dragged her out of the door and into the classroom where the tawse lay on the desk. He shut the door firmly behind them.

"If you thought you could deceive me for any longer, you were very much mistaken. How dare you? I will be no cuckold." His gaze was steely. "I will thrash you until you beg for forgiveness. You are hardly even worth words. You deserve to be…"

And he threw her to the ground, picked up the tawse and began to beat her on the back, again and again, on her legs, and on her shoulders. She cowered, arms over her head for protection, but soon she became so weak. She collapsed and her head hit the floor, blood seeping from a gash on her forehead. Then her husband stopped. He stepped over the comatose body of his wife and put the tawse back in his drawer. He went to the door and headed outside into the cool night air to return home.

A couple of hours later, when she felt able to move, she dragged herself to the desk. She found a piece of paper and a pencil, and, with great difficulty as she was in so much pain, scribbled a note.

My darlings Helen and Euphemia, it read.
I have to leave for now, but I shall be back to get you as soon as possible.
Your loving mother.

She dragged herself outside and felt her way along the wall in the black, moonless night to find her daughters' bicycles. She tucked the note deep into the basket at the front of Nell's bike, then lurched off towards the road. Her legs were covered in welts, she was bleeding all over, and she was in such pain when she walked, but she had to get away; she had no choice. Staggering in the pitch dark, she knew she could not risk waiting to see what he did next.

As she walked down the glen, wincing with each limping step, the wind began to get up, and she pulled her thin cardigan tighter around her bruised shoulders as the chill of the night seeped into her bones.

Back up at the schoolhouse, a small piece of paper fluttered out of the basket of a child's bike, then flew over the handlebars and drifted away on the wind into the woods that led towards Loch Brandy.

PART 6

Nell

Chapter 37

October 1943

Nell had a sleepless night. She kept going over and over what Effie had told her about what happened in May of 1915. Mathilde hadn't stayed long the previous evening; she clearly felt the tension in the schoolhouse, and once they'd settled on a date to invite her friend round for tea, she'd left. Then, Effie had told her sister about her time in Glen Prosen and what happened after the baby was born. Nell presumed that no detail had been missed out.

As she got out of bed and went to put on the kettle, Nell remembered that Effie had wanted to call the baby Manon, after Ma. It made Nell think back to all those years ago, in 1910, when her mother had died and how their father had told them the news.

The morning after he had lashed out at Nell with the tawse and she was still sore from the blow – the girls came out of their bedroom to find their father alone at the breakfast table. His usual clean-cut, spruce demeanour was absent. He looked haggard, his face grey, his eyes red and puffy.

"Where's Ma?" Effie had asked.

"She was taken ill in the night. She's in the hospital; the doctors are trying to treat her."

The girls gasped. "But she'll be all right, Pa?"

Their father's expression was unfathomable. "We shall have to wait and see what the doctors say."

"What's wrong with her? She was perfectly healthy yesterday." Nell was frowning.

"A serious pneumonia came upon her in the night. The doctor said it would be unwise to try to treat her at home." His voice was still dispassionate.

"Which hospital, Pa? Can we go to see her?"

"It's the cottage hospital in Forfar and no, you cannot go. I shall go this afternoon after class is finished. You girls can make supper for my return. And if I'm not back before your bedtime, then you will take yourselves off to bed. You are no longer little girls; it's about time you started to look after yourselves."

"But how will we manage without Ma?" Effie wailed.

"We will manage just fine." Their father leant in close. "It's as simple as that." His spittle was visible as he spoke.

He pointed over to the stove. "Get the porridge on the go, Helen. We have only one hour until lessons begin."

That day they did not see their father at all after class finished, and though they had left a pot of soup for his supper, he was not back by their bedtime.

"Could we go and ask the minister for help? Or the nurse?"

"Effie, Pa told us not to speak to anyone about Ma until he was back." She shook her head. "In the kind of mood he's in, we can't disobey him again. Look what happened yesterday."

"How's your back?"

"It still hurts." Nell grimaced. "Anyway, maybe it's good news he's not back yet. Maybe they're trying to get the right medicine to make her well." Nell forced a smile. "Come on, we'd better get ready for bed."

Even though neither of them felt tired, by nine o'clock they could not fight sleep any longer. They did not hear the door creaking open many hours later, just as the sun was beginning to rise down the glen.

That morning, their father was once more sitting at the table when the girls emerged from their bedroom. Their father looked as if he had not slept at all. His skin was ashen, eyes sunken.

"Sit down, girls. I have something to say to you both."

Nell put her arm around her sister's shoulder as they went to sit down. They both stared at their father.

"I'm afraid to say, your mother died in the night. The pneumonia was chronic, and she could not survive, even though she put up a good fight." He licked his lips and went to get a glass of water.

"Of course she did," he muttered.

The girls sat, immobile, watching him sit down again. Then Effie began to sob. "It's not true, Pa, you're lying. She's going to be fine. Ma's going to…"

Nell patted her sister's hand. "Why would Pa lie, Effie?" And she too began to weep. Their father sat opposite them, watching but not moving, hardly even blinking his dry eyes. Then Nell looked up and wiped her tears on her sleeve. "Were you there when she died? Did she know you were there?"

He looked away, towards the tiny window by the door, where the first light continued to brighten up the hills and the fields to the east. Then he turned back to his daughters. "Yes," he said, "she knew I was there."

Chapter 38

November 1943

"You'd think we'd never had anyone round for a cup of tea before," Nell said, sighing as she laid the table with the good tablecloth.

"Well, Mathilde seems to want to create a good impression. And it's rather lovely that she wants us to meet him, don't you think?"

"Of course."

"I mean, we've only known her for, what, just over three months, but it feels like we've known her forever."

Nell nodded then sniffed. "You're sure the scones aren't ready yet?"

"I do know how to bake scones you know, Nell. I admit you're the queen of treacle scones, but I can do a plain scone fine, thank you very much."

Nell screwed open a jar of jam and peered inside. "Oh, it's got mould on it. Did you not wait till the jam was completely cold before putting the wax seal on?"

"I like that," Effie said, tutting. "You were the one who sealed the jam after I made it."

"From the brambles I gathered."

"All right, all right," she said, pointing to the jar. "Just scrape off any mould, it's not going to kill us."

Effie bent down and opened the oven door. She pulled out the tray of scones. "Are they not a bit overdone?" Nell asked, frowning.

"No, nicely tinged with golden brown, I'd say," and she put them on the wire rack to cool.

"So do we know how long Doug's going to stay at Clova kirk?"

"No idea. What are they saying in the village about when Mr Johnson might get back to preaching?"

"It's Mrs Johnson who's more of a worry. She's never been out of bed all this time, since they heard the news. He must be so worried about her."

"Doug might have some more information, I suppose." She frowned. "Why isn't he in the forces, by the way? Surely they need chaplains?"

"Again, I've no idea. Maybe he's not medically fit or something? Do they have to be?"

"Who knows? Maybe that's something we can ask him." She looked up at the clock. "Half an hour till they're here, Nell. Are you going to leave your hair hanging all limp like that or push a comb through it?"

"Yes, I thought I would actually, Miss Perfect Hair," and off she stomped to the bedroom to find a brush.

* * *

"Did you hear last night on the wireless about the Vatican being bombed?" Nell said. "I thought that wasn't allowed?"

"Yes," Doug said, buttering his scone. "Luckily there weren't any casualties."

"But I thought Vatican City was neutral?" Nell continued.

"It is, and I don't think they know who did it. Or why."

"Let's not talk about the war," Mathilde said. Her English had come on well now she was good friends with Doug. "It's all so horrible. Surely it has to finish as soon as possible. Too much sorrow, too many deaths." She looked at Doug. "Let's hope it's all over before you have to go."

"Oh, are you going to join up as a chaplain?"

He nodded. "Ever since I was ordained as a minister I've tried to enlist, but until recently I was too inexperienced. I'm still hoping there'll be a vacancy soon. Until then, though, the Presbytery's confirmed I can stay on at Clova kirk. Certainly until Mr Johnson is able to come back to work."

"But how likely is that?" Nell asked. She had seen Mr Johnson at the post office the day before and he was grey. He could hardly even speak to her or to Mrs Bell. He looked utterly exhausted.

Doug shrugged. "I don't know. I've obviously had many conversations with him. He's desperately worried about his wife. She's terrified her other sons will be killed too."

"You can understand that, poor woman." Effie glanced over at Doug again. It was the first time she had spoken since Mathilde had introduced them at the door and they'd sat down at the table. It was unsettling how similar he looked to the Douglas Harrison she'd known all those years ago. Only his hair was different – and this man smiled more, with such a genuine smile. "What does your mother think about you going to war, even as a chaplain?"

"My mother died four years ago."

"Oh, I'm so sorry," said Effie.

"And your father. Is he still alive?" Nell asked.

"Yes, he is," Doug said, drinking his tea.

"Does he live locally? I keep thinking I can detect a bit of a Kirrie or maybe a Forfar accent?"

"He lives near Forfar."

"Do you… do you look like your father, Doug?"

"My mother used to say I did, yes." He looked down at his plate. "Unfortunately…"

There was silence as the two sisters continued to stare at him. "Doug does not see his father very much," Mathilde offered.

He nodded. "We're very different people," he mumbled. "He's not interested in my work, and there's some things he's done, I find I just can't…"

Effie gawped at him as his voice trailed away.

"Forgive him?" Nell suggested.

"Nell!" Effie snapped.

Doug smiled. "No, it's fine, Miss Anderson. And it's true, there are some issues. He was not always very…" he hesitated "hmm… kind to my mother."

"Let's change the subject," Mathilde said, standing up to put on the kettle again. The conversation was clearly bothering her.

"So, Doug, if you're not called up or the war ends soon, where would you like to go – if you had a choice obviously – for your parish?" Nell asked.

"Oh, well now, that's a big question."

Mathilde sat down beside him and turned to face him. She was looking lovely today, her hair loose around her shoulders and wearing a new dress Nell had helped her sew. Nell still somehow caught glimpses of her sister in Mathilde, though of course she'd not mentioned it to Effie.

"I suppose," he said, looking round at Mathilde, "if Mr Johnson feels he's not able to continue here, then Clova would be ideal."

As the young couple shared knowing smiles, Nell glanced at her sister. "Well, that would be lovely. Here's hoping that might happen soon, or at least after the war's over."

Effie nodded as she continued to stare, incredulous, at Doug's face, and tried to suppress memories of his father.

Chapter 39

December 1943

It was a bitterly cold morning when Nell set off from the schoolhouse on her bike. It was still dark when she arrived at the post office, and Mrs Bell had only just lit the fire.

"Come nearer the hearth while we sort the letters, it's still freezing in here," Mrs Bell said.

Nell pulled off her gloves and took a pile of post. "Hopefully no telegrams today?"

The postmistress shook her head. "Let's hope there's no more in the village."

"Did you hear on the wireless last night about the Cairo Declaration?"

"Yes, though my mother-in-law kept talking all through the bulletin. Remind me what they said, Helen?"

"I can't remember all the detail, but Mr Churchill and Mr Roosevelt – and I think the Chinese leader – demanded the surrender of Japan and also that it gives up all the Pacific islands it's taken since the last war."

"Well, well. But they won't do that, will they?"

"Who knows. We'll be able to read more about it in the papers later."

Nell pushed all the letters and parcels into her post bag and swung it over her shoulder. "It's not too heavy today."

"Oh, Helen, when you're delivering the letters to the big house, can you tell them I couldn't manage to get that parcel away last night in time, but it'll be in today's afternoon post. They were far too late yesterday."

"They clearly think normal post office opening hours don't apply to them," Nell said, smirking.

"Mind how you go, Helen, there's still a lot of frost." Mrs Bell came to the door with her and looked up at a threatening sky. "I think it might snow later. Take care on the road, won't you?"

She began to cycle, cautiously at first, noticing as she breathed out that her breath was a cloud of icy fog. It was so cold. She swerved to avoid someone crossing over to the bus stop, and Nell waved as she passed an elderly lady, who shivered a little and pulled her thick fur hat down to meet her coat collar.

After a couple of deliveries along the road up the glen, she soon came to the big house. She rang the doorbell. It was Mrs Clark who answered.

"Hello Nell, what have you got today, then?"

Nell delved into her bag and brought out three letters, which she handed over to the housekeeper while giving her the message from Mrs Bell.

"I knew it would be too late. I told them," she said, shrugging. She pointed to one of the letters. "Good, that's a Dundee postmark. Her Ladyship'll be pleased to hear from Isabella. She's been waiting for news about how they're settling into their new house in Broughty Ferry."

"It's nice when there's good news in my post bag," Nell said as she swung her leg over her bike and headed back down to the road towards Glen Doll.

* * *

The fields were covered in a blanket of white, and the branches of the trees were stiff with frost. She was trying to warm herself up, pedalling faster than usual. As she cycled, she thought of the letter with the Dundee postmark and was reminded of the family from Dundee who had wanted to adopt Effie's baby all those years ago: they had lived in Broughty Ferry too. It still tormented her to remember Effie's pain a few weeks previously when she told her sister more about that awful period of her life; she had suffered so much – and been so alone. If only Nell had known about the baby all those years ago.

"Nell," Effie had said, "I only managed to see her once, when Aunt Winnie was out and Betty was away. But then, in early June, only a few weeks after she was born, Aunt Winnie told me that she'd agreed on a date with the family she'd found in Dundee. They were due to arrive at the house in the middle of June. She'd wanted to meet them somewhere a bit away from Glen Prosen, but that spring was unusually cold and she didn't want the baby to be waiting about outside for too long, in case it was still chilly. The Dundee family had a covered carriage, unlike our aunt's pony and trap, so the baby could be taken straight from the warmth of her crib into the carriage, and then on to her new home in Dundee."

As she told Nell this, Effie's tears continued to flow. It broke her sister's heart to hear about the secret she had carried all alone for so long.

"It was grey and cloudy the day she was due to leave us, and I'd been allowed over to the Belgians' cottage for only the second time since she'd been born. As I nestled her dear little face close to mine and cuddled her close to me, I was broken. She was such a little thing – so dainty, so vulnerable. Our aunt had reservations about even allowing me to have one last hold of her, but Madame Dubois had told her it was unhuman not to allow a mother one final embrace.

"Then I was dispatched back over to the kitchen to look out from the window. Betty was watching over me, making sure I didn't try to bolt outside. The designated time arrived and there was no sight of a horse trotting into the courtyard, nor the sound of creaking carriage wheels. Aunt Winifred, who had been waiting inside the Belgians' cottage, emerged about an hour later, scowling. She swept into the kitchen and muttered something about how ill-mannered it was for people to be late. After another hour, she stormed back over to the Dubois' and told Madame just to feed the baby and continue their day as usual; there had clearly been a hold-up.

"By this time, I had no tears left. I simply sat, dejected, on the chair by the window. Betty tried to get me to join her at the table for some soup, but I shook my head. After another hour it was clear they were not going to turn up at all, and I went upstairs to bed. I lay down on the covers and could not even cry. I simply stared at the ceiling all afternoon until Aunt Winnie came to fetch me down for supper. She said she presumed there would be a letter of explanation soon, but until then, we all had to go about our normal business.

"Two days later, as we sat at lunch together, Betty brought in a letter. 'It's got a Dundee postmark,' she said, holding it out to Aunt Winnie. She opened it and removed the letter, then read it as I stared at her, waiting. She put it back in the envelope and turned to me. 'Euphemia, it turns out that the adoption I so carefully set up cannot now proceed.' She was trying to control her anger. 'The couple, as you know, had no children, even though the wife was in her twenties and the gentleman in his forties. It was the wife's mother I had been corresponding with. It seems her husband, Mr Donaldson, found out about it just as the carriage was being prepared and forbade it.'

"I remember bellowing 'Why?' and she explained that the older man was an eminent jute baron, and the extended family all lived in one of the seafront mansions in Broughty Ferry to the east of Dundee. He took his public profile very seriously. When he heard about the planned adoption, he decided to intervene and prohibit it. Though she did not expand on his reasons and I was not allowed to see the letter, Aunt Winnie implied that he did not want an illegitimate child as part of his family."

Though Effie's eyes surely had no more tears, she began snivelling again. When Nell then asked her what their aunt had decided to do, she said that the Belgians would keep the baby until another suitable family was found. But, after another three months of nothing happening, it was time for Effie to leave and return home to Clova, since Pa needed her to help him at school.

Just thinking about it all again, how her sister had suffered, alone, made Nell so sad. She looked around at the hills shrouded in mist, but the joy she usually felt when gazing at them, in any weather, was absent.

When Nell arrived back at the post office, Mrs Bell was standing by the fire. "Come away in, Helen. You must be freezing. At least the snow never started."

"I'm fine actually, I was cycling really fast. My hands are a bit cold, but that's all. Anything else?"

"I missed this one," she said, handing over a letter to Nell.

"Oh, it's for me," she said, looking at the address. "It's from France, it will be from my friend Paul." She smiled. "Thanks Mrs Bell, see you tomorrow."

Chapter 40

December 1943

The house was cold. Nell placed more logs on the fire and pulled the armchair nearer the flames. She wrapped her hands around a cup of tea, took some sips, then put it down at her side and pulled out the letter.

Chère Belle Hélène

It was wonderful to have your last letter telling me about the French woman staying with you. I wonder if you have found out more about her.

Not enough, Nell thought. There followed some paragraphs about the windy weather in Provence and the challenges of this year's olive harvest with so many young men away fighting, then the main news was about his family.

Paul and Nell had said goodbye to each other when Royaumont Abbey closed its doors as a military hospital on the last day of 1918. They'd both been emotional. The final pantomime two weeks earlier – a triumphal 'Cinderella', to which all the locals had been invited – was a high note to end on. And with the war over, they should have been overjoyed. Yet the two were apprehensive, knowing that nothing would ever be quite the same. The friends promised to write regularly, and even though their letters were intermittent, depending on Paul's family situation – he and his wife Monique had five daughters – they remained good friends.

As you know, my eldest daughter got married last spring. Well, now we are all awaiting the arrival of their baby. My wife and I are so excited to meet our first grandchild. Can you imagine me as a grandfather, Hélène?

Actually, she could. She could almost see his warm face breaking into a huge smile, revealing those beautiful dimples, as he dandled a chubby baby on his knee.

And also, my middle daughter has just become engaged. Her fiancé is still in the army, but after the war is over they will have a wonderful wedding. I will of course make the croquembouche: you remember I told you about this towering cake we often have at weddings? And you will be invited! Please say you'll come, Hélène. And your sister too, of course. We have all been waiting for you here in Arles for too long.
Your friend,
Paul

* * *

Máthilde knocked on the door, then came in, beaming as usual. Ever since she had met Doug Harrison, she was a different person.

"Nell, is it all right if I borrow your sewing things again, please? I thought I'd try to make another couple of aprons for the hotel kitchen. The ones there are so tatty."

"Of course, help yourself, Mathilde," Nell said, pointing to the sewing box. "Take the whole box with you if you want, there's nothing I need in it for the moment."

"And Effie?"

Nell shook her head. "She's busy practising carols on the piano for the children's Christmas concert next week. She wants it all to be perfect."

"And it will be. Doug's going to be there. Mr Johnson still doesn't feel up to doing the readings and prayers."

"Well, it'll be nice to have a young face there anyway." She glimpsed Mathilde's smile, then added, "And a handsome face too. You know his father was a teacher at the school with our father?"

"Yes, he told me." She frowned. "It's such a shame he's estranged from him. I thought it would be good to meet him, at some stage, but Doug really does not like him."

"I can understand that, Mathilde. He's not a good man, like your Doug seems to be."

"How can a son be so different to his father?"

"Clearly he takes after his mother." Nell shrugged. "Mathilde, do you think that if Doug ends up staying in Clova you would want to as well?"

"I'd like that very much."

"You're very fond of him, aren't you?"

Mathilde nodded.

"It's obvious he adores you. Do you mind me asking, how much younger is he? Even though obviously you don't look any older."

Mathilde was silent. Dear God, it was none of Nell's business, why did she sometimes just blunder in?

Nell sighed with relief as she realised Mathilde was silently counting.

"Only about four or five years I think, but… well, who knows what may happen." Mathilde picked up the box and headed for the door. "Thank you again. I'll hand it back over when I'm finished."

"It's all right, I know where you live," Nell said, winking.

Mathilde grinned.

"I've still not seen any letters arrive at the post office from France for you, Mathilde. You sent your mother a letter telling her your address, didn't you?"

Mathilde nodded. "Ages ago, more than one. I'm trying not to think about what could have happened. Ever since my uncle died, there's only Maman to write to, and I've not heard back."

"Yet. I'm sure you'll hear soon."

Mathilde bit her lip. "I hope so. But the post has been really difficult all throughout the war, and the restaurant's not that far from the Belgian border. There are so many Germans there."

"You must miss her so much."

"I really do," said Mathilde, forcing a smile. "See you soon, Nell."

Nell went to pick up Paul's letter again, then stopped as a thought occurred. She tried to work out exactly how old Mathilde was. Neither sister had wanted to ask her; it seemed rude somehow. Doug was surely in his early to mid-twenties, having finished his theological training fairly recently. So Mathilde must be in her late twenties or perhaps even early thirties, which would mean she could have been born any time from, say 1911 to about 1915...

And as she thought of those dates, Nell gasped out loud.

She thought back to what Effie had said about what had happened to her baby, back in 1915. She had not been taken by the adoptive family to Dundee, which had been a severe disappointment. And that was when Effie told her sister she had to stop talking about her past; she didn't have the strength to carry on telling Nell what had happened nearly three decades before. Perhaps the Dubois' had taken the baby back to their home in Belgium after the war.

Nell went to fetch a glass of water and took a gulp. She had difficulty swallowing. Mathilde had said that her home in France was not far from the Belgian border. Nell had never mentioned to Effie that she thought Mathilde looked exactly like her sister at that age, but with certain expressions, the similarity was uncanny.

Dear God, could Mathilde be Effie's daughter? As she swigged down the last of the water, Nell thought about the implications. Her eyes opened wide as she realised what that would mean for her relationship with the young minister. The glass slipped out of her hand and she stood completely still, staring trance-like at the broken pieces strewn across the floor.

Chapter 41

December 1943

The following day, Nell cycled away from the post office on roads still thick with frost. As she passed the manse, she could see Mrs Tweedie round the side feeding the hens. She slowed down and rested her bike against the wall. The woman came towards her as she walked across the garden.

"How is Mrs Johnson doing today?"

She shook her head. "Same as usual. I really don't like to leave her alone for too long."

"And Mr Johnson, how's he coping?"

She shrugged. "Fine on the outside, of course, but he's hurting too; he's almost as upset about his wife as he is about Jimmy."

"Is he going to be able to carry on as minister d'you think?"

"There were people from the Presbytery visiting him yesterday, so I presume that's what they were discussing." She pulled out a handkerchief to blow her nose.

"Was the young minister Mr Harrison there too?"

"No, but Mr Johnson's very fond of him. He'd be a good replacement if needs be."

"But surely he'll be off overseas with the army soon? I thought he was just waiting for his post."

"I really don't know, Nell."

"You're doing a great job, Mrs Tweedie. It must be hard."

She smiled a rueful smile. "It's certainly not easy, but look how good to me she was all those months before my Bill died."

"I know." Nell shivered. "Sorry to keep you so long in the cold. Send Mrs Johnson my best, please."

The woman nodded, then plunged her hand into the bucket of feed and turned back to the hens clucking around her feet.

Once Nell was back at the post office, Mrs Bell gave her

another letter. "Sorry, Helen, I must have missed this earlier. It's for your sister."

"Thanks, I'll pop it in now on my way down to Wheen farm with the parcel."

As she put a hand onto the handlebars, she turned the letter over to see if there was any indication of who might have sent it. It was the same handwriting as the other letters Nell had delivered to her sister since she'd taken over as postie. As she put it in her pocket, a thought occurred, and she decided not to post it through the schoolhouse letterbox; Effie sometimes popped home at lunchtime, and there were a few things Nell wanted to check herself first.

* * *

Nell looked at the clock. It was only half past two. She had at least an hour, possibly longer, before her sister was due home. She hung up her postbag and coat, then took the letter over to the table. She was not about to steam open the letter; that would be a step too far. But perhaps she could locate the already opened ones, if only to confirm Nell's worries.

She opened the door to her sister's room and began to pull out drawers in her tallboy. Compared to Nell's drawers, Effie's were so tidy, everything folded neatly in piles. In the bottom drawer where she kept her undergarments, Nell slid her hand underneath the pile and felt something. She pulled out four or five envelopes, all opened in one clean cut along the top with their father's paper knife.

She took them through to the table and compared them to the new letter. Just as she'd thought, they were all written in the same handwriting. Nell swung back on the chair, debating what to do. It would be a betrayal of trust to actually read the letters; she could not do that, surely. And yet she had to know if it was indeed the man from Effie's past trying to get back in touch.

She took out the top letter and read it through, feeling her heart sink as she got to the end.

And so, my dear Euphemia, I look forward to welcoming you here to Restenneth. Send me the details of when your bus arrives in Forfar and I shall collect you there.
Yours,
Douglas

She let out a long breath, then pushed the letter back into its envelope. She put it back on the pile and returned the envelopes carefully to the bottom drawer, just as the front door began to open. Dear God, Effie was back early.

She darted out into the kitchen and headed for the sink just as Effie came in, her heavy coat billowing behind her.

"I think it's going to snow, don't you?" Effie said to her sister, who by now was filling the kettle.

"No idea. I hope not. It's been dangerous enough on the bike today." She pointed to the letter. "A letter for you, Effie. I'm just putting the kettle on, do you want a cup of tea?"

Effie shook her head. "I don't have time," she said, grabbing the letter and pushing it into her coat pocket. "I'm still copying out the carols for the concert. You're going to manage to come along, aren't you?"

"What time is it?"

"Two o'clock."

"I'm sure I'll be finished with the first rounds by then. I'll definitely try."

"Good," Effie said, rushing into her room. Nell held her breath until her sister emerged with a warm scarf. "It's freezing in the classroom, I've no idea why; the fire's on. Maybe I'm going down with a cold or something."

"Shall I bring you round a cup of tea to warm you up?"

"Thanks, Nell," she said, heading for the door.

Once Nell had taken her sister's tea to the classroom, she came back into the schoolhouse and went to sit at the kitchen table, thinking over what she could do, if anything. Her heart was beating fast; she had no idea whether to confront Effie. Surely that would not be sensible, but there was no way her sister should meet this man, this brute who, good God, could be Mathilde's father.

PART 7

Mathilde

Chapter 42

February 1944

Mathilde picked up the photo by her bed and looked at it. Pierre was in his uniform, one shoulder slanting forwards and his eyes gazing directly into the camera, a serious look on his face, but somehow she still saw the twinkle in his eyes. She had had his picture beside her bed since she arrived at the hotel, but now it seemed like a betrayal. She and Doug were in love – her head wanted to say it was too soon after Pierre, but her heart knew otherwise. She tucked the photo into the drawer of her bedside table.

Doug was not only handsome, his deep-set eyes crinkling charmingly when he smiled, but he was also such a good man, just like Pierre had been. And on the few occasions he discussed his father, he was not as condemnatory as he could have been. He was a man of God; perhaps that was why. The father sounded like an awful person, treating his wife so badly. Nell had confirmed what an unpleasant man he was, though she had not elaborated on how she knew that.

She wondered what Doug's mother had been like. Was she as loving and caring as her own had been? Even when Mathilde had turned eighteen and her mother had revealed the truth about her past, she was empathetic and kind. She remembered that day so well: her mother had started by telling Mathilde about her own family in Provence, something she'd never talked about before. Her grandmother, who was dead, had lived with Mathilde's aunt in a town called Maussane, where both sisters had been brought up. Maman had moved to the north when she was quite young – to start a job at the school and also helping in the restaurant where her uncle was the chef.

That was when the real facts about her parents came out: Maman had sat her down and said she was old enough to know the truth. Mathilde remembered being shocked as she heard the story of who she actually was.

She and her mother had just finished dinner and as usual, after she'd done the dishes, Mathilde was getting ready to go next door and say good night to her uncle at the restaurant. It had been a daily ritual since she was little.

"*Chérie*, I have something to tell you," her mother had said. "And though it's a little complicated, I think you must know the truth." She started telling her about her family in Provence. In retrospect, Mathilde wondered why she'd never asked her mother where she was from before. But her life was so happy and stable at the restaurant with her mother and her uncle, she'd never felt the need to ask about her actual father, who she knew had died when she was little.

She had asked the day before if she could see her mother's wedding certificate.

"Why?"

"I was at Myriam's house, and she was showing me her parents' certificate and I just thought I'd like to see yours. I don't even know Papa's age, just that he died when I was little."

Her mother told her she'd try to find it but wasn't sure where it was.

The following night, taking Mathilde's hand gently in hers, Manon looked into her daughter's eyes and told her that she didn't have a certificate because she and her father were never married.

"For two years before you were born, Mathilde, I was in love with a man, your father. We moved to live with his family near Paris, and that's where you were born. We never married, but his family were accepting of that." She sighed. "I'm sorry darling, but your Papa and I loved each other very much; we did not need some official document for that."

Mathilde frowned. "I don't understand. So you had a baby – me – out of wedlock?" Mathilde's eyes opened wide. "What did the priest say about that?"

"I didn't care. Yes, we were shunned by some of the people in the town, but mostly they were fine."

"But why didn't you marry, if you loved each other so much?"

"I said it was complicated and it was. I could not marry him."

"Why not?"

"I…" she sighed. "You just have to trust me, *chérie*. It was not possible." She stroked her daughter's cheek. "And then in 1914 there was the war. He was one of the first to enlist and one of the first…", her mother swallowed, "… to die. He lost his life in the Battle of Lorraine, only a couple of weeks after France entered the war." She shook her head. "Such a waste of a young, beautiful life."

"Maman, sadly I can't even remember my father, and my uncle has been like a father to me all these years, so my life has been full of love. But is it not shameful that I was born out of wedlock – does that not make me illegitimate?"

"Uncle has indeed been like a father to you. He adores you as if he were your father, you know that." Her mother stretched out to reach Mathilde's arm.

"Let go of me." She yanked herself away. She needed space to process this. "I just don't understand, Maman, why you didn't marry? This burden – of being a… a bastard – will hang over me forever." And she began to cry softly as her mother patted her back to comfort her.

"It doesn't change a thing, not a thing, *chérie*. It's only a piece of paper. You know that."

"Does Uncle know you were going to tell me all this tonight?"

She nodded. "Yes, he's expecting you in the kitchen as usual."

Mathilde wiped her tears.

"Shall I come to the restaurant with you?" her mother asked.

"No, I'll go over myself." Mathilde stood up. "But why did you take so long to tell me all this, Maman?"

"I know, I'm sorry, darling, I just couldn't. I wanted to keep the illusion of a happy family going, even though your father was no longer with us. But then I realised you'll perhaps find someone to love soon, and so it was unfair to not tell you the truth about the past. I'm sorry."

Mathilde nodded, went to grab her coat from the hook, then headed for the door. She turned around and saw her mother's eyes were filled with tears; she was clearly trying not to cry. "It's all right, Maman, it's better to know the truth." She ran over to her mother and kissed her lightly on the cheek. "Even though I wish I'd known earlier."

She headed outside, and as she rushed up the road towards the restaurant, she mulled over the conversation. The revelation had seemed shocking, but maybe it wasn't that bad. Her mother was right: perhaps it was only a piece of paper. She slowed down as the lights came into view ahead. She always loved this time of the day, when she'd go to the restaurant to say goodnight to her uncle. When she was a little girl, he'd sit her on a high stool at the counter and feed her all sorts of delicious tasters from the kitchen while they giggled and laughed together, the most perfect little family.

* * *

When she remembered that conversation all those years ago now, how shocked she had been at her mother having a baby out of wedlock, she thought of her relationship with Pierre: all those nights they'd spent together and the fact that she too could have had a baby without being married. It was only with Pierre that she'd come to know love.

Mathilde took one last look at his photo and pushed the drawer shut. Her mother had met Pierre, and she had adored him. How could she not have done? But he was dead, and she knew – well, she hoped – that he would want her to be happy again. It was her dream that her mother would also meet Doug. If only Mathilde could hear from her. Why had she not had a letter? Perhaps she hadn't received hers and did not have the Clova address.

She sighed. This war was awful, not only for the dreadful loss of life and the enforced separation of families, but also because communication had become so hard, especially in Occupied France. She remembered when, a few years after the revelation about her father, her mother had left Lille to go to Maussane to see her sister, the first time that mother and daughter had ever been separated. During those long two months apart, she wrote to her daughter every week, and those letters took only a couple of days to arrive. She loved reading them, hearing about the relentless sun, the wide blue sky, the welcome shade of the olive trees and the chirping and clicking of the cicadas. Then, sometime after her return, there was the start of the fighting. And then she met Pierre, and everyone was busy helping in whatever way they could. But now, all she wanted was a letter from her mother. Had she moved back down to Provence, perhaps? Surely that would not have been allowed by the authorities, especially while the Italians occupied most of Provence.

Mathilde began to get washed and ready for work. She was in charge of the kitchen herself today as Mrs Mackie was away in Kirriemuir for a great-niece's wedding. She smiled at the thought of a wedding. Of course she had no right to presume Doug might want her as a wife, but, if he asked, she already knew what her response would be.

He had told her he was expecting an official letter about his overseas posting in the next few days, and then he would be leaving Clova until the war was over. But he kept telling her the Allies were making such progress; it wouldn't be long till he was back home. Mathilde blinked back her tears and tried to smile. There had been too many false promises in the past four years.

As she looked out the tiny window towards the schoolhouse, she thought about the sisters, her guardian angels. Mathilde had noticed that they had not been quite themselves for the past few weeks – since before Christmas, actually, that day she'd walked into the schoolhouse to see if she could bring Doug for tea, and they had clearly both been crying. Perhaps they'd had sad news of a friend or family member – or even a previous lover. She always wondered why neither of them had married nor had children.

Although, having heard how strict their father was, perhaps he had considered no one good enough for his daughters. Just like Doug's older namesake, the teacher was a father who clearly was not decent. She was outraged when she heard how he had beaten both his daughters with that instrument of torture which they called a 'tawse'. Her loving uncle had never raised a hand to her, unless it was to comb out her tight curls after breakfast when her mother had left for her job at the school.

She went to the tiny mirror to brush her hair, then headed downstairs, ready to start her day. Since she was seeing Doug that evening, it was going to be a good day.

Chapter 43

April 1944

It was a warm spring morning, and Mathilde was strolling back from an early walk over to the other side of the glen. She'd just crossed the bridge and was looking into the church graveyard when she thought about her mother. What if she had died? She'd been extremely fatigued before Mathilde had left for Scotland; perhaps that had got worse. She had no way of knowing, now that her uncle was dead. When he had died the year before she met Pierre, she was heartbroken. But he had died at work, a sudden heart attack, doing what he loved: cooking for others, sharing his passion for good food.

He had been the only one who could have told her any news of her mother. Everyone else she'd known at the restaurant had left, either conscripted or sent elsewhere to help the war effort. She never did get the address in Maussane where her mother's sister lived; how she regretted that. She had just assumed that her mother would live forever.

She smiled when she thought of how Maman told her she cooked Uncle's famous beef casserole for her younger sister Laetitia during her two-month visit to Provence, braising it with beer instead of red wine, which was more common in the south. The family could not believe that something cooked in beer could taste so good. It was not as delicate in flavour as the Provençal daube with its wine, dried orange peel and olives, but they all loved it. How could they not: her uncle had diners coming to the restaurant for miles around just to taste his famous *carbonnade*, northern France's answer to beef bourguignon.

Mathilde was meant to visit the Provençal family with her mother, but the war had intervened, and now here she was in Scotland instead. And what if she were to marry Doug? She would want her mother there. Yet how could she invite her if she was not receiving her letters?

She heard a noise of wheels on the road behind and realised it was the bus. She ran ahead towards the bus stop by the hotel and stood waiting. She had an order to collect for the kitchen.

The bus door opened, and an elderly lady wearing a large fur hat stepped out. The fur was brown with a silvery-grey tinge. She'd never seen such beautiful, glossy fur. It wasn't rabbit; perhaps it was hare. As Mathilde reached out her hand to help her down the steps, she was aware the old woman was staring at her, frowning. Then she took Mathilde's hand, mumbled "Thank you," and strode off towards the hotel's main door.

"Morning, Mathilde," Jim the driver said. "I'll just get your box. It's heavy today. What on earth have you got in it, then?"

He went to the back of the bus and eased a large box forward with his foot.

"I'm not sure you'll manage to carry it, it's pretty weighty."

"I'll be fine," Mathilde said, reaching down to pick it up.

"There's ox tails and cows' feet in there, that's why it's heavy."

"Can't you get them locally?"

She shook her head. "Only mutton. The beef carcasses are from the Kirriemuir butcher. He charges me very little."

"I bet you make something delicious from them, Mathilde." Her reputation for being a good cook had spread.

She waved him off, then lugged the box round to the back door of the kitchen, where she dumped it on the table, and went to wash her hands before starting her prep.

* * *

After the lunch service was over and her stock was bubbling away over a low heat, she turned to the lad who did the washing up. "I won't be long. I'm just heading up into the woods to look for some wild thyme." He nodded, and she patted him on the shoulder as she headed for the back door.

She set off into the woods behind the hotel, heading up the path towards Loch Brandy, through the trees towards the open hillside where she knew she'd find mountain thyme. She wanted to add it to the oxtail stew. She hadn't gone far when she looked over towards the burn and saw a bank of white: it was an array of beautiful snowdrops.

Until she had arrived in Clova, she'd never seen so many snowdrops, and she found them incredibly pretty. She loved the fact that in French they were called *perce-neige*: even though they were delicate and slender, they really did push through the early spring snow. She remembered Doug was taking a funeral service two days later, so she decided to pick some; perhaps she could brighten up the church with a vase of them.

She clambered over some tree trunks and knelt down behind a larch tree. She removed her paring knife from her apron pocket and began to pick some snowdrops, some single, some double. Then she heard voices and turned her head towards the path.

She could see a man coming toward her, talking in a deep voice, hardly stopping for breath. She leant forward to see more clearly. The man was middle-aged, his hair grey but otherwise unremarkable, yet for some reason she could not take her eyes off him. Then she realised why: he had such a look of Doug about him, something about the eyes. His face, though, was ruddy, his skin almost blotchy. He was talking to someone following close behind, and as Mathilde watched, she realised it was Nell.

She was about to wave and shout over to her, but something stopped her. Why was Nell with this man, this stranger? Was it some sort of assignation? Nell had a driven look on her face; for once she wasn't smiling or laughing. If she didn't know better, Mathilde would think this was a stern, humourless woman, whereas the Nell she had come to know was always full of fun, a twinkle in her eye. Perhaps she was simply concentrating on what the man was saying. He was talking non-stop, hands gesticulating as if he was explaining something.

They could not see her, and Mathilde decided to stay hidden as they passed nearby and continued along the path to the open hillside higher up. Once they were out of sight, she gathered up her snowdrops and placed them carefully in her wide apron pocket. She got to her feet and returned to the path. She picked her thyme, then headed back down to the hotel. She must see how the stock was doing; the aroma would hopefully be filling the kitchen by now, and it was time she added the thyme to the stew.

PART 8

Chapter 44

Nell

April 1944

The first Sunday of the Easter holidays, Nell and Effie walked the Minister's Path over to Glen Prosen. They'd received a letter from Allan saying his mother's dementia was becoming worse, and she was now in bed most of the time. He wondered if they would like to come and see her, perhaps before she no longer recognised them. It was tragic. Winifred was a woman who had been so strong physically, and yet this awful disease had affected her brain so badly, and seemingly so quickly.

They decided they'd walk the six miles over to Prosen as long as it was dry. The spring had been unusually mild, with much of the snow on the higher slopes having disappeared already. The track over from Clova should be easy, provided it wasn't too muddy.

They left as soon as it was light. Since Nell had work early on Monday as usual, they wanted to be back before dark. As they passed through the woods, heading up towards Elf Hillock, Effie began to talk. Nell knew she always found it easier to talk when they were walking. When she'd told her more about what happened to the baby before Christmas, they'd been walking along the glen towards Corrie Fee. Effie had also said a weight had been lifted from her, having at last shared with her sister details of the awful time she'd endured all those years before.

The hills were dotted with sheep and their tiny, snow-white lambs. "These lambs must have only been born in the past few days. They're so small, aren't they?" Nell pointed at a dainty little lamb suckling from its mother.

"Lambing's been a bit earlier this year, though, remember? Some of the children were off school a couple of weeks ago to help. So these lambs could be a fortnight or so old. Unusual for lambing to start so early." Effie stopped and stared at the sheep with their young.

"Nell, I'll show you the cottage where the Belgians stayed with my baby for all those months. It'll be as freezing cold there as it was that winter, I'm sure." She looked straight ahead, and Nell nodded but said nothing. She wanted to let her sister speak.

"I told you about the second family, this time from Arbroath, who'd been keen to adopt her, didn't I?"

Nell nodded.

"Well, we couldn't believe it when we heard that they too had to pull out as the father was suddenly ill with TB. It was as if everything was going wrong. I began to think this might be God's way of telling me I should keep the baby." She stopped and took out her flask to have a sip of water.

"Are you all right? D'you need to stop?"

Effie shook her head, then strode on, looking straight ahead at the path as they walked.

"So I began saying to Aunt Winnie that I wanted to keep the baby, and of course she said it was impossible. What would our father say, the minister and so on…"

"When was that?"

Effie looked up towards the clear sky where a buzzard was circling.

"Do you know why they do that, Effie? Buzzards, I mean."

She shook her head. "Looking for prey?" They both stood still, looking upwards.

"Yes, and because they've got such good eyesight, they can spot prey from almost a mile away, so they use the thermals to kind of float up there till they swoop down upon their quarry."

The bird soared away to the south, and Effie pointed to the track on the right where the path separated. "This is where we go now, towards Glentairie. I wish I was as fit as you, Nell. I bet you could still run up the hills like we used to do as children. I'd find a climb hard these days. I was even out of breath just now walking up through the woods."

"Cycling for miles every day keeps me fit."

They began walking again on the track through the brown heather. "So when did you start asking Aunt Winnie if you could keep the baby?"

"It must have been the end of July, or actually, probably early August as both families had let us down by then. I said to her that I would get a job somewhere far away, even in Dundee, and hire a nanny so I could keep the baby, but of course she knew it was impossible." Effie glanced towards her sister. "So did I. And I admit Pa was the biggest drawback."

Nell nodded.

"So when we knew I had to return to Clova, in September, the decision was made that the baby would stay with the Belgians until another family was found. And that Aunt Winnie would write to me regularly and update me."

"But then there was that awful winter."

"Yes. Did I tell you I found out later that November 1915 was the second coldest on record?"

Nell shook her head. "But I remember Pa writing to tell me how bitter it was and saying there were people skating on the rivers and ponds."

"The night-time was the worst; there were severe frosts at night and the little cottage was cold and damp at the best of times. Well, you'll see later, Nell."

They were now heading along the ridge above Glentairie. Behind them to the east were the hills of Clova. There was a row of sheep just beneath the sisters as they walked along the path, their cream-coloured bodies heavy with wool. At the other end were tiny, snow-white lambs. "So when I got that letter from Aunt Winnie, I could not believe it; and yet sadly, I could." She sighed.

"Madame Dubois had got up in the night to feed the baby and had noticed she was very sluggish. Even as she tried to wrap a blanket around them both, she noticed her skin was icy. She'd always put the two wee ones to sleep together, so her own baby would give off some heat, but he'd become so big – he was nearly eighteen months – and there was by then a danger that he'd smother her. So my baby had been alone in the cot for a few days, and even though she had a blanket on, she…"

Nell patted her sister on the back. "You don't have to carry on, Effie, you've told me before how she died."

"I haven't told you everything. I wasn't able to. Even after all these years, it's like a stab through my heart."

Nell glanced round at her but said nothing.

"I said she'd died of pneumonia – like Ma – but she actually froze to death."

"What?" Nell grimaced.

"Can you imagine how awful that must have been? She was five months old but very small, rather frail, and her body just could not cope with the freezing temperatures. Madame Dubois said in retrospect she'd been lethargic the day before that, presumably beginning to suffer from some infection, or perhaps the hypothermia had already set in during the freezing cold that November night."

"Surely she asked Aunt Winnie to come and help?"

"Oh yes, she ran over to the farmhouse and banged on the door till Betty answered, then she and our aunt rushed over with blankets and more kindling, but it was all too late. There was nothing they could do."

"So when did you hear?"

"I got the letter two days later. Of course I couldn't be there when she was buried. The weather was so bad, and Pa needed me at the school. Besides, what excuse could I have given him? That's when I decided I would cut myself off from any news from Aunt Winnie and Prosen, completely. I've not been over to the farm again until today."

"Goodness."

"Yes. So I was thinking that once we've seen Aunt Winnie, I want to see my daughter's grave. If that's all right."

"Of course, Effie." Nell pointed ahead. "Are we nearly at the village?"

"Yes. See those rabbits running towards the woods? Prosen is just at the foot of the trees."

Chapter 45

Nell

April 1944

Nell and Effie sat on either side of their aunt's bed, each holding a hand. She had smiled when she saw them, her eyes opening wide in clear recognition. But then, soon after, she had asked them confused questions about her brother, whether he was still fishing with the boys down at the stream and if mummy would be making pancakes for tea. She had then fallen into a deep sleep, her snores so loud the sisters had to speak in raised voices.

"Did you two patch things up when she came over to Clova for Betty's funeral?"

Effie nodded. "Yes, I had to apologise for ignoring all her letters. I just couldn't reply to them, it was so upsetting. And in my young, selfish ways, I'd partly blamed her for the death of my baby. The opposite, however, was true. She had not only tried to protect me and my reputation, but she had also done her best for her. And I suppose had she not died that horrible winter's night, she might have become part of the Belgians' family. Who knows, she might even have ended up arriving on our doorstep, just like Mathilde did."

"Effie, I've never said, but sometimes Mathilde reminds me of you when you were younger. I don't know why. I actually thought she might be your daughter till you told me how she had tragically died."

"I would have been so happy if Mathilde was my daughter; I'm so fond of her. Well, we both are. I just hope Doug treats her well."

"Of course he will. He adores her. And he's a good man."

"It must have been terrible for him growing up, seeing how badly his father treated his mother. Mathilde told me he demeaned her all the time. When I asked her if he was physically abusive, she said Doug told her he had seen her with black eyes and bruises around her neck on more than one occasion, always giving some feeble excuse like having bumped into something." She shook her head. "It's awful. What kind of man does that?"

"Well, our father did not exactly treat our mother well either, did he?" Nell asked. "Though I don't think he used to hit her, do you?"

"From what I remember, Ma was a strong character, but he was so controlling. Verbally, she'd have given as good as she got, but physically, who knows if she was his match. Though he certainly used to belt us, as if we were the naughty kids in his class."

Nell peered down at their aunt, who was still snoring, mouth wide open. "Shall we go and see where your daughter is buried, Effie?"

She nodded. They stood and went to find Allan, who had said he would take them to the place. Effie now realised he had of course known all along about the pregnancy and baby, but had said nothing, either to his mother or to his cousin.

"Allan, can you take us to the grave, please?" Effie shouted into the milking shed.

"I'll be there in a minute," Allan said, heading over to wash his hands in a bucket.

Nell followed Effie as she crossed the courtyard towards a little cottage. "This is where she stayed for her all too short life." She pressed her hand to the stone wall. "It's so cold. Allan said the shepherd lives here when they're shearing, but apart from that it's empty."

"Probably just as well," said Nell as Allan joined them.

"Your mother said the grave's up the slope a little, by the burn."

He nodded. "I've not been up myself for a while, but I can show you where to go."

The three of them set off, and as they crossed a burn, Nell called out, "Look at those beautiful flowers. They look like primroses, but are they not really early?"

Allan nodded. "Yes, but it's been so mild. We started lambing much earlier than usual."

Effie stopped. "Allan, is it all right if I pick some of the flowers?"

"Of course, Effie, help yourself." He put his hand into his pocket and handed her a penknife.

"Thanks," she said and knelt down by the burn, then used the knife to pick a handful of the pale yellow flowers.

They continued up the slope for another few minutes before he stopped and headed towards the trunk of a birch tree.

"This tree's one of the oldest. Ma wanted the grave to be here." He pointed over beside the stream, just beyond the raised roots of the tree. He turned to Effie and put his hand on her arm. "I'm so sorry, this must be really hard for you."

Effie nodded and muttered thanks.

"I've got to head back to the shed," he said. "Let me know when you're leaving. Shall I ask Meg to make you something to eat for the walk back to Clova?"

"Oh that would be too much, your wife's already given us a lovely lunch and…" Effie began.

"Thank you, Allan, that would be wonderful," interrupted Nell, who was always hungry.

Effie walked towards a little plaque nailed to the foot of the tree. She stooped down and laid the flowers in front of it. Nell joined her.

Manon Anderson
April 30, 1915 – November 28, 1915
Much loved and gone too soon

Effie sighed. "She called her Manon, look Nell. Aunt Winnie put her name on it. I always wanted her to be called after Ma." She grabbed her sister's hand. "She said I mustn't give her a name, that it would make me even more attached to her, but look what she did for me. For her."

"For Manon," Nell whispered, nodding.

As she knelt down, staring at the plaque over the tiny grave, Effie's shoulders heaved with sobs and tears rolled down her sister's cheeks.

* * *

"D'you think that, if you hadn't had a baby, you would have married Gordon Findlay?"

Effie chuckled. "I don't know. He was sweet, wasn't he?"

"He was certainly sweet on you. And Pa was really keen on him. But you were only lukewarm with him, weren't you?"

"I just couldn't make myself fall in love again. I was terrified I'd get hurt. I decided I'd be better on my own, avoiding all pain and heartbreak forever."

As they strode back home along the Minister's Path, Nell pointed ahead at the greying sky. "It's getting a bit dark; we should have left sooner. But it was good that Aunt Winnie seemed a little more herself after she'd had her nap, wasn't it?"

Effie nodded. "Thank goodness, but she still looks so frail." She looked up. "Don't worry about the light, I know the way well. We'll be back home in an hour or so." She pointed over to the other side of the valley. "You see that house over there? That's Glentairie, the shepherd's cottage. We just have to continue along the ridge till the top, then head left along the track towards Elf's Hillock. We can quickly have our pieces there, then it's an easy walk back down through the woods to Clova."

Nell glanced at her sister. "Do you ever wonder what you would do if you met Douglas Harrison today, Effie?"

She swallowed. "Oh yes, I've thought long and hard about that. I used to think it would be wonderful to meet up, perhaps even take up from where we left off now that he's a widow. But then I remembered the agony of it all, coming to terms with the fact that I was expecting, giving birth, having my precious baby taken from me – and then her dying that awful death."

"So I presume that what happened between you was," Nell paused as she chose her word, "consensual. You both wanted it to happen?"

Effie was silent. Good God, as usual you've gone too far, Nell. "Sorry, you don't have to answer that. It's none of my business."

Effie stopped and took out her flask. "He wanted it. I had no idea what was happening and I just kind of gave in. He was too strong for me."

"So he forced you?"

Effie nodded.

"Against your will?" Nell muttered. "Held you down?"

"I suppose so, yes. But Nell, I didn't know what a man and a woman did. I had no idea what was happening or that I should have consented first. I was infatuated with him, you know that, but I realise now he hardly had any feelings for me at all. He never did." She took a deep breath. "And now look what we've heard from Mathilde about the way he treated his wife. I wonder if she died of his abuse?"

"Doesn't bear thinking about, does it?"

Nell glanced round at her sister. "What did you do once you came back down to the house after he raped you?"

There was a gasp from Effie.

"Well, that's what he did, clearly."

She sighed. "I know, I know. I somehow felt it was my fault, though."

"What?"

Effie shrugged. "There was no one I could speak to about it, so somehow or other I presumed I was the one in the wrong."

"You obviously weren't, Effie. So what did you do once you got home? I wasn't there, was I?"

"No, you didn't get home till after tea. Pa was still out too so, because I felt... well, dirty, I wanted to get straight into a bath. I was bleeding too. I felt the only thing that might make me feel better, less sore, was a hot bath. So I ran one and lay in it for quite a while. I didn't even cry while I was in the water. I was just numb. I didn't know what to think."

"Did you just go to bed early? I can't remember that evening at all."

Effie took a deep breath. "Pa got home just as the water was draining from the tub and I was in the bedroom, dressing. He bellowed at me from the bathroom to come out at once. I could tell by his voice what sort of mood he was in."

Nell frowned.

"It'd been bath night only two days earlier, and remember we were only allowed weekly baths. He was livid and…" Her voice faltered.

"And what?"

"He told me to hurry up and dress, and when I eventually came out of the bedroom, he was standing there, tawse in hand. He beat me, Nell."

"He punished you for having a bath when you shouldn't have?"

Effie nodded. "It's odd, though, when I think back to it. I seemed to just accept it; it seemed as if this was the punishment I deserved, since, as I said, everything seemed like my fault, all that had happened up at Brandy."

Nell let out a long breath. "Why didn't you tell me about either the assault up at Brandy or Pa beating you?"

"I made sure I was in bed by the time you got home, and I just knew I couldn't tell you about either of those things." Effie nodded. "I was ashamed."

Nell grabbed her sister's hand and squeezed it.

They were silent for a while, then Nell said, "I can't get it out of my head that he took advantage of you. You were so young, so innocent. Can you ever forgive him for that?"

"If the baby and all the heartbreak and sadness about her had never happened, I probably could have. But lately I've realised that I probably never can. Is that terrible?"

Nell swung around. "No," she cried. "For God's sake, no. That is totally and utterly normal. The man's a degenerate, a cruel beast without a shred of conscience. I hate him."

Chapter 46

Nell

April 1944

The following Saturday, Nell woke up early and lay staring at the ceiling as she thought about the day ahead. She got out of bed and pulled back the curtains. She smiled: though it was still not fully light, she could tell it was going to be another beautiful spring day – hopefully the third cloudless day in a row.

Once she heard Effie shut the door behind her, Nell quickly got herself ready. It was unusual for her sister to leave before her in the morning, but Effie and Bessie were off to Dundee for the day, and they had to get the early bus. The two friends were going to see a matinee performance of the Dundee Repertory Theatre, so were planning a morning of shopping, then tea afterwards. Nell had not seen Effie so excited for a while. She was pleased; she deserved a treat after a long and challenging spring term.

Today should be a short working day for her. She always finished earlier on Saturdays, and hopefully she would not have to venture too far. If she got back by lunchtime and the weather was still fair, she was keen to head up into the hills for the afternoon. She decided to take a chance, get out her backpack and fill it with the essentials: a flask of water, some bread and cheese, and even though she knew the way well, a map and compass. The weather on the mountains was liable to change quickly; you had to be prepared for everything.

Over the years, she'd learned from experience that the respect shown for the hills and the mountains did not stop at protecting their wildness and obeying the unwritten rules of nature. It also meant keeping a keen eye on the weather while you were out there. No forecast could truly predict the sudden changes, and no one wanted to be stranded up there in a blizzard or thick fog, not even someone like Nell, who knew the hills like the back of her hand. Weather permitting, she'd head straight off after her rounds.

She had been reading a book from her father's bookshelf the night before and was fascinated by a fact she'd just discovered. It was something she hadn't been aware of, even after all her years of climbing in the area. In the hefty tome Fife and Angus Geology, she learned about the origins of the underwater causeway in Loch Brandy.

She'd often heard locals say it was created in the previous century to make for easier fishing in the loch, presumably for the brown trout. But then, in the bar the other night, she'd heard a customer insist it was a natural causeway, a result of glaciation. It was only after reading more on the Ice Age in the book that she realised it could be what was called a 'pro-glacial recessional moraine' – a natural feature indeed, not man-made at all.

She'd seen the outline of it often from the cliffs above the loch, whenever she climbed up The Snub on days with good visibility, but she had no idea it had been there for thousands and thousands of years. Hopefully, if the sun was still shining when she got back, she would be able to go up and look at it again.

* * *

She propped her bike against the wall when she returned home and looked all around. The weather was still fine, a few clouds were beginning to form over to the west towards Driesh and Mayar, but hopefully Brandy would be cloud-free so she could investigate the causeway from the crags above. There were still enough daylight hours left.

She went inside to change out of her uniform and was just lacing up her boots when there was a knock at the door. She pulled on her warm jacket and grabbed her backpack as she went to open the door. A middle-aged man stood there, a faltering smile on his lips. His hair was thinning and grey, his cheeks blotchy. His smile widened on seeing her, but he said nothing. In the awkward silence, she realised he must have thought she should know who he was.

Then she noticed the eyes: those piercing blue eyes boring into her as he stretched out his hand.

"Hello, Nell," he said, taking her hand and holding it in a weak, damp handshake. And all the while, Nell stared at him, incredulous, now also recognising the oleaginous voice.

"Douglas Harrison, what on earth are you doing here?"

"Well, that's a nice welcome, after all these years, isn't it!" He shuffled from one foot to the other. "Any chance I could use your bathroom, Nell?"

Without speaking, she stepped aside and pointed to the bathroom door. When he was inside, door shut, she let out a long sigh. Good God, what was that man doing here? She had to get rid of him – soon. Certainly before Effie returned from Dundee.

"Is your sister around, Nell?" he asked as he shut the door, then sauntered over to join her.

"No, she's not." Nell snapped, still unable to be civil to this man who had hurt Effie so much. "What brings you to Clova?"

"I was at a burial not far away, along at Piper's Hillock cemetery. It's a fine place to be buried, there up on the hill, isn't it?"

"I suppose so, though if you're dead, you're dead."

"Anyway, since it's such a fine day, I thought I'd carry on along the road to my old haunt in Clova and see if much has changed here. I was trying to work out, as I motored along the glen, how many years it's been since I worked here. I realised it's over thirty years." He shook his head. "How is that possible? It's still as lovely as ever. The hotel looks as if it could do with a good lick of paint, mind you, but apart from that, little seems to have changed."

Clearly he had forgotten there was a war on, and such things as painting buildings were way down the list of people's priorities. Besides, dirty white was far less obvious during blackouts than glaring fresh white paint.

Nell kept staring at him. Dear Lord, how could Effie – and indeed most people in those days – have found him attractive? He had a bulbous red nose, and his hair, which had been thick and dark all those years ago, was now straggly and grey. He was clearly trying to cover his baldness by combing thin strands over the crown of his head. His deep-set blue eyes were now surrounded by dark puffy circles.

He smiled as he stared at Nell's face, as if analysing each and every one of the lines that made up her features. She was aware her face was wrinkled, but she did not care one jot about how she had aged.

"You've looked after yourself not too badly, Nell. Middle age suits you."

Don't rise to the bait. Keep calm, Nell. This man must be removed from their house as soon as possible.

"Douglas, I'd obviously love to stay and chat, but I'm off up to Brandy. There are things I need to check out and I've only got a few hours of daylight left." She tried to steer him outside.

He was clearly oblivious to her sarcasm. "Loch Brandy! I've not been up there for years." He beamed and watched her fasten up her backpack. "Tell you what, Nell, I'll come too."

Nell's heart sank. "The weather might change, you're not exactly dressed for the hills." She looked down at his polished brogues. "And you certainly can't walk in those."

"You can't put me off that easily, Miss Helen Anderson. I always have boots in my car in case I suddenly feel the urge for a walk. If you're ready, come over to the motorcar with me and I'll get them on." As he strode across to the hotel car park, Nell realised that in order to keep him away from her sister, she had no choice but to join this man whom she had merely disliked all those years ago but now loathed with a passion.

Chapter 47
Nell

April 1944

"Right, let's start heading up into the woods. We'll get on the path up to Brandy from there," Nell said, pointing towards the trees behind the hotel. The snowdrops were out and Nell usually paused to admire them, but today she was so agitated by her companion talking non-stop, she just continued to look straight ahead.

"Do you have a map, Nell? In case I've forgotten the way," he said, following her towards the small wooden bridge over the burn.

"Douglas, I know this route like the back of my hand." Her voice was curt.

"So what things are you checking out, Nell?"

As she began telling him about the underwater causeway, she remembered his obsession with geology, which he clearly wanted to boast about. "Oh, this is right up my street, Nell. You'll perhaps remember I'm a bit of a glaciation buff. I always wanted your father to let me take the pupils along to Corrie Fee to explain all about the Ice Age, but he never agreed." He pushed his not inconsiderable bulk through the wooden kissing gate after her and looked up over the open moorland towards the hills. "Where's best to see it from?"

"We'll head up to Loch Brandy, then climb up to The Snub – d'you remember? It's steep though." He nodded as he struggled to stay alongside. There was no way she was going to slow her pace down for him. "Then we'll walk along the ridge. Hopefully there won't still be snow up there as that could make it a bit tricky underfoot. From there we should have a good view down to the loch. Though I've seen the shape of the causeway so often, I never knew it could have anything to do with glaciation."

Douglas began to tell her that he could explain all about proglacial moraines and how the underwater causeway could have been formed all those millennia ago, but she cut him off. "Then we'll head east towards Green Hill and come down the other side of Brandy. Unless you want to carry on to the north of Loch Wharral and The Goet, then over to Muckle Cairn to visit the site of the accident? If there's still enough daylight left? I'm sure you know that's where the Wellington bomber crashed in August 1942."

"Goodness, yes," he muttered, shaking his head. "That was a terrible crash, wasn't it? An inexperienced pilot, they said."

Nell had to stop herself shouting at him that tragically they were all inexperienced pilots, most only in their early twenties and flying with only a few weeks' training as they did their utmost to defend the country. They had died up there on the hills – and were still dying all over Europe – far too young.

Instead, when he paused for breath, Nell said, "Let's stop here and have a drink. You're looking a bit puffed." Part of her hoped he would head back down to his car, but she was now worried that he'd catch Effie coming back on an earlier bus. Above all else, her sister must never meet this man.

"Not at all," he said, turning around to look back down at the hotel, which was now a small white speck. She could hear him wheezing.

After a few minutes of silence as he gazed down the glen, he began to explain about the effects of glaciation in that area. Nell did not say a thing, even though she had read all about it in her father's book. She was not even listening; she was simply deciding whether she ought to bring up the past. And if so, when.

* * *

"Can you see that steep ridge over there to the west? That leads up to Ben Reid and the corrie. And before the corrie there's a sort of cave – well, it's more of a hollow than a cave. It's called the Laird's Chamber."

They were now walking up the path on the open hillside, covered in brown heather. She pointed due west.

"It's over there somewhere, in amidst the boulders. Some folk say that's where the Laird of Clova sheltered after his castle was burned down." Nell was striding on, enjoying the fact that her companion was no longer talking. Then she saw that Douglas had stopped to catch his breath; he was still wheezing.

"This area up here is beautiful in the summer and early autumn, full of heather and cowberries," Nell said, waiting for him. She pointed ahead.

"You mean crowberries," he gasped. Even panting for breath, he was determined to correct her. The man was not only a brute, he was also highly irritating.

"No, I mean cowberries: red berries, sometimes called mountain cranberries. Crowberries are black and their foliage resembles a sort of pale heather."

"Goodness, you know a lot," he said, scowling, "for a woman."

"Douglas, as I've been trying to tell you, if only you'd listen, I am on the hills most days. I know them well. It's just the glacial information that I wasn't, well, quite so sure about." She tried not to sound annoyed as she realised that perhaps she needed to keep him onside for now, and perhaps would not disclose her newly acquired knowledge about glaciation.

"The clouds are building up ahead, can you see? I hope it's not going to snow." He was frowning.

Nell nodded. "Have you been up there when it's been snowing, Douglas?"

"No, even when I taught with your father, when I was much younger, I tried to avoid climbing in inclement weather. I'm not sure it's safe."

"Sensible," said Nell, a glimmer of a smile on her lips as a delicious thought floated into her head. She turned around to look back down the hill towards the glen.

"Don't the houses look tiny down there?"

"Yes. What's that white one at the back of the hotel?" Douglas pointed to a house at the far side of the trees.

"That's the manse. It's a good-sized house. The minister and his wife will probably be moving out soon. They've been devastated by their son dying. The wife in particular can't cope." She shook her head. "It's so sad."

They set off up the hill and looked towards the gathering clouds ahead. The wind was getting up and it was becoming much colder. Nell pulled her hat down over her ears.

"You presumably know your son is likely to take over the parish, unless he's called up soon?"

Douglas bristled. "No, I didn't know that. He doesn't share much with me. Indeed I haven't heard from him for a while."

"Oh, well, the last thing we heard, he was hoping to get a posting as chaplain on the 1st Airborne Division, but we don't know anything more yet. Well, obviously where he'd be sent is all classified information anyway…"

"It's bloody ridiculous that he didn't just sign up at the start of the war as a normal soldier. Why did he have to decide to continue his divinity studies and take the easy route?" Douglas puffed his way over some boulders.

Nell's eyes grew wide. "Easy? I really don't think it's the easy route at all. They're in just as much danger as their fellow soldiers. You must know that from your time in France, Douglas?"

She had a strange frisson of excitement as she thought about bringing up the time he had been at Royaumont Abbey, but perhaps not yet. That was for later, if in fact he stayed the course.

She changed the subject. "That wind's Arctic now, isn't it?"

They got to the top of the ridge and could see The Snub and Green Hill up ahead, veiled in cloud. The clear blue sky of earlier had all but disappeared, and now there was a fierce, sleet-laden blast howling across the water from the north.

"That weather's come in fast," she said, turning to see him fastening up another button of his jacket. "Well, there's Brandy ahead." They both looked at the dark water churning up in the icy gusts. "We'll need to find some shelter out of the wind if we want to have a bite to eat," Nell said, and headed left towards a couple of big boulders, where she crouched down out of the wind. Douglas was still standing in the heather, buffeted by the biting wind. She watched him look all around as if trying to locate something, or perhaps just a memory somewhere. Then, having seen where she'd gone, he followed on.

Once they were sheltered from the wind, Nell opened her pack and took out her bread and cheese. Douglas kept staring back up towards the loch and the ridge above. "We'll never see anything from up there, Nell. The water will be too churned up. This weather's not looking good at all."

"It'll be fine, Douglas. I'm going on up anyway – you can stay down here if you want." She handed him some bread and cheese. "Here, have this and we'll make a plan."

Chapter 48
Nell
April 1944

"We've got another few hours of daylight," Nell said as she began to pack away the leftover food and her flask. "I'm definitely heading up The Snub if you still want to join me. We can easily get up there, round the top and back down before it's dark."

As they'd been eating, she'd realised it was actually going to be better if he stayed with her, odious though he was. Otherwise he might arrive back at his car about the same time Effie was arriving home on the bus. But if he stayed up on the hills with her, Nell could arrange the timing for the descent so that he missed the bus arriving back at Clova and could ensure he got straight into his car and didn't call in at the schoolhouse.

She had the impression he was so full of his own importance and had such little respect for women that he would surely come with her, if only to show how manly and robust he was.

"All right, Nell, just let me button my jacket up fully. I'm not exactly dressed for the hills." He fastened everything up as high as he could over his black tie.

"You don't want to remove the black tie, Douglas? Seems a little too funereal up here in the mountains."

"It's helping to keep my neck warm," he said, attempting a smile.

He thrust his hand into his jacket pocket and once again took a swig from his hip flask. "You're sure you don't want a dram? Helps keep you warm, Nell." She shook her head and frowned as she wondered if he always drank so much whisky.

He looked towards Nell, studying her face. "Your sister was a good-looking girl, wasn't she? Is she still as lovely?"

Nell stared at him, her expression giving nothing away. "Yes, I do believe she is."

"We came up here one day, you know. I was looking over the other side of the loch to see if I could remember where we were, but now I think it was over there." He pointed to a bank of heather between two boulders behind them. "It was a warm day, though, and there wasn't a breath of wind, unlike today."

Nell clenched her teeth together. "Right. Let's get going."

"She was a game girl for her age," he said, smirking.

"What d'you mean by that?" Nell snapped.

"You know perfectly well, Nell."

"No, I don't. Enlighten me."

"Oh, I'm sure she told you all about our memorable walk up here that glorious summer's day. It must have been in August. I enlisted a week or so later, I think, just after the school term had started."

She glowered at him, trying to think whether she should shut down the conversation or go on the defensive. He just sneered, then took a final swig from his flask and got to his feet. "I can fill you in later. Need to get moving before I get cramp." He jiggled his legs about.

Nell decided to save any conversation about Effie till later. She tried to think of something to say.

"D'you always drink so much, Douglas?"

He chuckled. "There's only a couple of drams in this wee flask, nothing more. It just keeps me warm. Like your sister did."

Nell leapt to her feet. "Don't you dare say anything more about my sister, d'you hear me?" She swung her pack onto her back and began stomping towards The Snub.

"Hang on, I've just got to spend a penny, Nell. Wait for me at the foot."

And though she wanted nothing more than to slap his blotchy, drink-addled face and head up The Snub alone, she turned around and climbed back up to the path towards the beginning of the steep ascent ahead.

***

The wind was now laden with sleet from the north. It was beginning to make visibility intermittently difficult, but Nell was confident she knew the way well. Even though they probably would not be able to see the outline of the underwater causeway from the top, she was now determined to keep Douglas Harrison up here for at least another couple of hours, so that Effie would be back home and she could just wave him off from the car park, ensuring he and Effie would not meet.

"How long after the war did you marry, Douglas?" They were walking close together up the steep path, Nell pointing out sections where the ground was less stable underfoot, full of scree and loose stones.

"Not very long after. Her family had lived in the house I now live in, beside Restenneth Priory, for many years, so we took it over as a wedding gift from her father."

Nell found it strange he never mentioned her name. "What was your wife's name?"

"Elisabeth." He stopped to take some deep breaths, and Nell stopped too; it was becoming difficult to see far ahead and she didn't want to lose sight of him.

"We had young Doug after only a year, but since she had a delicate constitution, she never really recovered from the traumatic birth. She was always rather fragile."

"No doubt you looked after her really well. I'm sure you were a good husband?" Nell tried to look sincere.

"Exemplary, Nell. Though she used to irritate me rather often; she fussed such a lot. When the baby was born, it was a freezing winter and she became quite neurotic, kept saying he would die of the cold." He shook his head as he started to climb again. "What nonsense; babies are stronger than we think."

"Not always, Douglas," Nell muttered.

"So why did neither you nor your sister marry? I heard that

you and Euphemia lived in the schoolhouse with your father until he died, just the two of you, a couple of spinsters."

"Not all women need men to be fulfilled, Douglas. And indeed, if a woman has had a, let's say, less than positive experience with a man, it could put her off for life." She was trying so hard not to talk about what happened to Effie, nor the fact she knew they had recently been in correspondence.

He changed the subject.

"Have you heard what's going on with Royaumont Abbey these days?"

"I heard it was turned into some sort of artistic or cultural centre after the war ended, but then it had to shut with the fighting that's now going on again all around." He said nothing so she continued. "When I think back to my time there, I can't help feeling rather proud of what we achieved. You know we treated over ten thousand patients?"

"No, I didn't, but it's of no interest to me: I hated my time there. It was so bloody cold all the time, and even when I started to get better, I was never treated differently, as I should have been as an officer. I had the same foul wine as the others and…"

Nell burst out laughing. "It wasn't a luxury hotel, Douglas. You have no idea how we struggled to keep things going. Those doctors were incredible, as were the nurses, the orderlies, everyone. They all worked all night long, often operating on the wounded with only candles to see by." She scowled. "Oh, and you had one of the best chefs cooking for you all the time you were there."

"Ah, you mean your pal, that annoying little Frog." He shrugged. "Food wasn't bad I suppose. Better than rations."

Nell had to bite her tongue to not vent her anger. How dare he insult Paul?

Douglas pointed up ahead. "Are you sure it's wise to continue up here? The visibility isn't great, Nell."

"It'll be fine, just stay close behind me," she said, peering down to her right where the dark, churning water of the loch, now far below, was just visible under the low, fast-moving clouds. The cliff edge was barely visible, so she moved slowly to stand precariously at the top: it was a sheer drop below, and the heath was becoming slippy. But soon the ground to the north began to level out, and she could just make out the cairn.

"D'you want to shelter from the wind over by the cairn? I need a drink of water anyway." She headed off towards the pile of stones and sat at the south side. He came over to join her, and she offered him her flask of water. Sharing food and drink on the hills was not restricted to those who deserved it.

He shook his head and delved into the inside of his jacket. He brought out another hip flask.

"Good God, how many of those have you got?"

"I always keep a back-up in the motorcar, Nell. Thank God I brought it with me." He took a long swig. "We're not going to see much at all. Is it even worth going on?"

"Once we've passed the cliffs over there, it all becomes less dangerous. In fact, it's quite an easy walk down over the heather back around to the loch. It'd actually be harder turning around and going back down by The Snub as it's steep and could be treacherous underfoot." She pointed to the opposite side of the ridge. "That descent is gentler."

He took another swig. The man was unbelievable: did he ever drink water?

"Do you think there's a chance we'll see the causeway from over there?"

She shrugged. "If the clouds clear a bit, we might do. The sleet's making it hard to see anything right now, but it's all moving so fast: look at those sweeping clouds. Who knows, we may even see a glimmer of sun."

He turned around to face her, his blotchy nose now dripping, his eyes looking decidedly red, perhaps from the battering by the wind, perhaps from the alcohol. "Did you say your sister never told you about our assignation?"

Her body tensed as she thought about her answer. "Why? Why is it important to you, Douglas?"

"You know why, surely. You're a woman of the world, Nell Anderson." He was smirking now as he held his hip flask to his lips once more. Clearly, he wanted to talk about Effie and him by the loch. Perhaps he felt it made him seem more manly, more like a human stud. He really was a pathetic, perverted little man.

Nell got to her feet and began moving warily towards the cliff edge. She was too angry to speak to him. She looked down as the clouds cleared a little, and she could see some of the loch underneath. A chink of sun shimmered on the north end of the loch, though the causeway was still invisible in the dark waters at the south. The boulders just beneath her were bare. Usually there was some heather and other ground shrubs clinging in between the rocks; there had clearly been a rock fall since her last trip up here. She turned around to return to the safety of the path and suddenly became aware he was right behind her.

"Don't do that!" she yelled. "You're too close. It's dangerous up here on the edge." She pointed down to great fissures cleaved into the rock below. Nell moved to push past him, but he stood still. He grasped her hand. "Come on, Nell, tell me about your little sister. Did she tell you how she was not only willing, but ready? I've often thought about it over the years, and I realised I'd like to bring her up here again, even all these years later, and see just how…"

Nell flung her hand free and punched him. He reached up to his face to feel where the blow had landed. "Don't you dare, Miss High and Mighty, I'll…"

He was so close she could smell the whisky on his breath.

"What will you do, Douglas?"

He stretched his arm to try to grab her again, but she swung herself nimbly round to his other side and watched him stumble on the wet heath and stagger backwards.

He steadied himself, putting his arms out for balance. He had a strange, leering expression on his face; he was clearly drunk. "I'll tell you what I'm going to do, Nell. After we get down, I'm going to go and see your sister and see what she has to say for herself. She will still want to see me after all these years, mark my…"

"No! She will not! You raped my sister when she was only a girl, you animal. You left her without hope, without…"

"Rape? That's a strong word, Nell." He tutted. "I told you, it was consensual. She's clearly been lying to you. She was…"

And that was when, as Nell stepped forward onto her left foot, she felt her right foot slide on the slippery ground and make contact with his leg, so that he landed with a thump on his back. The ground where he fell was icy from the sleet, and his body too near the rocky crevice above the place where he had violated her sister.

Nell regained her balance by thrusting her hands behind her to grab the woody stems of some blaeberry shrubs. She landed safely on her rear, away from the cliff edge. As she did, she watched, horrified, as Douglas Harrison's head disappeared first, then his shoulders, his torso, and finally his legs. She heard sickening sounds as he bounced off the rocks and hurtled down towards the water. She waited for the splash, but it never came.

As she lay immobile on the frosty ground, Nell felt an emotion she had never felt before. It was a combination of horror, terror and… what? What was it? She got to her feet warily and peered down into the dense grey clouds below, shivering as a sudden chill surged through her. She began to realise what it was: through the heavy sense of dread came a lighter sensation – one of relief. Yes, that was it. And also, finally, a feeling of atonement.

Chapter 49

Mathilde

April 1944

Mathilde plunged a spoon into the oxtail stew and tasted it. It wasn't quite there yet – another hour or so – but the seasoning seemed good at this stage. It would perhaps need more salt later, but she must be patient. And yes, that thyme had made all the difference; there was just a *soupçon* of that woody, slightly floral flavour – though the thyme here was more subtle, less aromatic than she was used to. When Maman described how pungent the Provençal thyme was, she wished once again that she had gone to Maussane with her before the war. Where was her mother now?

After she had taken the snowdrops over to the church, she went to the post office to see if they'd received any letters from France. Perhaps there was a problem with all of the French post because of the fighting. But Mrs Bell assured her that there had been post from France. In fact, Helen had received something just the other week.

"Thanks, Mrs Bell. Please let me know if anything arrives for me."

She wandered back towards the hotel and saw someone cycling over the bridge towards her. It was Doug! She ran her fingers quickly through her thick dark hair, then waved as he came towards her.

"Mathilde, I've just heard," he said, panting as he leapt off his bike. "I've got my posting at last!" He bent towards her to give her a kiss.

"Where are you going?"

"Devon. I'm leaving in five days."

"Are you joining the 1st Airborne Division, as you'd hoped?"

"I can't tell you any more, darling. I'm so sorry." He was smiling, clearly delighted that at last he had a role in this awful war. Mathilde reached towards him and drew him in close so he could not see the tears welling up as she began to contemplate life without him... for however long that might be.

* * *

Doug and Mathilde spent her free hour that afternoon making plans for what they would do over the next few days before he left. He kept reassuring her that he would be fine, even though he was not able to tell her what exactly he would be doing.

"To be honest, I don't know myself. I just know where I've to report to, that's all."

"So how will I know you are all right, safe?"

"I'll write when I can, Mathilde. I'll be fine, don't worry."

As soon as he'd left for the church to start preparing for the funeral the following Monday, she returned to the kitchen and tasted the oxtail stew one final time. Yes, it was ready: the meat so tender it would fall off the bone, and the flavour was rich and wholesome. She looked at the clock. It was half past five; she had to hurry up and prepare the vegetables for the dinner service. She had just come back from the larder with a bag of potatoes when the kitchen door was flung open.

"Mathilde. Where's Mr Noble? I need to use the phone. There's been a terrible accident." Nell stood there, her usually ruddy complexion gone. She was deathly pale, clearly in shock, all colour drained from her.

"What kind of accident? Is it another plane?"

Nell shook her head.

"I was up on the hills just now... I went for a walk up to Brandy and was standing on the water's edge looking towards the ridge at the back. The weather was beginning to set in, but there was a sudden clearing in the clouds and I saw..."

"What?" Mathilde was frowning.

"I need to use the phone," she said, and ran out into the corridor.

Mathilde followed and watched as she ran up the stairs, taking them two at a time. She thumped on Mr Noble's door and stood watching as the elderly man emerged from his room, pulling on his cardigan, blinking against the light; he had clearly been having a sleep.

"Mr Noble, we need to phone Tam Campbell at once. There's been an accident on the hills." Nell stood shouting at him, beckoning him to follow her down the stairs towards the telephone. As they walked along the corridor, she continued.

"I was up on the hills, standing on the edge of Loch Brandy. The weather was closing in, the sleet had started and the visibility wasn't great. But then, while I was staring up towards The Snub, there was a sudden gap in the clouds and through the sleet I saw what I'm sure was a body dropping from high up on the cliffs."

Mathilde gasped and held her hands up to her face. Nell was not looking at either of them but stared at the floor outside the office where they had stopped.

"The sleet was getting worse. By then it was light snow so I couldn't see that well, but in that sudden clearing in those dark clouds, I'm positive I saw a man falling, bumping off the rocks like a loose boulder." She shuddered.

"Maybe it was a sheep. I believe they do wander up there sometimes," Mr Noble said, buttoning up his cardigan.

"It definitely wasn't an animal." Nell looked towards them both, blinking tears away. "I could see boots at the end of his feet and…" She was twisting her hands round and round. "And as I came back down the hill just now, all I could think of was that he must have slipped. It would have been treacherous up there." She stared at them both. "Surely he hadn't jumped. That would be…"

"Miss Anderson, please go and take a seat. You are obviously in shock." Mr Noble turned towards Mathilde. "Could you please make a cup of sweet tea for her while I phone the constable." He turned to walk away, then raised his hand. "And Mathilde, please can you then run and fetch Miss Anderson's sister."

As he shut the office door behind him, Nell reached out to grab Mathilde's hand and looked into her wide eyes. "Where is Doug?" she whispered.

"Over at the church. Why? D'you need to speak to him, ask him to say some prayers perhaps…?"

Nell continued to stand, immobile, all colour blanched out of her. The only movement was in her face as she began to bite her lower lip. Mathilde withdrew her hand, patted Nell gently, then went to put on the kettle. As she opened the kitchen door, she kept thinking, *But you were not by yourself, Nell. You had a man with you when I saw you. Why did you not say that – is he the man who fell?*

A noise behind her made her swivel round; the front door of the hotel opened and in walked Doug Harrison in his clerical collar. Thank God he was here. Mathilde rushed towards him and watched as his initial smile soon changed to a frown as he took in the scene. His brows furrowed and he went towards Nell, reaching out his hand to her shoulder. "I'm sorry, is something wrong?"

And that was when Nell's whole body started to shake with sobs and she began to howl, awful animal-like wails as she collapsed onto the chair Doug thrust behind her just in time.

Chapter 50

Mathilde

April 1944

Nell sat in the kitchen, her head on her sister's shoulder. Mr Noble, Doug and Mathilde sat on the opposite side of the table.

The teapot was in the middle, and Mathilde refilled everyone's cups and pushed some shortbread towards the women.

"Try to eat something, Nell."

Mathilde glanced up at the clock and saw it was already six o'clock; she must get on with the potatoes. She went to the sink and started to peel.

"But I don't understand, Nell. Who on earth could this man have been? Is it not unusual for someone to go up there alone, unless they know the hills really well, like you do?" Effie said, putting a piece of shortbread in front of her sister, who lifted her head, then began nibbling on the biscuit. The hotel's front door opened again, and Mr Noble got up.

Doug pointed towards the dark clouds through the window. "It's not snowing down here, but I don't suppose anyone will be able to go up there till first light tomorrow."

Nell took a deep breath and looked directly at Doug. "You've not heard anything about a posting yet, have you?"

"Yes, I just told Mathilde about it in fact. I leave in five days' time."

Nell frowned. "Could it be delayed if necessary?"

"No, I don't think so. Why?"

"I'm sure Mr Johnson would be up to doing a funeral, if that's what you're thinking about, Nell," Effie interrupted. "But from what's been said about lone climbers, surely it's unlikely the man who fell was a local. You'd have seen him on his way up. He must have come over to our glen from somewhere else. So why would the funeral need to be here?"

"No reason," Nell muttered.

Mathilde looked around. Nell was still clearly in shock; instead of being rosy cheeked in the warm kitchen, her face was grey.

The door opened and Mr Noble led Tam Campbell in. He removed his police hat and sat down beside Nell. He took out his notebook and pencil.

"Can I pour you a cup, Constable?"

"Oh yes please. My wife was just about to serve up my tea when I got the call."

"I've got a big pan of oxtail stew if you can wait till the potatoes are boiled. There's plenty for everyone…" She glanced at her boss. "If that's all right, Mr Noble?"

"Of course."

Effie poured his tea, and Tam Campbell began to take notes. Nell repeated what she had said before about standing on the edge of the loch when she saw, through a sudden glisk of sunlight penetrating the dark clouds, a body fall from the ridge.

"What sort of time do you think that was, Miss Anderson?"

Nell took another nibble of shortbread. "Well, I'd left home by half past two. It doesn't take me long to get up to Brandy, but I did stop for a piece and some water while I was up there, so… I don't know, 3.30? Or perhaps a bit later?"

"And when did the weather change up there?" Tam Campbell was scribbling in his notebook. "It was fine down here till only an hour or so ago, wasn't it?"

Everyone around the table nodded. "I went up to my room about three o'clock and there was only a handful of clouds in the sky then." Mr Noble looked at his watch as if to confirm.

"The weather changes so fast up in the hills. Nell's always saying that, aren't you?" Effie turned to smile encouragingly at her sister.

"Yes, that's true. So probably about 3.30."

Mathilde lit the stove under the pan of potatoes and returned to sit with them. She peeked over at Effie; she looked fraught. She was obviously worried about her sister, whose frail vulnerability was so out of character.

"And had you seen anyone else on your way up to Brandy on the hills?"

Nell looked down at the table.

"I'd had a brief chat with a man I met up at Brandy."

"Could it have been him? Do you think he walked up there from the hotel or over from another glen? Did he say?"

"It was such a short conversation, the weather was coming in. He was heading for The Snub," she mumbled as she stared at her cup.

"And you didn't try to dissuade him?"

"Why would I? It wasn't my place."

"What did he look like?"

"It was hard to see clearly, the sleet had become really bad, but I'd say middle-aged, middle height? Florid face…" She closed her eyes. "And I could smell whisky on him."

"I see," said the policeman. He turned to Mr Noble. "Do any of your residents match this description?"

"I don't think so, and we don't have any climbers staying at the moment, just some guests staying before the funeral on Monday," Mr Noble said.

Mathilde opened her mouth to mention the man she had seen Nell with; her description of him being middle-aged and middle height fitted. But she decided to remain silent. She would ask Nell about it when she was more back to herself. It seemed so odd she never mentioned it, but it was not Mathilde's place to contradict her evidence.

The policeman looked out the window, where the darkening clouds were making the room dimmer. "If it was a brighter day I could try to get a couple of the gamekeepers up there with me just now, maybe with a couple of ponies – and the stretcher. But as is we'll need to wait till early tomorrow."

"Good idea," said Mr Noble. He finished his tea and got up. "We'll need to put the lights on now. I'll away and put up the blackouts."

"Do you need any help?" Doug said, getting to his feet.

"It's fine, I can easily do it."

Doug looked up at the clock. "I'm meeting the family in the bar in five minutes anyway, to go through the finer points of the funeral service. Obviously tomorrow I'll be busy with the morning service – and I'm also going over to Glen Prosen kirk to take the evening service there, so can't be much help then. I'll come through with you just now."

Nell sprung to her feet. "I've just realised, I'm on bar duty tonight. Is there much more you'll need from me, Mr Campbell?"

Mr Noble put up his hand. "You will not be doing any such thing, Miss Anderson. I shall cover your shift. Once Mr Campbell here is finished, you are to go straight home with your sister." He glanced around at Mathilde. "Oh, though perhaps a plate of your oxtail for everyone would be a good idea."

She nodded and watched Doug follow Mr Noble out the door, then went to run the tip of a knife through the potatoes.

Chapter 51

Effie

April 1944

"Did you say it usually takes you no more than 45 minutes to get from here up to Loch Brandy, Miss Anderson?" Tam Campbell was on page five of his little notebook. Effie could not help wondering why he used such a small pad.

"Yes, usually."

"And surely coming back down takes less time than going uphill?"

Nell's eyes narrowed. "Yes, that's also usually true."

"So if that is the norm, I don't understand how you only arrived back down here at the hotel at…" he turned his page back, "… 5.35, as confirmed by the cook here," he said, gesturing towards Mathilde.

Effie stared at her sister. Was she hiding something? And if so, why?

"My knees have been playing up of late. I'm fine for all the cycling I have to do every day to deliver the post – and also for the uphill climbs, but coming down a slope I find more challenging these days. My knees seem to jar sometimes, so I take it more slowly on the descent."

Nell kept her head turned towards the policeman, as if refusing to look at her sister. What on earth was she talking about? Nell had never complained of sore knees, ever. But it was not her place to say anything… yet.

"We're nearly finished, Miss Anderson. It must be so difficult for you to re-live the awful moment when you saw a body fall. But would you feel able to perhaps come up to Brandy with us tomorrow, to indicate exactly where you saw the body fall? Just to help us pinpoint exactly where to start looking."

Nell's mouth hung open.

"Of course I understand you may not feel up for that."

"I'm sure my sister won't be up for that, Mr Campbell."

"No, no, of course. I understand."

Nell delved into her pack and brought out her map. "I can show you on the map, though." She pointed to the southern edge of Loch Brandy. "This is where I was. And I think the body must have fallen from somewhere along here." She pointed to the ridge of The Snub beyond the cairn.

"It's steep up there, and it could be slippery underfoot, so be sure to be careful too. You might want to take Jim Baxter as well as the gamekeepers with you. He's experienced on the hills, but also, I've seen him scale the rocks; he can easily get roped up if you need. You'll probably need someone to go down the cliff here."

"Or the body could be in the loch, which would be even more problematic," the policeman commented as he continued writing.

"I don't think it's in the water, I'd have heard a splash and I…" Nell faltered.

"But if you were over here on the southern shore, you would perhaps not have heard a thing. From my memory Brandy is quite a large body of water." He looked up from the map. "Was there wind?"

"Yes, certainly at the top. A fierce blast, laden with sleet and…"

"But you weren't at the top?"

Effie watched as her sister took a deep breath. "I meant the top of the hill, on the way up to Brandy." She forced a smile.

"We will head off up there at first light tomorrow, then perhaps you and I can continue our chat once we see what we find." He scanned his notes. "Is Jim Baxter still the beadle at the kirk? He'll have to miss the service tomorrow."

"Yes," Effie nodded. "He lives at The Drums, but I'm sure you know that, Mr Campbell." She looked round at her sister, anxious to get her home. There was something not quite right about Nell's account.

"I'm just serving up the oxtail. Everyone want a plate?" asked Mathilde.

"Would you mind very much if we take ours back over the road, Mathilde? It's been quite a day and I'm sure…"

"Of course, let me cover both of yours with a second plate on top."

"See you tomorrow then, Mr Campbell, if you have anything else to ask – or indeed to tell…" Nell bit her lip again.

And the policeman nodded as he turned towards the heady aroma of Mathilde's oxtail stew which was being set before him.

* * *

"What's going on, Nell?"

The two sisters were eating at the table. Effie looked directly at her.

"What d'you mean?"

"Saying what the weather was like at the top. Were you also up on the ridge?"

"No, like I said, I was down on the shore. Sorry, I was confused. I'm so tired. I think I was probably in shock." She forked up a little potato. "Did I sound a bit muddled?"

"Completely. But hopefully it's just the shock."

Nell nodded. "How was your day, Effie? So sorry to have stolen the limelight. Was the big city as fun as ever?"

"It was. We had such a good outing, and the bus was even on time."

She looked out the window at the fading light. "Oh, by the way, I noticed a car parked in the hotel car park that wasn't there this morning when I left." She pointed outside. "You can't see it from your seat I don't think, but it's a dark blue one – and it's still there just now. I'll mention it to Tam Campbell tomorrow, just in case it means something. It could even belong to the man you saw fall."

Nell started coughing, a choking sound. She glugged down some water. "Some of the oxtail went down the wrong way, sorry." She laid down her fork. "The car probably belongs to some of the family in town for the funeral on Monday. I think most of them had to come up today as it's Sunday tomorrow."

Effie nodded. "Also, Nell, why have you not told me about your knees? I'd no idea you struggled coming down the hill now?"

"Yes, I didn't like to grumble. It's obviously a middle-age thing."

"We're not middle-aged yet, Nell! Well, I'm certainly not," she laughed.

Effie let her sister finish her food in silence.

"That was so good, wasn't it? Honestly, I do hope Doug takes over Clova kirk after this bloody war's ended and marries Mathilde so we can keep tasting her delicious food," Nell said, forcing a smile. "Did he say where he's being posted?"

"Down south somewhere. He's not allowed to say any more. Another five days, he said, till he has to leave. Poor Mathilde will be heartbroken."

Effie removed the plates to the sink. "You go and have a nice hot bath, Nell. I'll tidy up here. You must be exhausted."

"Oh thanks, Effie. I really am shattered; I don't know why." She trudged towards the bathroom but stopped at the door when Effie called after her.

"Did you have any visitors here today?"

She turned around. "No. I came in from work, grabbed my pack and went straight up the hill. Why?"

Effie shrugged. "It's just that, when I got home about five, I went straight to the bathroom and the door was fully shut. You and I always leave it half open."

Nell laughed. "I was in such a rush to get into the hills while the weather was fine, I must have done that inadvertently." She turned back round.

"But also, Nell, the toilet seat was up."

Effie saw Nell's shoulders rise as she took a deep breath.

"That hasn't happened since Pa was alive," said Effie as she watched her sister continue on into bathroom and pull the door firmly shut behind her.

Chapter 52
Nell

April 1944

Nell woke early and lay there, just as she had the day before, staring up at the ceiling. Such a lot had happened in the past twenty-four hours. In her wakeful moments she had tossed and turned in the dark, hoping it had all been a bad dream, but now she was fully awake, and she knew it was not. In fact, it was a living nightmare. She went over to the window and saw a glimmer of light from the east, through the grey clouds. Hopefully it would at least stay dry for the men going up the hill.

She went into the kitchen and looked at the clock. It was only half past six, but she presumed the men would be gathering in the car park soon. She went into the bathroom, shaking her head as she remembered Effie's accusation about a visitor. She'd forgotten her sister had such good observational powers.

She washed, then quickly dressed, and put on the kettle. Once she had made the tea, she took her cup outside and sat on the bench. She had a good view of the hotel's car park from there. Douglas Harrison's dark blue car was still there. Once the men had gone up the path behind the hotel towards Brandy, she'd go and peer into the car and check if there was anything to be seen inside.

She had only taken a couple of sips of her tea when she heard the rumble of a car coming over the bridge. It was Tam Campbell's black police car; he did say they'd start at first light. He parked the car in front of the hotel, got out and went straight round to the boot. Nell watched him lever out a long stretcher. He had just placed it on the ground when she approached.

"Morning, Mr Campbell. Is that to bring the body down?"

"Hopefully not a body, but we have to be realistic. The stretcher's one of those you can use vertically, so it should be easier if we've got to recover him from the cliff."

Nell studied the structure's wooden laths and canvas straps. "Have you ever used that before?"

The constable sighed. "Yes, sadly. Last time we took it up the hills was after the Wellington bomber crash in '42. But of course there were only bodies up there, so we just used the ponies to carry them down. You must remember that day well. You were the first to see the survivor."

"Yes, that was quite something, he was so lucky to survive – and with remarkably few injuries."

"I'm still hoping that it's an injured man we bring down today, too, and not a body. Though if he was hurt in the fall, then had to spend the night up there, it's rather doubtful." He sighed. "It'll have been another cold night up there."

Nell nodded and pointed to Douglas Harrison's car. "I've just realised, that car's been there since yesterday, I think. I wonder if it could belong to the man I saw fall?"

He swivelled around and stared at the car. "We'll check that out later, once we've confirmed it doesn't belong to a hotel guest." He turned back round. "How are you feeling today?"

Nell shrugged. "Still rather shocked I suppose."

"My wife sends her best regards, by the way," he said as he removed his black uniform boots and put on his sturdy mountain boots. Mrs Campbell often offered Nell a cup of tea when she was delivering the mail as they lived at the far end of the glen, beyond Gella Bridge.

Nell turned to see two men arriving from the low road and one walking over the bridge from the high road.

"Ah, there's the keepers arriving. We'll be on our way shortly. Are you in all day in case we need to chat again?"

Nell nodded, and when she saw it was Jim Baxter approaching from the bridge, she said, "Shall I tell Mr Baxter where I reckon he should go down the cliffs? It looked as if there might have been a rockfall up there, so he'll have to be careful."

"Thanks. We'll see you later." He went to greet the two gamekeepers while Nell went to brief Jim Baxter about the possible location of the body.

* * *

"He's such a good minister, young Doug Harrison. Makes even a sermon gripping." Effie walked across the playground from church towards her sister, who was sitting on the bench eating a sandwich. The day was warm but cloudy.

Effie removed her hat and sat down. "He said he'd pop over after he's said goodbye to everyone at the service to see how you're doing."

Effie turned to look directly at Nell. "And how are you? Presume there's been nothing from Tam Campbell yet?"

Nell shook her head. "That's about five hours they've been up there. They must be back soon." She handed her plate to Effie. "Want a bite?"

"No thanks, I can make my own."

She had just gone inside when Nell was aware of noise coming from the path behind the schoolhouse. She got to her feet and stood, immobile, as she watched the men emerge from the trees. Jim Baxter led the way, Tam Campbell was at the back, and between them were the two gamekeepers, carrying a stretcher. Fastened inside the many canvas straps was something bulky wrapped in tarpaulin.

She began to walk towards them, but the policeman put up his hand and shouted, "Stay where you are please, Miss Anderson. We need to get the body into my motor." So he was dead.

She walked on anyway. Then she became aware that another figure was approaching. She turned around. It was Doug Harrison in his dog collar. He had a grave look on his face.

"Can I do anything to help, Mr Campbell?"

"Just keep Miss Anderson away, would you?" he yelled back. "It's not a pretty sight." He looked down the car park towards the church, where some people were still standing, chatting. "And anyone else."

She and Doug stood at a respectful distance, staring as the men placed the stretcher on the ground behind the car, then began to unstrap the tarpaulin bundle. One of the rope ties on the tarpaulin loosened as the main stretcher straps were untied, and part of an arm was revealed.

Every other part of the body was still tightly fastened under the covering, apart from one hand and some forearm. The fingers dangled, lifeless yet stiff, on the nearest side of the bundle to Nell and Doug.

Nell winced and tried to look away, but she was aware Doug had left her side. She presumed it was to ensure that none of the congregation witnessed what was going on in the hotel car park, but he strode off in the other direction, towards the stretcher. Jim Baxter held up his hand. "We've got to get him in the car, Mr Harrison. We can manage just the four of us, but thank you anyway."

The young minister ignored his beadle and continued marching towards the corpse. He knelt down beside it while the policeman was inside the car, moving things off the rear seats to accommodate the body. Nell watched Doug lift up a stiff right hand and stare at it, lifting a little finger towards him. She screwed up her face. What on earth was he doing?

Mathilde came out of the kitchen door and ran across to her, then stopped when she saw Doug. "What is going on?" She was frowning, but he ignored her and instead turned to the men who were about to lift the body wrapped in the tarpaulin.

"Stop! I know this man." His voice was louder than Nell had ever heard.

The two gamekeepers looked around as the policeman emerged from the back seat. The keepers were standing at either end of the body, so the people on the road could not see what was going on. Tam Campbell came to stand in front of the minister.

"Are you sure? How d'you know?"

He nodded. "That's my grandfather's signet ring." He pointed to the rigid little finger. "It's an unusual square shape, not the regular oval. Cushion shape, it's called." He reached his hand towards the gold ring.

"Can I see what he was wearing? Was there anything else he had on him?"

Jim Baxter delved into the deep pockets of his warm jacket and brought out two hip flasks. "These must have fallen out of his jacket as he fell. I found them just beneath him on the rocks."

Doug took them in his hands and turned them both over. He nodded. "That's my mother's brother's initials here, and this one has my initials on it. It was given to me by my maternal grandfather on my sixteenth birthday."

Tam Campbell frowned. "So can you formally identify the body, Mr Harrison?"

Nell looked over to the group of congregants; a hush had descended. They were huddling in front of the hotel, clearly aware something was going on but not wanting to get too close.

Mathilde put an arm around Nell's shoulder as the constable went towards one end of the tarpaulin.

"The head's a bit of a mess, I warn you," he said. "Are you ready?"

Doug nodded, and the policeman lifted the tarpaulin just high enough for him to be able to see the dead man's face. The women watched Doug's shoulders heave as he gagged. The policeman replaced the covering quickly, and Doug shut his eyes and breathed in deeply.

The three men were now motionless, their gazes turned towards the young minister as he let out a long breath. He opened his eyes, then said, in a quiet voice devoid of emotion, "Constable Campbell, this man is Douglas Harrison, my father."

Chapter 53
Nell

April 1944

Nell was cycling along the high road and had just arrived at the bridge beside the church when she came to a sudden halt. Four men dressed in black were carrying a coffin aloft. They were heading out of the entrance of the church towards the graveyard behind. She propped her bike against the fence and stood watching at a respectful distance.

She then saw Doug Harrison begin to walk behind the coffin, wearing his long black robes. The day was grey and the wind was getting up. The women now emerging from the church were holding onto their hats in the breeze as they headed towards the gate, where they stood in a huddle. Nell watched some of them raise their handkerchiefs to their eyes.

She watched the procession of pall-bearers, the minister and the men filing out of church towards the burial place, and tried to see Doug's face more closely. His expression was grave, but was it the solemnity of the service he was conducting or the fact his father had just died?

Earlier that morning, when she had set off to the post office to collect her mail, she'd spotted Mathilde tipping rubbish into a bin at the back of the hotel. Nell had gone over to speak to her and noticed how pale she was; she was usually so healthy looking, with her olive skin.

"How are you, Mathilde? Any news?"

"Doug is going to try to delay his posting for a few days so he can bury his father."

"But he surely won't take the service himself?"

Mathilde shrugged. "I don't know, Nell. He has been very quiet about it all. It's been such a shock, not only to know his father died, but in such awful circumstances." She replaced the bin lid, then turned to face Nell. "I saw you with someone at the foot of the hill on Saturday. I was over the bank, picking snowdrops for the service today. I didn't say anything, but I presume it was him?"

Nell swallowed. "Yes, it was. I didn't want anyone to know I'd met him in case they thought I had anything to do with, well, with the whole awful situation." She sighed. "He was drunk, the weather was shocking, and it was slippy and…"

Mathilde put up her hand. "You don't need to tell me any more. I'm not going to say a thing. For all Doug has told me, his father will not be a loss to anyone."

She began to walk back towards the kitchen. "But he still may try to take the funeral service. As I said, he's going to try to defer his posting, even until next week, if it's possible to have the funeral soon."

Nell ran to give Mathilde a hug, then cycled off towards the post office, churning over in her mind what she'd told the policeman and wondering why on earth she had not told the whole truth. Had she been in shock perhaps? But it was all too late: that loathsome man was dead, there was nothing else she could have done – and certainly nothing could have prevented that awful fall.

* * *

Effie set the tea things on the table and called Nell over. Once the sisters were opposite each other in their usual places, Effie spoke.

"Nell, I don't know why you said what you did to Tam Campbell, but there's certainly nothing wrong with your knees. So why did you take longer to get back down the hill? You could have sprinted down easily, you're so fit."

Nell poured the milk into her cup, took a sip, then leant against the chair back. "Effie, after I saw him fall, I just felt terrible, well of course I did; it was all so awful. And I felt I had to try to get to him, in case he'd survived." She took a sip of tea. "So I went to where I'd seen him fall, up on The Snub towards the northwest, and tried to lower myself down a bit to the rocks below. But the weather was so bad and I began to slither and slip on the rocks; they were covered with snow by this stage. And I was scared there'd be a rock fall." She walked around the table and rolled up her trouser leg to show Effie her shin. It was covered in livid bruises.

Effie winced. "That looks sore."

Nell took her seat again. "I managed to get back up to the top of the ridge, then went around and came down the hill on the eastern side, really slowly. It did take a bit longer. I was terrified I'd slip too." She frowned. "Should I tell Tam I was in shock and that was why I arrived down from Brandy later than normal?"

Effie shook her head. "He's gone, that vile man is no longer a danger to anyone. And you must not blame yourself." She took her sister's hand. "Nell, it's a terrible thing to say, but I'm glad he's dead."

Nell nodded. She was about to tell her sister that Douglas Harrison had indeed been at the house earlier, and that she'd actually walked with him all the way up to The Snub, when there was a knock at the door.

"Come in," Effie shouted, and Mathilde walked in.

"Are you busy, ladies? I have a favour to ask."

"Come in, there's fresh tea in the pot." Mathilde took a seat while Effie poured her a cup.

"Doug heard this morning that his posting has been delayed. His father's funeral will be at Kirriemuir next Monday, two days before he leaves."

"He won't conduct the service himself, will he?" Nell frowned.

Mathilde nodded. "He wants to. He says he can easily overcome his emotions as his relationship with his father was so poor."

"Goodness, well that's quite something. So he'll do the eulogy and everything?"

"No, he's getting the local doctor to do that, he was a friend of his father's. Doug just doesn't feel he can talk about how marvellous a husband and father he was, when he clearly wasn't."

"Will he want you to go along to it?"

Mathilde drummed her fingers on the table. "That's the thing. I would like to be there for him."

The sisters nodded.

"So I was hoping you might both accompany me?"

Nell glanced at her sister, whose face was grim. "Well, I'm sure we'd love to be with you, but I've got work and Effie…"

"I'll come with you, Mathilde," Effie interrupted. "I won't have you going to this by yourself. We can get the bus together."

Nell was drumming her fingers on the table and staring at her tea. She lifted her gaze towards Effie, whose expression was inscrutable. "I've not had a day off for months," Nell announced. "I'll get cover for my rounds and come along too."

"No, you really don't need to, Nell, it's…"

"I'll be there. For you both," Nell said, downing her tea.

Chapter 54

Nell

April 1944

The first thing Nell noticed on entering Kirriemuir parish church was how few mourners there were. Perhaps Douglas had not just been hateful to his family; it seemed his friends were few and far between too. As the three women walked down the aisle, Nell turned and whispered to Mathilde. "Do you want to sit near the front?"

She shook her head, and Nell turned into a pew about halfway down.

Once she had sat down and taken off her gloves, Nell turned to look around again. There were only a dozen or so people in the church. Was that not unusual for someone who had lived in the area for most of his life? And he was not that old, so surely he must have had contemporaries still alive?

The organist began to play. The congregation shuffled to their feet as the undertaker asked everyone to stand. They turned around to see Doug, dressed in his long black robes, walk slowly down the aisle in front of the coffin, which was borne on the undertakers' shoulders. Nell could see Mathilde biting her lips; she was clearly anxious for him.

Doug's expression was inscrutable. He looked directly ahead, his jaws locked tightly together even as he reached the front and turned to face the mourners. As the pall-bearers laid the coffin on the bier, he simply turned his gaze towards the organ pipes on the back wall.

The undertakers withdrew to the back, and Doug looked towards the scattering of mourners. He gave one brief smile, then took up the papers in his hand and announced in a solemn voice, "Let us sing. Psalm 121, 'I to the hills will lift mine eyes'."

As they began to sing, Nell could feel Effie tense up beside her at the words.

> *"I to the hills will lift mine eyes*
> *From whence doth come mine aid*
> *My safety cometh from the Lord*
> *Who heaven and earth hath made.*
>
> *Thy foot he'll not let slide, nor will*
> *He slumber that thee keeps*
> *Behold, he that keeps Israel,*
> *He slumbers not, nor sleeps…*

Were there no other songs Doug could have chosen? She knew it was a common psalm sung at funerals, but the words were rather too poignant.

* * *

The eulogy was well delivered by Douglas's retired doctor friend, who had made him out to be a fun-loving gentleman who adored his family. Though when he made reference to his son, the Reverend Doug Harrison, and how proud the father had been of him, he made no eye contact with the minister. It was clearly all fabrication, all for show. Even the part about his heroics during the First World War did not ring true. Nell had known him for those few months at Royaumont, and there had been nothing heroic or noble at all about his behaviour. She was sure he was not even awarded any medals other than for campaigns; she doubted he'd had any for gallantry or bravery.

She usually felt such a mix of contented emotions in the church – if not peace, then a certain calm. But today, a glorious Monday in spring, she felt very little at all. In fact, she just wanted to get out of there, to guide her sister and Mathilde outside and onto the bus home, to get away from the memories of Douglas Harrison forever.

At last it was the final hymn. As the congregation sang 'Abide with Me' as loudly as possible to try to fill the sanctuary, Nell looked around at her companions. Mathilde was staring down at the words of the hymn, which she had probably never sung before. Effie knew all the words by heart and was looking straight ahead, belting them out. Her head was raised as she stared at Doug, a benign expression on her face. Previously she had said how unsettling it was that he looked so like the Douglas Harrison she had known and thought she loved all those years ago. Now at last she could look at the young minister and just see a good man.

After the benediction, the coffin was lifted back onto the undertakers' shoulders, and the congregation was invited to follow, filing out from their pews from the front of the church. Nell walked behind her sister and Mathilde, who were arm in arm, but as she passed the final pew, she noticed an old woman sitting near the end, her head bent over in prayer. She wore a large fur hat which concealed her face, but at the entrance door Nell glanced back just as the woman raised her head from her devotions. She stared straight at Nell, a glimmer of a smile on her lips, before turning her head away.

Chapter 55
Nell

June 1944

The mellifluous notes of the rondo Effie was playing were crystal clear, even through the stone walls of the schoolhouse. Nell loved it when her sister played, and she knew just how this beautiful piece would proceed, the left hand taking over the melody while the right hand flitted about with the lightest of touches, before – and here it was – that glorious ending of alternating octaves. The tone was thundering, the result triumphant – such a perfect tune for today.

She and Effie had been reading about the successful landings in France the day before. The Scotsman's pages covered nothing else and the talk around the village that day was the same: at last, the Allies had begun to push the Germans back after the massive assault on the beaches in northern France. Surely this war must end soon?

Effie rushed in, beaming. "Sorry, there were a couple of mistakes, but I decided just to keep going, not to stop and correct."

Nell shook her head at her sister's modesty. "It was fabulous, Effie. Mr Mendelssohn himself would have been proud of you." She smiled. "Though I'm sure he would have allowed people to be in the same room to listen to him play!"

Effie hated when her sister was in the same room when she played the piano, so Nell had to listen to every note from next door.

"The piano could do with tuning, by the way, but I've no idea when Mr Robertson will make it over from Kirrie."

"Is he still doing it? He must be ancient?"

"He's not that old – eighty maybe? But his son died, remember? And his grandson is away fighting; he had just taken over the business from his granddad when the war broke out."

Nell poured the tea. "Let's sit outside, it's warm today."

The sisters took their cups and saucers out and sat on the bench, looking down the glen where the sheep were grazing in the fields and the high cirrus clouds in the blue sky promised another fine evening.

"Nell, I was thinking about Mathilde's ring."

"What about it?"

"Well, she only has a cheap one that looks like a curtain ring."

"They didn't exactly have time to go to a jeweller's before he left; it's just make do till he returns and can have his father's signet ring melted down."

"That's what's bothering me. I don't know why that man has to be involved in any way, even from beyond the grave."

"Don't be daft," Nell muttered. "They might as well use the gold. They won't have any money for a real gold ring once he returns."

"I wish we had a ring to give her to wear."

"Effie, even if we did have rings to give – neither of us were ever married, never mind engaged, so how could we? Besides, it's not our place. Mathilde is not family. She walked into our lives nearly a year ago a complete stranger. We can't interfere in her life even though we are so fond of her."

"I know, I know. But the issue with the ring made me wonder…" She turned to her sister. "Where did Ma's rings go? She had a wedding ring – and I'm sure there was a diamond engagement ring too?"

"Remember, I told you ages ago I'd asked Pa about that, and he said he had her buried with her rings on."

"But no one does that – they're always handed down to the girls of the family, surely?"

Nell shrugged. "I know, it makes no sense to me either, but that's what he said. We've got one of her brooches and a necklace each, that was all Pa said was in her jewellery box."

"I still wonder if Pa was keeping something from us about her death. D'you think that, like those boys said to you all those years ago, she did actually kill herself?"

"No. She was strong. Can't you remember? Why would she do that?"

Nell stood up. "Anyway, we've got Mathilde coming tonight for supper. We'd better get cooking. What did we decide on?"

Effie snorted. "From the vast array of possibilities, we decided on potato pie. Again."

* * *

"You must be so pleased to have got a letter from Doug, at last."

Mathilde beamed. "I really am. I was worrying so much, but now there's an end in sight for this dreadful war. He may even be home soon."

"I wouldn't hold out too much hope of it being over any time soon," Nell said, frowning. "The Allies still have a lot of ground to cover. And there's Japan too, remember."

"I suppose so." Mathilde sighed. "I guess I can't plan the wedding yet. I just need to get him safely home."

"Of course you do," Effie said, taking her hand. "Was he able to say much? I know they're all censored so I suppose not."

Mathilde shook her head. "The usual things – how are you, how's the weather, very little about him in case I was able to guess where he was."

Mathilde took a sip of water. "I've actually been wondering if he was with the airborne troops landing yesterday."

"Why do you think that?"

"I don't know. I just feel it's the kind of thing he'd have volunteered for, if they needed a chaplain to be with the men."

"He's brave, isn't he," Effie said, smiling.

"No more so than any of the other men," Mathilde said. "But when I think of Doug in one of those aircraft ready to parachute into France I can't help thinking of Pierre." She sighed. "I'm so afraid Doug will die too."

"Don't be daft, Mathilde – the Allies are on the ascent. The war could be over in a few months. Then he'll be home and you can have your wedding and…"

There was a knock at the door. Nell drew back her chair and went to open it.

An old woman stood there, a large fur hat on her head. Nell's first thought was to wonder why she was wearing a fur hat on such a warm evening. Then, as a flicker of a smile appeared on the woman's wrinkled face, Nell realised she recognised her from the funeral in Kirriemuir. She was the woman in the back pew.

"Hello, can I help you?" She looked again at her and became aware she had also seen her around the village before that; she looked somehow familiar. Nell had seen that hat before, and not just in Kirriemuir church. "Would you like to come in?"

The woman nodded and followed Nell in. Effie pulled out a chair at the table and motioned to her to sit down. The woman remained standing as she nodded thanks to Effie, then turned her gaze to Mathilde, who was smiling at her. As she continued to stare, she put her hand on the back of the chair as if to steady herself. Her smile now gone, her rheumy eyes were filling with tears. "You look so like her," she said as she sat down at the table, shifting her gaze from Mathilde to Effie. "You both do," she said, as tears began to trickle down her cheeks.

Chapter 56
Nell

June 1944

"My name is Edith Bain, and I was your mother's best friend," she said, taking a sip of the tea Nell had given her.

All three women stared at her. Neither of the sisters were able to speak; all the colour had drained from Effie's face.

Mathilde scraped her chair back. "I'll leave you. This is obviously a conversation just concerning you ladies." She began to stand up, but the old lady took her hand and looked at her. "No, Mathilde, please sit down too."

Nell turned to look at her. How did she know Mathilde's name? "Why have you come, Mrs Bain?"

"Miss Bain," she said, then smiled. "I have news to tell you all."

"All? Why would it concern Mathilde?" Nell asked. Should she perhaps ask her to leave anyway? Much as they adored Mathilde, it did not seem appropriate for her to be here if it was to do with their family. Unless this old woman had something to do with Douglas Harrison – why else would she have been at his funeral?

The woman gestured to Mathilde to take her seat again.

"Your mother and I were friends for years, even though she lived here in Clova and I lived in Kirriemuir, in the manse."

"Ah, your brother is the minister…"

Edith nodded. "My younger brother, yes; and my father before him."

"I can't remember Ma even having friends, can you, Nell?"

Nell screwed up her eyes. "Did you come here for tea one day, Miss Bain, during the summer holidays when Pa was over in Prosen?"

The woman smiled. "Yes. Do you remember, we went for a walk after tea and you got stung by nettles, Helen. And I had to clamber over a fence to get some dock leaves to make it better. Your mother was laughing so much at the sight of me trying to climb over the fence with my long skirt on."

Nell nodded. "I do remember the nettle sting and someone else being with us; that was quite unusual; Ma was almost always alone. Pa didn't seem to like her having friends." She looked at her. "And now I think about it, I do remember thinking how lovely it was that Ma was laughing. She seemed so happy. She never laughed at home."

"I was there on the day she met Emile. It was at the Wateresk picnic. He was such a handsome man, also a very kind person. They would have been such a lovely couple, though it was not to be, obviously."

"Who on earth is Emile?" Effie raised her hands.

"Your mother's lover for two of the happiest years she had here in Clova. Their clandestine relationship lasted for a good while, until your father found out."

"What?" Both sisters gawped at her.

"I don't believe it," Effie said, shaking her head.

Miss Bain turned to Effie and Nell. "Your father did not treat your mother terribly well, perhaps you knew that?" She continued.

"Well, he was…" Effie began.

"Yes, we did know that, Miss Bain. But what's that to do with why you're here?" said Nell, willing this stranger to come to the point.

"On that awful September night in 1910, when your father almost beat your poor mother to death, she managed to walk – Lord knows how – to Kirriemuir, where she stayed in my room in the manse for several days, till she recovered enough to head to France."

"Beat her?" Effie's eyes were wide.

"Yes. When she had recovered, my mother helped to plan the trip for her, but no one else even knew she was staying with us."

"Hang on," Nell said, raising her hands. "Ma died in September 1910."

The woman shook her head. "Your father told everyone that, but it's not true. When he realised she had escaped his clutches, he announced that she was dead."

"But why would he…"

"He was a complex man, James Anderson. I never actually had much time for him, but he was clever, an intellectual in fact, and he somehow charmed your mother into marrying him. But he was a bully and controlling. Any other woman might have been scared of him, but she stood up to him." She sighed. "And that last time she did, he almost killed her – he actually left her for dead, she was convinced of that."

"What happened when she left your house in Kirrie?"

"She managed to get over to France, to Emile's hometown, near Paris, and they were happy together, though unmarried, until he was sadly one of the first killed in the last war."

Mathilde had put her elbows on the table and was resting her head in her hands. She looked up. "When was this, Miss Bain?"

"It was just before the war started." She looked at Mathilde, who was now sitting up straight, shaking her head. "And that was where her third daughter was born. So even though she was constantly distraught that she'd had to leave her daughters behind in Scotland, she now had another. And she began to plan how she could come over to Clova to take you both back to France with her."

All three women were staring at her, mouths open.

"But then Emile died, and there was the war, and she had no choice but to go to the family restaurant her uncle ran to the east of Paris, near the Belgian border, and it was he who helped her bring up her little girl."

Mathilde let out a long breath.

"I don't understand," Effie scraped back her chair and got to her feet, "Why did she not come back for us? I don't believe you. I think you're lying. Why are you telling us this now?"

"Effie, let Miss Bain continue. Did you not hear – she wanted to come back for us."

"Then why didn't she write?"

"That's true," Nell said, turning to the older woman. "Surely after the war ended, in 1918, she could have come for us..."

"Are you perhaps forgetting how strict your father was? His teaching methods were draconian, and that was reflected at home I believe?"

Nell and Effie nodded.

"She knew that if she dared set foot anywhere near Clova, he'd have her institutionalised, or worse. And he most certainly would've got rid of any letters that arrived from her. His reputation would have been in tatters, everyone knowing he had lied about his wife. He was a hypocrite, a respected dominie on the outside, but at home, a coercive tyrant." She paused. "She said she had written a note to you both before she left, but clearly you didn't get it."

Nell shook her head.

"So, what have you got to do with all this?" Effie was frowning at Edith Bain. "If you live just along in Kirrie, could you not have told us well before now that our mother was alive?"

"I was forbidden. She knew she could do nothing until your father died, but when he did die, in 1939, the war was just beginning, so there was no time for her to travel, even though she was desperate to seek your forgiveness."

"Forgiveness?" Effie gasped. "For abandoning us for all these years? And does she expect us to accept her now with open arms?" Her eyes were filled with tears.

"Effie, sit down!" Nell turned towards the old woman. "So where is Ma now and what happened to this other daughter, Miss Bain?"

"Is there any more tea, Helen, please? I have more news to convey," Miss Bain said, removing her hare fur hat and placing it on the floor beside her.

* * *

"I was tasked with writing to her a couple of times a year, with news of how you both were."

"And how were you able to do that? We've only just met," Effie said, sniffing.

"I got the bus to Clova regularly, checked what you were doing and reported back in my letters to her. And during that year you were over in Prosen, Euphemia, I saw you there too."

"You were spying on us?" Effie said, wiping her tears. "I just don't understand why you couldn't have told us earlier."

"Your father: I had to make sure he never saw me. He'd have recognised me; I was your mother's only friend. Besides, you were still young. You might have blurted out inadvertently that we'd met and that your mother was still alive. It was awful – for me, but mainly for your mother, who had to get through all those years with the only news of her beloved girls coming from my letters."

"Why didn't she write to us at your house?"

"I suggested that, but we both realised it would be too dangerous for me to be seen giving something to either of you; your father had eyes everywhere."

"Did Aunt Winnie know you were snooping on us?"

"Effie, stop being so rude!"

"Well, I can't believe this stranger has just arrived and is telling us all this now. Why now?"

"Your aunt knew nothing. Her brother had told her your mother was dead, why would she doubt him?" She shrugged. "And those first three years of this war, after your father had died, I wanted to come and tell you your mother was alive, but as soon as the war began I had to go to Dundee to live with my niece. Her husband was one of the first to join up; I looked after her four small children while she ran the family shop. Then he was invalided out, but not injured badly enough to stop him working in the shop again. So I came back to Kirrie in the autumn of '42, but by then it was almost impossible to get letters to and from

Provence, because of the occupation."

Mathilde, who had been silent, spoke. "So, what happens now? Can she come over now the Allies have started their invasion and…"

Miss Bain raised a hand. "I should probably come to the crucial piece of information."

She delved into her handbag and took out a large envelope. She laid it on the table and pulled out a letter from inside. "It's in French so I don't know if one of you wishes to read it out loud or for you all to read together."

Nell and Effie pushed their chairs together.

"Mathilde should read it with you," Miss Bain said, and they made room for her to join them.

"Dear Edith,

My darling sister Manon has been writing to you now for so many years, I feel I know you well.

When she came here to stay with me in Maussane in September 1943, she seemed fit and well, and we began making plans for her to travel back to Scotland to see her daughters. Please tell Helen and Euphemia that she wanted so much to come and take them away, but even though she was a strong character, she decided that their father posed too much of a threat to their safety. She worried they would come to harm if he knew she was still alive and could make a claim on them – he was more dangerous than any of us could have believed. She was convinced he might take it out on her daughters if he knew she was alive. And so she loved them – in fact adored them – from afar.

When she was bringing up Mathilde,…

Here the sisters gasped.

… caring for the daughter who so resembled her other girls helped in a small way to mitigate the pain of their absence.

Please let them all know how very much she loved each and every one of them.

Effie dabbed her eyes with her handkerchief. Nell and Mathilde were staring, open-mouthed, as the page was turned over.

"*When we heard about her husband's death, we began planning for her return to Clova as soon as the war finished, but instead of things getting better, they got worse. Though most of Provence is under Italian occupation, Maussane is on the western edge of Provence, and it's the Germans who're occupying our town. Things have been tough, very tough. The resistance around here is strong, but no one trusts anyone anymore. My nephew, a maquisard, is taking this package to post somewhere he assures me is safe.*

It was only in December 1943 that Manon began to truly suffer from her illness. She had been fatigued and in pain for some time but kept brushing it off. When the doctor diagnosed cancer before Christmas, she began to get her affairs in order, and when she died, in March of this year, everything was in place.

I enclose letters, one for each girl, and a small token for each of them: her old wedding ring for Helen, as she said she used to like trying it on, even though it was far too big for her; her pearls for Euphemia, as she always took them to bed with her when her mother was late home, as she missed her; and her old engagement ring for Mathilde, in case she is ever fortunate enough to find love.

Manon is buried here in our little cemetery in Maussane. If ever this war ends, it would be so good if any of the girls were able to come and see me – and visit their darling mother's grave.

Thank you again, dear Edith, for your friendship,
Laetitia

Epilogue
September 1946

"Are you sure the train isn't late, Nell?"

"No. I told you, we arrived far too early. We've a long way to go, so please don't start getting anxious at the very start of this journey!"

Nell and Effie stood on a platform in Waverley station, each with a small case at their feet. All around them were people waiting for the train to London. Beside them a lady was holding on tightly to a child who kept trying to pull her towards the rails. A man in a heavy overcoat stood stock still, gazing up at the clock as the hands moved slowly towards the hour. A young woman held an old lady in a large hat by the arm, whispering to her as she pointed to the far end of the platform as if willing the train to arrive.

At last a noise made everyone else turn towards the west, where a plume of smoke heralded the arrival of the train. The noise of the steam engine became louder as it approached the station.

"Right, you go on first and get the seats. I'll carry the bags," said Nell, pushing Effie towards the door as the train came to a halt.

As Nell picked up the luggage, she watched Effie dart through the waiting crowd and step onto the train. Nell soon followed, a small case in each hand. She joined her sister, and they both swung their bags overhead, then sat down in the carriage, Effie at the window and Nell beside her. They smiled as a young couple got into the carriage with a baby.

"It's such a same Mathilde couldn't come with us," Nell whispered. "But it's understandable that she and Doug thought the journey would be too long for baby Manon." She looked over at the baby who was sound asleep in his mother's arms. "Though, at two months old, she'd probably just sleep most of the way, but I suppose it can be a bit sooty and dirty on trains. The fresh air of the glen is better for a newborn."

"And Doug couldn't possibly leave. He's got too much to do, and we're away for a whole month, remember. He's just settling into his full time position at Clova kirk; he can't just take a long holiday whenever he likes."

"I know, but it would have been so lovely to show off our beautiful niece to Paul's family at his daughter's wedding."

"Another time, Effie. I know Mathilde will want to bring her daughter to visit our mother's grave. And Doug's French is coming along; perhaps he'll be able to get longer leave in a year or two."

Effie nodded and turned to look out the window as the train puffed slowly out of the station.

"Next stop London. Then Provence, here we come."

"With rather a lot of stations in between," Nell said, riffling in her bag.

"What are you looking for?"

"The sandwiches, I'm hungry."

"We'll be going to the dining car for lunch in an hour or so, can't you wait?"

Nell pulled out a string bag and opened it out on her lap. "No, I can't," she said, unwrapping a cheese sandwich.

"You're impossible," Effie muttered as she watched her sister take a large bite of sandwich. A broad smile spread across her face, and she took her sister's free hand in hers and squeezed it tight.

* * *

Nell and Effie stood in the cemetery side by side, staring at the headstone. Their aunt Laetitia had walked to the graveyard with them, but had then gone home to prepare the celebration lunch for the extended family.

"Though Aunt Laetitia is shorter than Ma and her features are a bit different, she still reminds me so much of her."

Nell nodded. "It's the accent as well as everything else, isn't it?"

Nell pointed to the stone. "I'm pleased the inscription has no reference to Pa or to Emile, aren't you?"

"I was just about to say that, but I thought it might seem a bit mean. He was Mathilde's father after all."

"I know." Nell shrugged. "But then it wouldn't be right not to mention our father, who doesn't deserve to be on it."

Effie stepped forward to place her flowers in front of the stone, and Nell followed. They moved back and bowed their heads for a moment.

Effie sighed. "I know we promised we'd take a picture of it for Mathilde – and Miss Bain of course – but it doesn't seem right somehow."

Nell nodded. "I know, but they both need to see it. Mathilde for obvious reasons, and then Edith Bain deserves so much from us. Only through her did Ma know how we were doing all those years in Clova." She took her camera out of her bag and gestured for her sister to stand aside, out of the way.

Nell crouched down and peered into the camera lens. The silence in the cemetery, broken only by the steady, high-pitched buzzing of the cicadas in the olive trees behind, was interrupted by a click as she pressed the shutter and their mother's memory was captured forever.

À la mémoire de Manon,
mère adorée de Helen, Euphemia et Mathilde
3/3/1875 – 9/3/1944
Dans nos cœurs pour toujours

Author's Notes

In my quest for remarkable women from the past, I came across **Jean Cameron, a postwoman in Glen Clova** in the Second World War; the usual male postal workers were away fighting, so women took over their jobs. She refused to wear the standard uniform skirt, insisting on wearing trousers on her bike as her rounds involved scaling walls, clambering over stiles and cycling along bumpy farm tracks in all weathers, even knee-high snow.

It took a special request from Jean to the Head Postmaster, who eventually agreed, and by 1943, 14,000 pairs of uniform trousers were being worn by rural postwomen across Britain. They came to be known as 'Camerons'. There is a wonderful old short film from 1944 about Jean Cameron doing her round on her bike, called 'Coming of the Camerons'. It is available from the Moving Image Archive at the National Library of Scotland.

I first came across the role of **Royaumont Abbey** in the First World War in a book recommended by the Australian writer Kate Morton. In Falling Snow by Mary Rose MacColl is a historical novel whose twentieth-century narrative includes the location of Royaumont Abbey as a Scottish Women's Hospital (SWH) in the First World War. Dr Elsie Inglis set up the Scottish Women's Hospitals for Foreign Services in 1914, providing doctors, nurses, orderlies and ambulance drivers – run exclusively by women. By the end of that war, fourteen medical units had been set up in many countries, including France, Corsica and Serbia.

It was a truly magnificent achievement, with more than a thousand women working for the SWH, especially given society's attitudes towards medical women at the time. Interestingly, only the medically trained personnel, such as doctors, nurses, lab technicians and x-ray operators, received a salary. Orderlies, ambulance drivers and administrative workers were expected to pay their own way.

The women medics treated 10,681 patients at Royaumont Abbey and its nearby ancillary hospital at Villers-Cotterets. Most patients were soldiers, but some civilians were also admitted. Out of 8,752 soldiers registered as patients, there were only 159 deaths, a remarkably low figure considering the circumstances.

I had begun researching this novel before I found out about the **Vickers Wellington Bomber crash above Glen Clova on 9 August 1942,** though I subsequently heard from a couple of my cousins that they'd been taken up there by my uncle years ago. Gary Nelson, a hillwalker interested in historical aircraft sites, had visited the crash site on Muckle Cairn with Gayle Ritchie, a journalist from DC Thomson. Gary helped fill in some details that had not been readily available.

The Wellington L7845 crashed on a test flight from RAF Lossiemouth; after this flight, it had been scheduled to take off on a bombing mission, presumably over Germany. However, during the test flight, the aircraft lost part of a cowling, and the dislodged section damaged one of the propellers, leading to engine failure, which caused the bomber to crash in the hills above Glen Clova only an hour or so after take-off. Some say the pilot was attempting a forced landing, but there is no evidence as to exactly what happened high on those hills (the crash site is over 800 metres from sea level – almost a Munro).

Tragically, all crew members except the rear gunner died in the accident. Three of those killed (pilot, observer and air gunner) were from the RCAF (Royal Canadian Air Force).

I read the journal of a Dr Jessie Learmonth from Kirriemuir, citing a letter sent in 1942 by a total stranger to one of the Canadians' parents. In the letter, Miss M J Robertson writes how their son was laid to rest in a cemetery nearby (this was Fettercairn Cemetery, which has nineteen Commonwealth war graves from the Second World War) and she poignantly describes the location of the cemetery and the wreaths on each of the three graves. She says she 'wished she could have taken a snapshot to send, but they can't get film for the camera at present' – it wasn't only food that was rationed in the war. She also writes that on Sunday their minister spoke of the 'gallant lads and prayed for the loving hearts out in Canada'.

The other casualty was an RAF observer, and the only survivor an RAF tail gunner.

I climbed up to see the crash site one chilly, damp October day, along the east side of Loch Wharral, then alongside Ben Tirran and The Goet, over the moor towards Muckle Cairn. Even through the mist and low cloud, melancholy and gloom hung in the air. The sight of so much metal from pieces of propeller, engine, fuselage and the almost intact tail fin scattered across the desolate terrain was heart-wrenching.

I heard from an elderly Glen Clova gentleman that locals said the survivor had probably climbed down the hill from the crash site towards either Wheen Farm or the Glen Clova Hotel, which had previously been named the Ogilvy Arms Hotel.

Since I have known and loved **Glen Clova** for so long, an idea formed for a story based there. It was always known as **my family's favourite glen.** When my dad and uncle were teenagers, they used to cycle up there from Dundee (a not inconsiderable thirty-mile trip each way) or catch a bus (sometimes the post bus), then stay in the youth hostel there and climb the hills. The climbs were often the nearby Munroes of Driesh and Mayar, but also Loch Brandy and The Snub, Loch Muick, Craig Mellon and so many other hills around Clova.

Even in the Second World War, while Dad was too young to sign up, he visited Clova often, without his older brother, who was already away fighting. Dad recorded in his journal that he stayed overnight at Clova hostel every few months from August 1939 until June 1942, just before he was allowed to join the Marines.

Unc, Dad's older brother, continued to walk and climb the hills into his nineties. Indeed, after he died aged ninety-nine, the family scattered his ashes near Clova, some on the top of Driesh, a Munro of 947 metres.

Glen Clova is a place of nostalgia and history, of beauty and challenge. It is a place of legend.

Come by the hills to the land where legend remains
The stories of old fill our hearts and may yet come again
Where the past has been lost and the future is still to be won
And the cares of tomorrow can wait till this day is done

W Gordon Smith (1928–96)

Acknowledgements

Paul Blackford
John Boyle
Jen Falconer, Angus Archives
Hamish Gray, Curator, Tayside Police museum
Celia Greig
Graham Henderson
Ross Henderson
Colin MacDougal, retired officer, Tayside Police & Search Rescue
Gary Nelson
Gayle Ritchie, DC Thomson, Dundee
Cathy Tingle

Heartfelt gratitude to Iain Spink for his unrivalled knowledge of the Clova hills and to Su Spink for her invaluable local history contacts – and for delicious bakes en route up the glen.

Special thanks to MaryAn Charnley, Anne Dow and Isabelle Plews for such assiduous and patient reading of early manuscripts and for commenting so wisely, and to Angie Harms for editing.

Thank you to Judi and John Matheson for agreeing to be dragged up to Loch Brandy in weather that was more than a little inclement…

Thank you to Jim Donaldson at the Stanley website (stanley-perthshire.co.uk), for kind permission to reproduce the front cover photograph of Kate Gairns and Hilda Crawford, taken in 1940, when both worked at Stanley Cotton Mills.

Thanks to Aidan Smith for kind permission to reproduce a verse from the poem 'Come by the Hills', © W. Gordon Smith.

Thanks to Glen Clova Hotel for the warm welcome after a long day on the hills.

As always, thanks to Pat not only for accompanying me on many walks and climbs in our favourite glen, and for his aviation expertise, but also for patiently waiting as I stopped to take yet another photo…

And thank you, as ever, to Jenny Brown for encouragement and boundless enthusiasm during the writing of this book.

The Author

Sue Lawrence is the author of gripping historical thrillers that cast fascinating light on the perils and injustice that characterised women's lives in Scotland through centuries past – whether they were born into penniless or powerful families: *Lady's Rock, The Green Lady, The Unreliable Death of Lady Grange, Down to the Sea, The Last Train* and *Fields of Blue Flax*. She is also one of the UK's leading cookery writers and broadcasters. Having studied French at Dundee university, she then trained as a journalist. After winning BBC's *MasterChef* in 1991, Sue wrote regular columns in *The Sunday Times, Scotland on Sunday* and many leading magazines. She has appeared frequently on television and radio and has written twenty cookery books, winning awards for her food writing. Born in Dundee, Sue has lived in several countries – France, Finland, Germany and Australia – and now lives in Edinburgh.

Also by Sue Lawrence

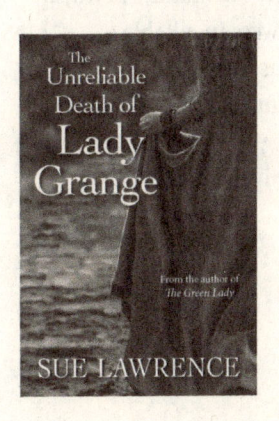

A thrilling historical novel based on the extraordinary true story of Lady Grange, who in 1732 was kidnapped on the orders of her powerful husband, who faked her death and secretly exiled her to a remote island beyond the Scottish Outer Hebrides.

"The wronged lady finally has her say."—*The Times*

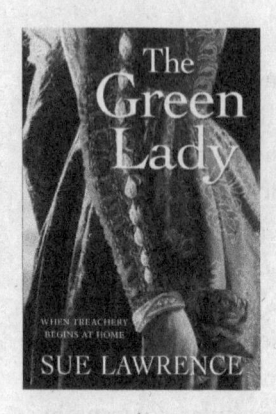

A gripping tale of court intrigue, secrets, treachery and murder, based on the true lives of Lilias Drummond, Alexander Seton – 1st Earl of Dunfermline and Lord Chancellor of Scotland – and his aunt Marie Seton, one of the "Four Marys" who were ladies-in-waiting to Mary, Queen of Scots.

>"Compelling."
>—*Historical Novels Review*

As 16th-century clans battled for power, Catherine Campbell was betrothed to Lachlan Maclean to forge an alliance between two powerful chiefs. But when she failed to bear a son and her husband made an impossible demand, betrayal and revenge were inevitable.

>"Gives a fascinating insight into the murderous clan system"
>—*The Scotsman*